"Please, just drive." Joy said quietly, and Molly did, back through the quiet streets, down the boulevard of expensive homes, and through the commercial district. Once they were on the highway, Molly stole a look and saw that Joy was staring straight ahead, rigid.

"It's got to help to talk about it," she said.

Joy covered her mouth with her hand, as if she was afraid to say.

"What is it? What's wrong?"

Joy took several deep breaths and let her hand drop. "Something awful happened there," she said slowly, in a whisper. "Everybody knows it and no one will say. I know it but I can't see it. I can't see what it is."

"It's going to come," Molly said gently, handing her a tissue. "When the time is right, it's all going to come."

BURIED LIVES

Nancy Star

FAWCETT GOLD MEDAL • NEW YORK

A Fawcett Gold Medal Book
Published by Ballantine Books
Copyright © 1993 by Nancy Star

All rights reserved under International and Pan-American Copyright Conventions. Published in the United States of America by Ballantine Books, a division of Random House, Inc., New York, and simultaneously in Canada by Random House of Canada Limited, Toronto.

Grateful acknowledgment is made to Frank Music Corp. for permission to reprint an excerpt from the lyrics of "THUMBELINA" from "Hans Christian Andersen" by Frank Loesser. Copyright © 1951, 1952 (Renewed) Frank Music Corp. All rights reserved. Used by permission.

Library of Congress Catalog Card Number: 93-90092

ISBN 0-449-14823-8

Printed in Canada

First Edition: July 1993

For Larry

CHAPTER ONE

THE BLACK DOOR slammed. Buddy stared at her somberly through the rear window. The car inched down the hill, taking him away.

Leaping through the air Joy grabbed onto the back bumper, the sharp edges digging into her palm, slicing her fingers. Her canvas sneakers turned black, then disintegrated as the car dragged her down the road. Bleeding, her clutch tightened, and she shrieked, "Stop!"

The bumper popped off. Joy fell to the curb. The dull metal landed at her feet. She wanted to run after him. But her legs were Jell-O. Her bottom was cemented to the ground.

"Joy," her brother yelled from inside the car. He grabbed at the collar of his blue and green flannel shirt as if it were strangling him.

She sat bolt upright, awake and sweating, as Lanny turned off his alarm clock. He scooted out of bed to the shower. The water blasted on full force. The plastic rings squealed on the rod as he drew the vinyl curtain shut. The echoes of exuberant humming drifted toward her.

She closed her eyes and struggled to hold on to the dream. But it was too late. All that was left was the afterglow of a forgotten terror.

"Hey. Uncrease that brow," Lanny called out when he returned from his five-minute shower, clutching a plush white towel around his middle. Letting the towel drop, he tousled the fiery crown of her long wavy hair. He loved to play with her hair, streaks of red and blond and amber that he said reminded him of flames.

Joy smiled, her anxiety dissolving. She was home, safe with her husband in her new house. Her hands traveled the contours of her belly, feeling the shape of the rest of her family. After seven years of marriage and two miscarriages, they had finally conceived again. She was big and round and hard; six months pregnant with twins.

"We are going to be nauseatingly happy here," Lanny whispered in her ear. He kissed her neck, then disappeared into a room adjoining theirs. The night before, their first night in the house, while Joy unpacked their clothes, Lanny had turned the small connecting bedroom into a giant walk-in closet. With oak shelves he'd discovered in the basement and a stack of dusty closet rods he'd come upon in the attic, he sawed and drilled into the morning hours, constructing a perfect haven for his trove of navy blue suits and his collection of weekend crewneck sweaters.

"I'll be fired," he announced as he returned with a starched white shirt, carefully checking to see if the collar was pressed right. "Because I'm bad for morale. Because everyone's life will pale next to ours." He slipped his arms into the shirt, then disappeared to choose a tie.

"We'd better get a little misery in our lives," he joked, popping his head back in the room. "We don't want our tombstones to read: Joy and Lanford Bard, so happy no one wanted to be their friends."

He left, and Joy thought, maybe that's why we don't have many friends—our happiness scares them away. It scared her, some days. Pregnant with twins, married to a doting husband, in demand as a free-lance illustrator of horror novels; it was all so perfect. Yet she didn't trust it. Didn't trust that it wouldn't disappear suddenly. That she wouldn't wake up one day and find herself where she was before she met Lanny. Alone.

Lanny returned, pulling tight his carefully knotted navy

and red striped tie. As Joy lifted her heavy body out of the bed, he raised his chin, revealing the full breadth of his wide neck. She lumbered toward him, then with her fine thin fingers, buttoned down his collar. He kissed the palms of her hands.

Do I really deserve this, she thought, letting her head fall forward slightly, to rest on his shoulder. She shook the doubt away, but not before he noticed.

"What? What's up?"

It was uncanny. Lanny picked up on her moods as if they were a part of him. She had only to touch her hair for him to ask if she was nervous. If her shoulders raised a quarter inch, he'd tell her she was getting mad.

"I just had a bad dream," she admitted.

Lanny sat at the edge of their rosewood bed, his parents' bed, the ornately carved headboard crested with what looked to Joy to be the face of a child in pain. He tied his laces with perfectly even loops. "What kind of dream?"

She shook her head. "I don't know. I can't remember." She considering telling him the rest, that it was nothing new. That as a teenager she'd been plagued by bad dreams. That she used to force herself to stay awake at night so they wouldn't come. She'd never mentioned the dreams before because they'd stopped, abruptly, on her wedding night. And this was not the day to tell. Not on their first day in the new house.

"It's just a dream," she said, smiling, as she grabbed Lanny's wide wooden brush. She turned her back to the gilded mirror, another inherited antique, this one with a carved head so angry and grotesque it forced her to look away. She turned back to Lanny and ran the soft bristles through his golden waves.

"You're just uptight about work," he posited, rubbing his cheeks with the back of his fingers to check the closeness of his shave. "With the move you haven't been able to work. It's probably a work dream."

She accepted his theory and handed him his brush so she could slip into her navy maternity sweats. Without looking in the mirror, she pulled her hair up into a ponytail.

"God, you're gorgeous," he blurted out, grabbing her in a tight hug.

She slithered out of his hold, avoiding looking at her reflection. She didn't feel gorgeous. She felt as misshapen as a raw potato. She felt like her nose was too long and her hazel eyes too small and that they looked frightened all the time.

"And the best thing is you don't even know it."

"Go to work," she said. "Go do lawyer things. Help companies get bigger or avoid bankruptcy. Go win a case."

Lanny checked his smile in the mirror, then ran his tongue over his teeth. "And you finish your painting and tell Anna-Marie you're done until the babies are grown. So you don't have any more bad dreams." He grabbed her again, so tight it took her breath away, and kissed her, hard, on the lips. Before she could say good-bye he was downstairs, the door slamming behind him.

She was alone with the sounds of her new home. The pipes whined quietly, then stopped. The iron radiator clanked intermittently, letting her know the fall morning was cool enough to call for heat. Her eyes scanned the room, taking in the open door to their new walk-in closet, the window seat overlooking the front lawn, the dark oak floors. It felt so comfortable. Already she could barely remember why she'd resisted when Lanny proposed leaving the city.

He'd been insistent, claiming Manhattan was a dangerous place to raise kids. He wanted them to have a yard to play in, a basement with a Ping-Pong table, a vegetable garden where they could grow pumpkins. He was convincing enough that they put their co-op on the market the week after they found out she was pregnant. Three months later they sold at a sizable loss.

They chose Edgebury because of the forty-minute commute, and because Berger, the senior partner in the firm, lived there.

"Imagine," Lanny said as he tried to convince her it was the place for them, "being invited to swim in Berger's indoor pool in December. Playing paddle tennis on his own private court. We can't afford that kind of place, right now. But wouldn't it be nice to be a quick drive away?"

Since all the towns seemed the same to her, Joy agreed. After six hectic weeks of searching, she found their house.

But when Lanny walked through the tall, pale blue Victorian, his disappointment was obvious. She tried to see it through his eyes. The rooms were small; the walls had cracks; the yard was seriously overgrown. Yet it was the only house, out of nearly forty she'd seen, where she felt comfortable, instantly at home.

So he went to see it again. Joy waited in their small Gramercy Park apartment, oblivious to the Saturday morning golf game on TV, certain Lanny would walk in any minute even more convinced that the house was wrong for them. Instead he returned holding a bottle of Moët and a dozen red roses. With the second look he'd been won over.

He negotiated a good price and got a quick closing. In another month they were in.

Now the nightmare was back.

CHAPTER TWO

IT TOOK TWO trips to the hardware store to stock up on all the things they hadn't noticed they'd needed their first week in the house. Lanny had made the list: light bulbs for the garage, batteries for the smoke detectors, phone jacks, giant garbage bags, raccoon-proof trash cans, a heavy-duty Dust Buster. Things they now had room to store. The

house was old, the closets small, but there was a rabbit war-
ren of a basement and two spacious attic crawl spaces for
tucking things out of sight. There was even room for both
bikes in the garage. In the apartment the bikes had hung on
hooks in the narrow front hall, the greasy chains catching
and snagging Joy's sweaters every time she passed by.

Finally finished with the morning errands, Joy stood on
the porch at the front door, balancing two bags filled with
industrial strength cleaners on one knee, and fumbled for
the key. When it flew out of her hand, she put down her
parcels and crept around the porch, looking for it. She
found it hidden in a dusty corner. Then a flash of white
caught her eyes, leading her to the mailbox.

The mailman used the brass slot in the front door—she
didn't even know the cast-iron mailbox existed. Painted the
same pale blue color as the shingles, it hung camouflaged
in a corner, invisible, until the white envelope caught her
eye.

She pulled the jammed envelope out. There was no way
to know when it had been placed there, but the invitation
said the tea party was to be held the next day.

That evening as Lanny lay in bed beside her, massaging
the hard hill of her pregnant belly, Joy was annoyed to discover he knew about the party already.

"Why didn't you tell me? Why didn't you get me out of
it?"

"You'll be glad you went," he reassured her as his fingers felt around for the bumps that marked the babies'
growing limbs. "I just forgot to mention it. Barb caught me
on the way to work last week to ask if I thought you'd go.
I said sure, and then I forgot all about it." He squeezed
some more Vitamin E cream on his palms and began rubbing her belly with firm, circular motions. "You want to divorce me, you got to give me the kids."

"A tea party. I hate the idea." Joy shivered. The babies
shifted. She raised herself up to watch the mound move.

"An elbow," Lanny whispered, pointing to a protrusion

that was disappearing back into her. He kissed the spot. Joy lay back down, a restful smile on her face.

"It's a great way to meet the neighbors," he continued. "And it will be good for you. You spend too much time by yourself."

It was true. She preferred her own company to that of most people, except for Lanny.

"You come," she said, grabbing him.

He laughed and held her tight. "I can't. You go."

"I have no choice. I have to go. You already said I would." She sighed. "Now what in the world do I wear to a tea party?"

Before she had time to decide, Lanny had hopped out of bed and returned with three maternity outfits from her corner of the walk-in closet. He laid them out at her feet, then passed her the bowl of vanilla ice cream he'd brought upstairs for her. She swallowed a big spoonful and pointed to the dress she liked the least. "That's the one. The one that looks the most polite." She swallowed another spoonful of the icy cold dessert and tried, unsuccessfully, to convince Lanny to take the next day off from work so he could come with her.

But the next morning she stood alone at her neighbor's front door, dressed in a subdued gray-blue tent, clutching a bouquet of orange chrysanthemums. She rang the bell exactly on time. As the door opened, she heard Barb call out, "Stop that, she's here."

Barb Cast was the perfectly put together real estate agent who cheerfully led her through what seemed like half the houses in Edgebury before Joy decided on the house right across the street from where Barb lived. In their dozens of quick jaunts in the sporty red Mercedes, she'd learned a lot about how Barb thought Mercedeses were better than Jaguars, but little about her new neighbor's life. All she knew was Barb was happily divorced. She was chirpy as a bird. She was nosy as a cat.

"You know," she said now as she grabbed Joy's hand and led her through her stark white living room into her dining room, where a glass table was covered with trays of fruit and cheese and crustless triangular sandwiches, "we were just talking about how your husband is such a doll. When I told him I was going to have a few neighbors over to meet you, he was worried. He told me you're shy." She let go of Joy's hand and pointed to a chair. "That man is a find, my dear, and you'd better hold on to him with both hands."

Joy's cheeks reddened, but she kept a smile plastered on her face. She nodded hello to the two other women seated across from her. One of them lifted a glass and drained it in a long gulp.

"The only time my husband ever worried about my being shy," she said in a gravelly voice, "was on my wedding night."

"That's our Sue," Barb sang out as she took her place at the head of the table. "Everybody, this is Joy."

Sue lifted her glass again in an empty toast. The other woman stood up and reached her pudgy hand across the table.

"I'm Donna. I'm normal. Don't worry."

Sue coughed out a hoarse chuckle. Barb looked at her reprovingly.

"Sue's a bit of a troublemaker," she added with affection. "She doesn't know how to beat around the bush."

"Oh, I remember." Sue snapped her fingers, ignoring the comment. "You're the ones who paid Charlie twenty bucks to help you unpack, right?"

The red color in Joy's cheeks deepened to burgundy. Halfway through the move, when the skies had opened and monsoon-strength rains began to drench them, Lanny had enlisted Sue's son Charlie and two of his teenage friends to help the movers unload the truck. The boys had stomped through the house in muddy sneakers like they owned the place, dragging rugs over piles of wet leaves, carrying cartons of dishes as if they were filled with indestructible bricks. They'd ignored Joy's pleas to be careful, making her feel like a piece of overstuffed furniture.

Charlie was the worst offender. He looked so sweet with

his bright rosy cheeks, his thick, shiny black hair, and his wide smile. But he paid no attention when she asked him not to leave a carton of glasses in the middle of the kitchen floor. And when she chased after him, grabbing out of his hand the Tiffany vase he was carrying casually by the handle, he rolled his eyes and thought she didn't hear when he muttered to his friends she was a wacko.

"What can we do for you next, Mr. Bard?" he'd asked Lanny, ever so politely, looking right through Joy.

Lanny put an arm around the boy's shoulders. "Let's see," he wondered aloud, his eyes taking in the cartons stacked around the perimeter of the living room. "Why don't you start unpacking that one."

"That's our china," Joy interrupted. "I want to unpack that box."

"Come on, honey," Lanny insisted. "You shouldn't be doing any lifting. The boys will be careful. Won't you boys?"

"Sure thing, Mr. Bard," Charlie replied, smiling broadly as he began slowly tearing apart sheets of crumpled newspaper, looking for teacups.

His friends watched, smirking. They had Joy pegged— nervous, tentative, an easy mark. Charlie had tested the waters, played out a quiet battle, and won the first round.

"Charlie helped us move, yes," Joy said, trying to sound like she meant it. "He was very helpful."

"Hah," Sue's laugh shot out, her eyes managing to look at her and through her at the same time. "Helpful. Nice try. Helpful." She swirled the ice cubes in her glass and sucked down what little water had melted.

Conversation jerked forward uneasily while Joy remained heedful of her promise to keep an open mind.

Finally the other guest of honor arrived. They had prepped her about Molly. She was also new to the block, having moved in three months earlier with her four-year-old daughter and her dog. Rumor had it her late husband had had a lot of money, but no one knew anything for sure because Molly was now busy going to law school and hadn't made much effort to get to know them. Barb had made it clear, this was her last chance.

Despite the warning, or because of it, Joy was drawn to her instantly. It was obvious Molly was an outsider. Even her clothes refused to blend in. In a room filled with mint green sweatsuits and hot pink warm-ups, she wore a long black skirt, black turtleneck, black boots, and bluntly cut short black hair. But most of all, with her arrival came a change in the air, a coolness that made Joy rise to her defense.

It was because of her dog, Cookie, and the boys, Charlie, Seth, and Dennis. Molly brought it up straight on, without rancor, as soon as she sat down at the table.

"I have to ask you all a favor."

Barb's face opened in a wide smile. Sue stared down into her glass. Donna raised her over-plucked eyebrows and waited.

"Could you tell your kids to try to remember to close my backyard gate when they cut through on their way home from school? Cookie got loose again. That's why I'm late."

Barb stiffened instantly. "You're supposed to keep her on a leash." She poured milk into a cup of tea and passed it down to Molly, unsolicited. "Isn't there a leash ordinance in town?" She looked at Donna who nodded. "Donna works up at town hall," Barb whispered to Joy with manufactured intimacy. "So if you need to know anything, you ask Donna."

Molly took a deep breath, then went on. "I really don't want to have to keep her on a leash when she's in my yard. So if the boys can't remember to close the gate, maybe they just shouldn't cut through back there at all."

The only sound was the tinkle of ice as Sue swirled her glass. She set it down, gently, and lit a cigarette, sending the smoke swirling up to the light fixture above her. "What makes you so sure it's our kids, anyway?" she got out between puffs, staring at the cloudy air.

"Well, you can ask them," Molly replied. "But I have to tell you, Sue. You may think I'm dumb, but I'm not blind. I've seen them from my kitchen window."

"You won't have a problem with Seth," Donna said quickly. "I'll see to it."

"What's the big deal, really?" Barb asked, beginning to pout. But before she could conjure up a serious frown, the front door slammed and she shot up out of her seat. The thud of a basketball hitting carpet drew closer until Dennis, Barb's son, appeared in the archway to the dining room.

Joy recognized him at once as one of the boys who'd helped with the move. His hair was like his mother's, the color of vanilla ice cream, and his eyes were such a pale shade of blue they were almost transparent.

"Don't bounce that ball in the house. And what are you doing home?" Barb's gray eyes narrowed into an angry squint.

"Half a day," Dennis said. "Hello, Mrs. Fischel," he said to Molly in a sing-song voice. "Hello, Mrs. Bard."

Joy hadn't even known he knew her name.

"Seth didn't say anything about half a day," Donna piped up. "Seth," she called. "Are you out there, too?"

The third boy who'd helped unload the truck appeared, a skinny kid with tight curls, as unkempt and nervous now as he'd been on the day she'd moved in, when he almost dropped the papier-mâché clock case her mother had given them on their first anniversary.

"Half a day?" Donna asked.

Joy saw Molly try to hide her smirk, and she saw Donna notice.

"Could we discuss it later, Ma?" Seth whined.

"Sure," Donna said. "We'll discuss it this evening with your father. Since you'll be home. Since you're grounded."

"Come on, Ma."

Molly untangled her lanky limbs and stood up. "I just came by to say a quick hello. I have to pick up Trina from nursery school."

Joy looked at her watch reflexively and then took a quick breath. She met her neighbor's stares with a weak smile. "I forgot. My mother's coming this morning. By train. You went to all this trouble. And I can't stay."

"Well," Barb said, her dimples deepening as her smile stiffened slightly. "We'll just have to do it again real soon then, won't we?"

Joy thanked everyone and followed Molly out as Barb waved from her front door.

"They really are a bunch of witches with juvenile delinquent sons," Molly said under her breath as they walked across the street. "The Weird Sisters in person."

"I'm glad you were there," Joy admitted. She was happy at the prospect of telling Lanny she'd met someone she wanted to befriend.

Molly smiled warmly. "Me, too. Why don't you give me a call? Maybe we can get together sometime. Do you know any single men?"

Joy thought of Lanny's associate, Ray, and then shook her head. "No one I could recommend."

"Great," Molly laughed. "I'm not ready for the rejects yet. Call me," she yelled as she ran up the block.

Joy watched her disappear into the dark brown house up where the road curved. Then she swung open her front door to the sound of a ringing telephone echoing angrily off the naked walls.

CHAPTER THREE

"I'VE BEEN CALLING for half an hour," her mother, Dorothy, announced in a clipped voice. "I'm standing in the middle of nowhere. Thank God there's a phone. Did you forget I was coming?"

Joy promised to be there in a minute, grabbed her silver heart key chain from the dish on the antique secretary in the hall, and ran out of the house. The automatic garage door was halfway up when she remembered Lanny had taken the car in to be inspected. She ran all the way to the train station, holding her stomach to try to stop the sharp tightening of her uterus, practice contractions that had just begun.

From two blocks away she recognized the erect posture, the perfectly coordinated green wool plaid suit, the sensible heels that clicked on the concrete as her mother paced in front of the train station steps. There was no greeting. They simply plunged into arguing over who was going to carry Dorothy's heavy leather case, stuffed with wallpaper swatches and fabric samples. As usual her mother won.

They walked in silence, Dorothy awkwardly moving her case from hand to hand, sighing just loudly enough for Joy to hear. When they got to the house, she touched her mother's arm. Dorothy pulled the case away and snapped, "I said I'd carry it."

"We're here," Joy announced. "My house."

Dorothy stretched back her long neck, taking it all in while Joy waited, resigned. If Lanny had picked the house, Dorothy would have gushed with compliments. But he had already boasted that Joy had found the house on her own. The criticism was going to come swiftly and cut deeply.

She followed her mother inside, watching the back of the swanlike neck shift from right to left as she glided through the rooms, a motorized china doll. Her large suspicious eyes scanned the faded floral wallpaper, the worn oak floors, the paint-chipped chair rails.

"Do you want to see the rest?" Joy asked when they circled back around to the foot of the stairs.

Dorothy shook her head dramatically and retreated to the small parlor off the front hall, to the dark green velvet sofa that Lanny had just gotten out of storage. She tried to settle into the couch, but it was firmly uninviting to human shoulders. "I'm not sure I can take anymore," she announced wearily.

Joy sat stiffly in the wing chair facing her, her legs crossed tightly.

"I'm amazed," Dorothy muttered.

Joy glanced up at the high ceiling and waited.

"It's a shock, really," Dorothy went on in her disappointed voice. "That you didn't tell me. You could have told me."

"Told you what?"

"How it's practically identical to our house."

Joy felt the room get close, stuffy, no air.

"What house?"

"What house? The house in Toney's Brook. What other house was there?"

Joy laughed nervously and then caught herself and stopped.

"What's so funny? Are you making fun of me?"

"No," Joy said. She fought the urge to giggle as it bubbled up inside her, inappropriate and unstoppable. The half-suppressed laugh burst out and Dorothy glared. "I'm sorry. I'm just laughing because it's crazy. I'm crazy. I haven't thought of that house in years. If you asked me what the house I grew up in looked like, I couldn't tell you. I don't remember it. And now you tell me it looked like this."

"Don't start that memory thing with me," Dorothy said in an angry monotone.

The subject was a sore point between them. There were things Joy couldn't remember, big chunks of her childhood. As if everything that had happened before she moved into the Upper West Side apartment that Dorothy still called home was lost in a fog. She'd moved when she was a teenager, and ever since then the memories had faded, like patterns of old wallpaper, getting paler and dimmer until they vanished, without her noticing they were going. Without her noticing they were gone.

It was Christmas vacation, her first year at the Rhode Island School of Design, when she came home and angrily reported that her roommate Liv remembered all kinds of details of her childhood and adolescence. She remembered her first sleep over, getting her first period, the day her mother explained about sex. "Why," Joy demanded to know, "don't I remember anything like that?"

"Things are forgotten for a reason," Dorothy barked, her anger flaring up like a wooden match struck on a brick wall. "You haven't forgotten anything worth remembering. There's absolutely no good to come from looking to the past." She had refused to discuss it further.

Lanny was no help either. He was one of the few things Joy did remember. He had been their next-door neighbor in Toney's Brook, her brother's best friend, growing up. They'd lost touch when she'd moved away, until Lanny, just out of law school, surprised her by appearing one night at her mother's front door. Dorothy welcomed him in, thrilled with the visit, gushing over him as if he were her long lost son. Then she retired to her bedroom, leaving Joy alone with her guest, hoping for the impossible, that they would fall in love.

They did. While they caught up on the years gone by, they shared the excitement of discovering a kindred spirit. It was a nice surprise for Joy: the boy next door, who'd had dirty nails and ants in his pants, had turned into a handsome, charismatic man. For Lanny it was as he'd always suspected. Buddy's feisty skinny sister had flowered into a delicate beauty.

That first night Joy probed the tender spot, sliding the question in while Lanny was looking through her portfolio, at the sketches she was compiling to submit to publishers. "Do you remember much about Buddy?"

"If we're going to be spending any time together," he jumped in quickly, before she could ask more, "which I've always hoped we would, then we have to have an understanding. We have to promise each other that we'll forget about Buddy, about talking about what happened, about dwelling on that part of our lives. Otherwise, his ghost will drag us down."

It was easy to agree to give up talking about what she couldn't remember, so that she could have what she knew she wanted. With Lanny she found instant peace.

* * *

"Trust me." Dorothy called her back to the present. "The houses are identical. Let's leave it at that." She looked around the room at the old cracked walls and sighed. "It even has the same smell. That old house smell. You know you can never get rid of it."

Joy breathed deeply through her nose. There was an odor of damp walls and old plaster. Lanny had mentioned it the first time she'd taken him through the house. He said it reminded him of dead worms and was surprised to hear that Joy liked it, that the smell comforted her. He'd never mentioned it looked like her old house in Toney's Brook. She giggled nervously.

Her mother's harsh voice lashed out, "This little game is not the least bit funny."

Joy tried to swallow her laugh. "Why didn't Lanny say something? He must have noticed it. Why didn't he say?"

"Because he's probably as irritated by your selective memory as I am." She set her case down on the coffee table and snapped open the latches. "You've bought the house so that's that. Now let's just try to do something about the way it looks." She laid several large swatches out on the mahogany coffee table. "Let's start with these awful walls."

Joy scanned the room, waiting for some memory to click in. "Did our house really look like this?"

Dorothy stood up. "You know, people pay me a lot of money to decorate their homes. So if you'd like my help, which, I might add, you desperately need, you'll have to treat me like a professional. I am not interested now, nor have I ever been, in dredging up the past with you. Is that understood?"

Joy closed her eyes and tried to imagine herself as a young girl, tried to conjure up an image of her brother, but she couldn't. When she opened her eyes again, her mother was anxiously staring back at her. Joy pushed on. "How come I don't have any pictures? Don't you have any pictures from when I was growing up?"

"Oh, Lord. I don't know." Dorothy sighed loudly, pulling

the last of the swatches out of her case. "Will you please stop upsetting yourself?"

Joy laughed again, a dizzying nervous laugh. "Why don't I remember that house?"

Dorothy sighed again, losing several inches of her height. "Joy. Let it go. Leave it be."

"Just tell me. How old was I when we moved to the apartment in Manhattan?"

Her mother's mouth twisted into a tight circle, as if that would stop the conversation, stop the words from coming. "I will answer this one last question if you promise this is the last question you'll ask."

Joy nodded and drew her teeth over her bottom lip, waiting.

"You were thirteen," Dorothy said. "End of discussion."

It must have been a busy year, Joy thought, the year I turned thirteen, the year that Buddy was kidnapped.

"Joy. Look here," her mother called.

And the thought was gone as she looked at the pale rose swatch Dorothy held before her, and tasted the salty flavor of her own blood, where she had just bitten her lip.

CHAPTER FOUR

DISTRACTED, SHE WENT through the motions but got things all wrong. Touching squares of flannel, she called them silk. She passed the primrose swatch when asked to hand over the linen white.

Finally, disgusted, Dorothy grabbed her swatches, threw them in her case, and snapped it shut.

"It doesn't matter to me," Joy explained wearily. "They're all lovely."

"I will not decide on your walls for you," Dorothy declared, "only to have you complain about them forever after."

Joy was about to suggest they finish another day when Dorothy snapped, "Where's my coat?" As Joy held open the tweed jacket, her mother slipped her arm through the silky sleeve lining and muttered, "This was a huge mistake." Then she let herself out, pulling the door closed behind her with a double-handed yank.

Joy watched through the front door peephole as her mother disappeared up the block to the train. Then, unnerved and jittery, she roamed the rooms, waiting for some feeling of familiarity to come over her. She walked through the small living room, the only room filled with their own furniture. Their Gramercy Park module couch looked completely out of place here, but she still preferred it to the dusty, dark furniture in the parlor that Lanny had inherited from his grandmother, or the heavy rococo pieces from his parents that made their bedroom feel so claustrophobic.

Slowly she moved past the empty breakfast nook and the old butler's pantry, still crowded with unpacked cartons. She stepped around the boxes and continued on, pausing in front of the tiny pale pink powder room. Sliding closed the thin pocket door, she thought, this was the broom closet. It had whisk brooms and dust mops leaning against the wall, cleaning supplies stacked on high shelves, ironed kitchen towels piled below.

She shook off a chill and the memory went with it. Lanny was right. She was overwrought. Anxious because she had fallen behind in her work. The babies shifted, and her stomach tightened with another Braxton-Hicks contraction. She had to calm down. She lifted her heavy body up the creaky stairs to her third-floor studio.

When she opened the door to the odd-sized room that

made up the finished half of the attic, she felt instant relief. It was bright, with windows beneath the sloping ceiling from which she could see the street and the yard. Two more windows, half-moons made of leaded glass, sent a speckled pattern of late afternoon light over the hardwood floor. Lanny had set up her drafting table in the sunniest spot, next to the biggest window facing out back.

As if he'd been able to predict what she'd want to do, he'd dug out her X-Acto knife and left it lying in the middle of the drafting table. With it she slashed through the packing tape of the nearest box and lifted out the coffee cans she used to store her brushes. Underneath she found the brushes, carefully boxed. She unpacked them gingerly, touching her cheek with the soft bristles of the biggest one. Her shoulders unhunched.

She stuck the brushes in the cans and placed them on top of the paint-splattered bookcase next to the wall. On the shelf below she lined up the squashed tubes of oil paint, carefully arranging them by color. On the bottom she placed the jug of mineral spirits and the small bottles of oil of cloves and cobalt dryer. She pulled her glass palette out of its newspaper envelope and breathed in the smell of the oil paint. As she placed her scraper on the drafting table, the muscles in her neck began to unknot.

The two cartons of reference books and old contact sheets and photographs would have to wait to be unpacked another day. Anna-Marie, her art director, was waiting for a completed pencil sketch. As soon as that was approved, Joy could start her book cover painting. She was itching to start painting.

After digging around through two more cartons, she found the folder with the photographs of last week's modeling session. She pulled out the art instructions, two typed pages that told her everything she needed to know about the book at hand. The capsule synopsis refreshed her memory.

"Occult novel, beach setting, summertime, summerhouse.

A corpse dangles from a rope swung around the nozzle of an outdoor shower, neck slit, blood already dry."

She found the tin box that held her mechanical pencil and lead. The thinnest lead was her favorite to start with. She filled the pencil and began to draw. Her hand traced the lines of a room, a small room, the outdoor shower, but bigger, more like a shed, an old wood shed. A figure emerged, running in the trees in the distance. She looked up, and back.

There was no moon, just hundreds of stars, and all around her fireflies blinked and vanished, leaving trails of fading light behind.

"This is our clubhouse," Lanny whispered, and she struggled to see. "Do you want to come in?"

Something was going to happen. Lanny touched her thick braid, tugging at it gently. It was so dark she could barely see him. She stepped into the clubhouse slowly, her feet hitting the plank floor with hollow thuds, as if the shed was lifted off the ground.

It was too hot, too dark. She opened her mouth, about to speak, when a figure leapt out of the blackness, screaming wildly. It brushed up against her, and she felt the soft flannel of Buddy's favorite shirt, the one he wore every day; the green and blue plaid faded, both elbows worn through with holes.

She tore away from him and ran down the street, while from behind she could hear Buddy mimicking Lanny's hearty laugh. But she didn't turn around, and she didn't stop running until the sound had faded, his laughter replaced by the chug of an oncoming train.

The tip of the mechanical pencil dug into the page, tearing it, and then broke off. She stared at the picture before her, running her finger over the images, as if to make sure they were real. She hadn't thought of the clubhouse in years. It surprised her that the memory was unsettling. Staring at the picture now made her cringe, as if she were re-living an old insult she hadn't realized still hurt.

She stuck the drawing inside a book at the top of the nearest carton, a coffee table collection of old horror movie stills. Then, feeling calmer, she adjusted the lead in her pencil and looked back at her notes.

"Beautiful woman, dead, in her bathrobe in the fore-ground; man looming in the shadows, gaunt demonic face; in background, the house, and farther beyond, the sea."

At the bottom of the page Anna-Marie had stapled a two-by-two photo, cut out from a magazine, of a sinister-looking man with hollow cheeks and bad skin. A yellow Post-It note was stuck on top, obscuring one hooded eye, instructing her to "make him look something like this, only younger."

She closed her eyes to clear her head and then began to draw. She gave the roof a turret and the windows thin shut-ters decorated with half-moon crescent cutouts. On either side of the house she added a wide brick chimney, for cold night fires. This is no beach house, she thought, as she drew the tops of the chimneys, spiked with ridges like chess piece castles. But she went on.

With her gum eraser she turned the front deck entrance to pink dust, replacing it with a wide porch that wrapped around one side. On the other side she added an addition, a square box of a room with six small windows along the top and a metal handle at the bottom. It was a garage door. She had given the house an attached garage.

One by one she blackened the windows until the lead snapped again, leaving the last square with the look of jag-ged glass. She picked up the paper and stared at it. This was no beach house. This was her house, the house she was in now, but something was off.

Slowly she moved out of her studio, down three flights of stairs, out the front door to the street. Clutching the drawing in one hand, she scanned the pale blue shingles on the house in front of her. There was only one chimney, not two, and the shutters didn't have crescent moons. The detached garage sat, like a distant cousin, on the other side of the backyard. But everything else—the slope of the roof, the wrap-around porch, the windows, the shape, the style, the size—was exactly the same.

"You're the house in Toney's Brook," she said to the sketch, and then she looked up, suddenly aware that she had spoken aloud and that she wasn't alone. Across the street, on Barb's front steps, Charlie, Seth, and Dennis sat, watching her.

In slow motion, Charlie stood up and lifted his head to gaze at his house. Then he turned, slowly, like a top winding down, a dazed expression on his face. Dennis joined him next, then Seth. The three boys lazily spun in place, staring blankly at the house, the trees, the sky, at Joy. Suddenly she realized they were imitating her.

Her face flushed, she retreated to the house, her eyes stuck to the drawing in her hands. She grabbed the phone and dialed quickly, surprising herself with her urgency.

"This is Dorothy Ash," her mother's over-articulated, phone-machine voice greeted her. "I do want to talk to you, so please leave your name and number and I'll call you back."

"Mom, it's Joy." She paused to better frame her thoughts. "I have a question about our house, in Toney's Brook." Suddenly she knew how silly it would sound, but she pressed on. "Were there half moons on the shutters?" She laughed at herself, nervously, forgetting for a moment that she was being recorded. Then she caught herself, sobering instantly. "If you have any photographs, can I see them? You must have some pictures," she added, as if Dorothy had already balked at the request.

When she hung up the phone, gently placing the receiver in the cradle, she felt a rush of adrenaline. For the first time in years the memories were close, within reach. Then abruptly they were pushed aside by the sound of pounding rain.

She was racing to close the dining room windows when she noticed the sheets of rain were only falling on the front of the house. She grabbed her umbrella from the over-stuffed closet, leaving the two winter coats that slipped off their hangers lying on the floor.

Hiding under her umbrella, she walked down her front path to look at the freak storm. Then she saw the boys. They stood at the edge of her lawn, holding her garden hose pointed up to the sky. The water careened down the front of the house, drenching it.

"What are you doing?" she shouted as she moved away from the spray and tried to close the umbrella. It fought her, stuck half-open.

Charlie motioned to Seth who disappeared to turn off the faucet. When the arc of water dropped to a tiny sputter he said simply, "Mr. Bard hired us to do some yard work."

"What kind of yard work was that?" she asked, her voice tight, wound up.

Dennis stepped forward. "We call it watering the lawn." The boys all laughed.

"I'll water my own lawn, thank you." She grabbed the nozzle away from Charlie. He looked at his empty hand as if he didn't know what to do with it.

"Mr. Bard asked us to rake the leaves and clean up the yard," he reported, not budging.

"And I'm telling you not to bother." Her voice cracked, but her eyes were unblinking.

"You two better get it together," Dennis said. Then Charlie turned and walked across the damp grass. His friends stepped in the squashed imprints of his footsteps, bouncing along as if they owned the world.

When they reached the sidewalk, Charlie stopped and swiveled to face her. "Mr. Bard paid us ten bucks each to rake up the leaves in front and back, and we're going to rake up the leaves in front and back."

Joy watched him saunter away. She thought of calling the police, but she knew it would sound silly, complaining of being threatened with having her leaves raked. So instead she went in to make dinner. As she sautéd onions and garlic and rinsed the chicken under warm water, she let ev-

erything else fade away, forgotten. Including the drawing of
the house she grew up in that lay on the kitchen table like
a blueprint of her mind.

CHAPTER
FIVE

"I MEANT TO call you, but I didn't have time,"
Lanny whispered as they huddled in a corner of the kitchen.
"We have to finish writing this motion tonight. At least this
way I get to see you for dinner." He grabbed her in a tight
bear hug.

She pulled away and eyed the chicken suspiciously. "I
don't think we have enough food. All I have to go with it
are mashed potatoes and peas."

"Hey. Not to worry. Ray's single. He's been dying to eat
a home-cooked meal for a change."

The stairs creaked under Ray's heavy weight as he came
down from a self-guided house tour. "What a place," he
called out as he joined them, looking everywhere. "You two
are a couple of lucky ducks." He walked the circumference
of the kitchen, his eyes wide. "And this kitchen. Big
enough to eat in. With a microwave and everything."

"Lanny tells me you've got a terrific place in the Village."

"Come on. Get out. It's a closet." Ray pulled a piece of
crisp skin off the chicken Joy had just finished carving. He
grabbed a paper napkin and wiped his fingers, his mouth,
then blew his nose. "Put it this way. I could reach the stove

from the toilet, if I wanted to. But I never eat there. I don't even know if my toaster works." He wandered to the kitchen table. "Great drawing," he said, lifting up the sketch of the house Joy had left there, forgotten. "Is it for a book cover you're working on?"

Lanny walked behind him to get a look.

She ignored Ray's question. "Lanny, don't you recognize it? It's my old house in Toney's Brook."

Lanny took the picture from Ray who grabbed another piece of chicken off the platter and then helped himself to a bottle of beer to wash it down.

"So it is. What did you do? Copy it from a photograph?"

Joy drew a deep breath to stop herself from asking why he hadn't seen the similarity in the houses either. She struggled to keep from telling him about the feeling she was having, of her memory tickling her, teasing her. She desperately wanted to describe how the sketch of the house had poured out of her, unsummoned. She just didn't want to say any of it in front of Ray.

"What are you two now, the most talented couple in Edgebury?" Ray asked, interrupting her thoughts.

Lanny threw his arm around Ray's shoulder. "Hey, guy, what do you say we have a drink, relax, eat dinner? Then we can get to work."

The men wandered into the living room, leaving Joy alone. She considered calling Lanny back in, but when she heard his easy, untroubled laugh, she decided she would wait until later. She shook a can of Le Sueur peas, to get out the ones that stuck to the bottom. But she couldn't shake off the feeling of dread that inexplicably enveloped her.

Adding milk to the mashed potatoes, she whipped them creamy and smooth, the way Lanny liked them. Then, while the peas heated, she sat down at the kitchen table, turned over the sketch of the house, and began to draw on the blank side.

A face came, a long face, with small, oval eyes, freckles, and a full mouth. It was herself as a girl. But as she added short curly hair, and made the face a little fuller, it changed into her twin brother, Buddy.

A hand touched her shoulder. She dropped her pencil and tipped over the glass of club soda Lanny had poured for her.

"What's wrong with you?" he asked. "Are you feeling okay?"

He knelt down next to her, ducking under the table to help mop up the spill. She looked into his piercing blue eyes, then whispered, "they're coming back."

"Who is?" He put his hand on her cheek and held it there.

"The memories. They're coming back."

Lanny got up, banging his head on the corner of the table. "Now is not a good time. We have a guest." He took her hand and pulled her up.

"It's because of this house," she went on. "Why didn't you tell me this house looked like my old house?"

Lanny looked around. "I don't know. Lots of houses look alike. Why are you so upset? Come on. We have company."

It wasn't what she wanted. She wanted him to tell Ray to go home.

"Honey, look. The peas are turning to mush." He stirred the mixture with a wooden spoon, his back to her. She had failed him again.

She grabbed the spoon. "Go inside with Ray, and I'll bring everything in." For a moment she stood watching him glide out of the room. Then she dumped the overcooked peas in a glass bowl. As she carried it past the kitchen table, she picked up the damp sketch of Buddy and stuck it in the pocket of her dress.

"Now, Ray," Lanny said as Joy took her seat at the foot of the table, "You've got to admit, this is home cooking."

"I'll tell you," Ray said to Joy as he scooped a double portion of mashed potatoes on his plate. "Lanny said he wanted to get home so he could see you, which I'm sure is true. But I also think he asked me over because he wanted to rub in my face what a life he's got here."

"What do you mean, Ray?" Lanny asked, unable to conceal his eagerness to hear more.

"Come on. Get out. You know. This house. This wife. This life. A kid on the way."

"Two," Lanny reminded him, looking at Joy with affection, as if nothing was wrong.

"Two kids on the way. It's perfect." Ray looked at Joy for confirmation. She forced a small smile. A foot kicked her under the table. When she looked over at Lanny he was busy pressing microscopic lumps out of his creamy potatoes.

The conversation didn't take long to turn to the office. The three-million-dollar merger Lanny was trying to close was looking unsteady again. Berger was leaning on them hard. The mergers and acquisitions department was nearly at a standstill. If this one didn't work out, Lanny could end up transferred two rungs down the ladder, to the corporate work-out group.

They finished trashing the litigation department's overspending and bragging how Ray was the only associate who wasn't afraid of hard work. When they settled down to discuss the details of the latest sexual exploits of their paralegal, Joy pushed back her chair and began clearing. She ducked out of the room without anyone noticing she was gone.

In the pantry she found an unopened box of chocolate chip cookies and laid a dozen out on a small plate. Then, as she waited for the coffee to brew, she sat down and started drawing again on the yellow legal pad Lanny had left on the counter. She had never drawn him like this before: Lanny as a teenager.

"What are you doing?" Lanny asked, breaking the silence as he pushed in the kitchen door. He glanced over his shoulder and watched the door swing back and forth, rhythmically. "We have company here. What are you doing?"

Quickly Joy scribbled over the face, hiding it under a tangle of circles and jagged lines.

"You're talking business," she said casually. "I thought you wanted to be alone."

"If I wanted to be alone I would have stayed at the office. I brought Ray here to work so I could see you."

"Here I am."

Lanny compressed his forehead into a web of creases. He sat across from her and grabbed her hand, running his finger over the lines in her palm, waiting for the door to settle, quietly, at rest.

"What's going on?" he whispered. "You're not yourself."

"I keep trying to tell you, but you don't let me." Her voice rose, her anger surging. "Being in this house. I have the oddest feeling. Moments of my childhood suddenly pop into focus and then, before I can hold on to them, they disappear."

Lanny sighed, looked at his lap, and leaned closer. "I'm not sure that's such a good thing."

"What do you mean?"

"Well, look at you. You're all agitated. You're snapping at me. You're not yourself."

The door swung open and Ray walked in carrying two plates and a picked-clean platter balanced on his forearm.

"Oh," he said, sensing something. "Sorry. Didn't mean to interrupt."

Lanny got up out of his seat. "Hey. Don't worry. We were just grabbing a second together." He turned to Joy, his eyes flashing brighter. "Honey. Why don't you leave the dishes? I'll take care of the coffee. You relax. Go to bed. We'll clean up."

"I'm not tired," she said as she started scraping the leftover food off the cream-colored dinner plates.

"Well then, why don't you go watch some TV?"

She stared at Lanny wishing he would read her mind and get rid of Ray.

"Go ahead. Lie down. We have work to do." He patted her belly. "Give those kids a rest."

"I'm going for a walk," she said.

Lanny pressed his lips together, then managed to smile. "Okay. Just don't get lost."

Ray's eyes traveled back and forth between them. Then

he laughed. "Don't get lost," he repeated, pretending he got the joke.

Lanny laughed, too. "Let's go, guy." He elbowed Ray. "Let's get that sweetheart letter out of the way, and then we can work on the motion."

Joy didn't join in the shared laughter. It was a dig that hurt. She did get disoriented easily. Just last week when they went to buy art supplies, she'd walked up to a woman in the store, stepped aside to let her pass, and discovered, to her embarrassment, she was deferring to her own reflection in a wall of mirrors.

Lanny and Ray disappeared into the dining room while she took the long way around to the upstairs bathroom, to avoid them. But even through the closed door she could hear the electronic beeps coming out of the phone on Lanny's night table. They were in the kitchen again, calling colleagues, bouncing off ideas, checking facts, picking brains.

Suddenly, she hated that phone. At first she'd found it funny. A housewarming gift from Kelly, Lanny's secretary, it was shaped like a man's loafer so you had to hold the toe to your ear and talk into the heel. But as if simply being ugly wasn't bad enough, there was a glitch in the circuitry so that whenever anyone dialed from another phone in the house, the bedside phone beeped, tiny electronic hiccups, loud enough to have woken her from a dead sleep on two occasions.

The first time it happened, she'd gone to bed early while Lanny stayed up in the living room to watch the news. But unable to do one thing at a time, he'd started working and ended up calling Ray from the kitchen phone at one A.M., to straighten out some details. The electronic beeps had cut through her sleep and sent her flying out of bed in a muddled stupor as she tried to locate the source of the irritating noise.

She would have thrown the phone away right then, but Lanny insisted he could fix it. It was something he was proud of, his ability to fix things. His father had been a mechanical genius whose favorite pastime was taking apart the kitchen appliances. Then, after unscrewing the ceiling bulb, he'd watch Lanny struggle in the dark to put them back together. It was one of the few stories about his father Lanny liked to tell. How their kitchen was a veritable fix-it shop where toast was burned, clocks were stopped, and radios rattled while Lanny battled wires and nuts and heating elements, trying to find his way, blind. Lanny learned eventually, his hands still bearing scars of several electrical burns. But now there was nothing he was afraid to put back to together. And nothing he was afraid to break.

She returned downstairs, stopping in to wave good-bye. Lanny was still deep in conversation on the phone. She let the back door bang behind her.

Halfway down the block she heard footsteps, then heavy breathing, coming closer.

"Joy."

She swung around to see Lanny coming toward her, his white face emerging out of the blackness like a disembodied head.

"Here." He handed her his old denim jacket that now barely covered her full breasts. "I'm worried about you."

She softened and replied, "I'm all right."

He brushed her hair off her face, away from her eyes. "Are you sure?"

She took a deep breath and sighed. "I'm sure. I just want to remember, that's all. Because the babies are coming. I want to be able to tell my children about my life. Is that so crazy?"

"What's crazy is, if it upsets you, you shouldn't push it. You should just leave it alone."

Her spine stiffened with the echo of Dorothy's words. "Lanny, I need you to help me with this."

He stared down into the blackness that had wrapped around his feet. "Sure," he answered quietly. "I'll help you. I'll help you pack, and I'll help you move. Because I think this house is bad for your health."

A Braxton-Hicks contraction squeezed her, the worst one

yet. She forced her body to keep still, but even in the black night Lanny noticed her eyes narrow with pain.

"And the health of your babies," he went on. "Don't you care about that? Are you that selfish?"

"Lanny?" Ray's voice boomed into the silent street. "Lanny? Berger's on the phone for you."

"Shit," Lanny said. "Come in soon," he called as he ran back to the house. "It's cold." His voice was hard and tense. His strong frame disappeared into the shadows.

A tentative smile nervously stretched itself across Joy's face. It wasn't like Lanny to get so worked up. Yet in a way, his sudden bad temper was a relief. It humanized him. It meant even the hardest worker, the best friend, the most considerate neighbor, Lanny Bard, wasn't perfect.

In the morning, reason would prevail. She would help him see that working to collect her memories wasn't selfish. It was important. It was for the children. She thought of them, two little infants, a boy and a girl, with blank faces, patiently waiting for their mother to tell them the story of her life. She stopped walking and looked around. She had no idea where she was.

Authentic gas lamps dotted the slate walks with low flames that burned like dim candles. A faint glow struggled to illuminate the iron posts. The darkness was now nearly complete. She was swallowed up in it. It took her a moment to figure out she had walked, lost in thought, around the block.

She turned back toward home, quickening her pace until she rounded the corner. Another contraction came, and she forced herself to slow down, pausing to massage her swollen belly in front of a large house that blazed with lights and the sounds of children's laughter. Spotlights lit the elaborate swing set in the backyard, the empty swings swaying gently in the wind.

There were swings in her backyard in Toney's Brook, she thought suddenly. Steel frames painted forest green. A matching set of monkey bars sat beside it, on clumpy uneven grass. She could see herself hanging upside down, knees and feet hooked under the middle bar. She could see Buddy on the swings, pumping crooked, yelling something, sounding desperate. She could smell the ground up close, her nose tickled by dandelions, the blood rushing to her forehead.

Suddenly she felt nauseous. The street was too quiet, too dark. She was dizzy and weak-kneed. Her footsteps echoed loudly as she hurried toward the dark outline of her house.

"Joy."

The unfamiliar voice reached out to her as softly as the breeze, so softly at first she thought she'd whispered it herself. Then it came again, a young voice, a taunting voice, coming from the bushes or the trees.

"Joy Bard," once more, out of the darkness.

She froze. A branch scraped the roof of a garage. Her shallow breathing sounded too loud. She cleared her throat, then turned her head slowly, to one side, to the other. She spun around quickly, to confront the presence she felt behind her. But she was alone in the black night of a new moon.

Her feet flew through the oppressive blackness until she stumbled, nearly falling over a large warm mound. As she found her balance, the mound moved. Something wet touched her hand. She pulled away and tried to scream, but her throat was so tight her voice came out like a weak whimper. Then she heard panting. It was a dog.

Cautiously she approached the animal, making out the friendly shape of a Golden Lab with a collar and a license, dragging a leash. The Lab's tail wagged excitedly as he licked her hand again. She picked up the end of his leash, and he fell into step beside her, as if she'd always been his master. When they were directly under the street lamp, she was able to make out the name on the license. It was Cookie.

"Come on, girl," she called. Cookie walked obediently at her side as she led her home.

"I thought she was still out back," Molly said when she opened the front door and watched Cookie run into the kitchen to her water dish. "Thank you for bringing her over. Do you want to come in?"

"I can't," Joy demurred. "I have to get home. It's late."

"I'm sure I closed the gate back there. I know I did. It's those damned kids again."

Suddenly Joy thought of the voice calling her name, only now there was a face to go with it. It was Charlie's face.

Molly followed her down the front steps. "I'll watch you till you're inside."

On another night Joy would have told her not to bother, but tonight she just said, "Thanks."

She was only steps away from Molly's house when a car pulled up alongside her and slowed down. Keeping her eyes straight ahead she pretended to ignore it. Then she glanced at the road. It was her car. It was Lanny.

"Where the hell have you been?" he called through the open window. "You said you were coming right home. I've been worried out of my mind."

"I am coming right home. I found a dog. That's all. I returned a dog."

"Don't you think about anyone but yourself? Didn't you think about how worried I'd be?"

"Joy? Are you okay?" Molly jogged over with Cookie, who made a poor watchdog, panting merrily, her enthusiastic tail wacking Joy's leg.

"Oh, Molly. I'm sorry. It's just my husband."

Lanny turned off the car and hopped out.

"Hi," he said. "I'm Lanny. Just her husband. Out looking for her. It's amazing how hyperactive your imagination can get when your wife is six months' pregnant with twins."

"How chivalrous," Molly responded, clearly impressed.

"What do you say we call it a night?" He walked around to the passenger door and swung it open.

"Thanks again, Joy," Molly said. "And call me. I'd like to get together."

Joy smiled her thanks and watched Molly disappear into her house. Then Lanny slammed the car door shut. They sat enveloped in thick silence.

"Something is very wrong here," Lanny finally said as the car coasted into the driveway. He pressed the electric garage door opener. "You're acting like a child. Completely irresponsible."

She began to tremble, a mixture of exhaustion and anger, but she held back her tears. Lanny didn't have patience for emotional scenes. If she cried it would only get worse.

He swung open the front door, and Joy disappeared up the stairs to the bedroom. She undressed and washed quickly, settling in under the weight of the heavy down quilt.

She was floating at the edge of sleep when she heard her name called out again. Her eyes snapped open, and she listened. But the only sounds were the distant chatter of the television, and an occasional creak, the old house breathing, contracting, and expanding in the night.

It was after three when Lanny came to bed, crawling in carefully and curling his body around hers, a sleepy attempt at reconciliation. Then he felt something wet and cold on his thigh. He threw back the covers with a wind that woke Joy with a start.

Her eyes snapped open. "What is it?"

He pointed somberly to the circle of blood on the sheet where she had just been lying.

CHAPTER SIX

"LET'S LEAVE THE worrying to me," Dr. Wayne said as he drummed his fingertips together.

His nurse, Madeleine, hovered in a corner against the

wall, staring at her thick white shoes while she fingered the slit at the top of a box of latex gloves.

"How's Lanny?" he asked.

"Fine," Joy got out, unable to make small talk. "Why did I stain?"

"Well, many of my patients stain," he went on, back on track. "Although at this point in the pregnancy it is more serious." He flipped through the pages of her file, holding them inches from his nearsighted eyes. Then he dropped the file on the counter.

"We have a problem."

She felt herself sink, heavy and tired.

"I understand you're still working with paints and chemicals in a small room. At all hours of the night."

Her spine stiffened. "Did the chemicals cause the staining?"

"I'm not saying that. But you may be working too hard. Your mother is worried."

It wasn't the first time she regretted her decision to use her mother's obstetrician, the same man who'd delivered her thirty years ago.

"Lanny is concerned, too. He tells me you've moved, and that you're under considerable stress."

"Can stress cause bleeding?"

"Let me ask you a question. Do you feel all right?"

"No. I'm worried. About the staining."

"Well, no more worrying for you. From now on I'm the only one allowed to worry around here. You have to stay calm. Remember, your stress is your children's stress. Your worry is their worry. So no more worrying. Just go home and relax. Go to bed. Stop working. Don't upset yourself. Just relax." He looked at Madeleine and chuckled. "How many people would love for their doctor to order them to relax."

The nurse smiled, as if on cue.

"Why did it take so long for Madeleine to find the heartbeats?"

The nurse looked back at her shoes.

"Who's the doctor here?" he snapped.

Joy didn't answer.

"Twins are tricky. Maybe they're playing hide and seek. Trust me, we're going to find out. But you have to stop worrying."

Her toes curled under as he brought his hands together as if in prayer.

"Tell me, Joy, did I do such a bad job of bringing you into the world?" He rested his hand on her shoulder for a second, then picked up the chart and opened the door. "Madeleine will call to get you an appointment for a sonogram. By the time you walk over to the radiologist's office, they'll be ready for you."

But when she got there, they weren't ready. There were two dozen people anxiously waiting before her. Under orders to have a full bladder, she sat for an hour with her legs tightly crossed. Barely able to walk, she made her way to the receptionist and borrowed the phone. Lanny had left word with Berger's secretary to get him out of the meeting the minute she called.

"So? What happened? Is everything okay?"

"I don't know. I guess so." Joy tried to walk away, to find a corner of privacy, but she was held in place by the tightly coiled phone cord. "I'm still waiting to have the sonogram."

"Hang in there, honey. And call me as soon as it's over. I'm sorry I can't be with you."

"Joy Bard?" An overweight technician in a snug white lab coat and lime green pants that matched the walls surveyed the crowd, fanning himself with her file.

"Love you," Joy said quickly. Clumsily she reached through the receptionist's glass window to pass back the phone. She couldn't afford to lose her turn. Her bladder ached so badly now she could barely stand.

Following the technician she waddled down a narrow hallway to a cubicle the size of a phone booth. Grabbing a paper gown from a tall stack, she put it on backward twice, before figuring out its simple configuration. She could see the technician's shadow as he hovered on the other side of the louver doors. When she emerged he was already pointing the way to the small windowless exam room where the sonogram equipment sat, awaiting her.

"Relax, relax, relax," she chanted to herself. But she couldn't stop wondering how long it would take to find a new doctor, one who listened to her, not her mother or her husband.

As she tried to imagine what she could say to convince Lanny and Dorothy that this late in the pregnancy switching doctors was a good idea, the door opened. The technician walked in, followed by a short, squat man.

"Hello, I'm Dr. Blau," the man introduced himself in a flat, disinterested voice. He offered her his limp hand. "Lie down, please," he instructed, letting his hand drop to his side.

Joy lay on her back on the cold exam table, the waxy paper crinkling as she shifted her weight. The technician rubbed something greasy and cold on her stomach.

"What is that?" she asked.

The technician looked over to the doctor, who was washing his hands at a small sink.

"I'll be with you in just a minute." He washed slowly, rubbing the liquid soap up and down each finger, spreading his fingers wide to rinse. He dried them with a brown paper towel, then stood on his tiptoes to look in the mirror at his bloodshot eyes. He turned to Joy. "Why don't you just hold your questions until we're done?"

But Joy had already forgotten what she'd asked.

The technician placed the cold probe on her exposed skin while the doctor pressed several buttons on the sonogram machine. Joy turned her head to see.

"Please lie perfectly still," the doctor instructed.

She settled back on the table. The technician rotated the probe. Joy could make out streaks of gray and white on the screen next to her. She craned her neck to see more. The doctor turned to her again.

"When you move, I can't image the fetus."

He punched more buttons, and out of the corner of her eye Joy saw numbers flashing on the screen.

"Does everything look all right?" Her throat was closing. She could barely get the words out.

Dr. Blau tilted the screen away. "I cannot do my job and talk to you at the same time." He paused for effect and then turned back to his work.

The technician continued to move the probe in circles around her greasy belly. Joy closed her eyes and concentrated on her breathing. Then, abruptly, the weight of the probe lifted off her.

Her eyes blinked open. The doctor was already standing, extending his hand. "Thank you very much."

Joy sat up. "That's it? Is everything all right?"

"Your doctor will have my report by the end of the day, and he'll be in touch."

"Is there a problem?"

"It would be premature to discuss the data before I've had a chance to study it. Your doctor will call you by the end of the day."

He turned and left, the technician trailing behind, their eyes to the floor.

Her loose dress clung to the front of her sticky stomach as she wrote out her check and asked if she could use the phone again.

Berger's secretary answered on the sixth ring. "They broke for lunch, Mrs. Bard. Do you want me to call the restaurant and get a message to him?"

"No," Joy got out between shaky breaths. "Just tell him if he gets back before I'm there, I'm on my way."

CHAPTER
SEVEN

SHE SAT IN the black leather visitor's chair, swiveling gently back and forth, her eyes fixed on a photograph of herself, not seeing it.

"Honey."

Feeling drugged, she got up and lumbered over into Lanny's open arms. He squeezed her tight, then lifted her chin so her full, sad eyes met his. "Hey. Everything is okay. Dr. Wayne called. It's okay."

As if she'd been uncorked, deep guttural sobs lurched out of her, surprising her. Lanny shut the door.

"Come on, now. It's okay." He pulled his handkerchief out of his breast pocket. "Here you go. Come on. Calm down."

She dabbed her eyes with the white pocket square, then looked at Lanny again. Something wasn't right.

"Get a grip on yourself now." He was pacing the room. His mouth was puckered. He was lost in thought.

"Lanny?"

"Just calm down."

She couldn't tell if he was talking to her or to himself. His pace quickened as he strode from the door to the window and back to the door. She clutched his handkerchief, now rolled into a hard ball in the palm of her hand. "Lanny, you've got to tell me what's wrong."

He stopped, suddenly, then looked at her as if he'd only

just noticed she was there. "Everything is fine," he said, his
voice curt, clipped, cold. "Dr. Wayne said everything is
fine." He stared at her from across the room, weighing
something. Then he pointed for her to sit down in a chair.
He took his position behind his black wood desk. She sat
at the edge of the seat and leaned forward.

"Something is wrong," he admitted finally.

Automatically Joy's hands went to her stomach, pressing
in on her hard belly, concentrating on feeling for movement. Her uterus tightened its grip; one of the babies rolled
slightly.

"First, you start in on the house. On this schoolgirl idea
of yours to go around collecting memories, like it's a trea-
sure hunt or something."

"It's not like that at all," she protested.

"So, okay, I agree to go along with it. And then what
happens? I wake up in the middle of the night lying in a
puddle of blood."

Joy's breathing became shallow. She leaned back in her
chair, remote, shut down, watching Lanny as if he was nar-
rating a documentary on PBS.

"Do those sound like the actions of a healthy mother to
be to you?"

Her answer was nearly inaudible. "What are you saying?"

"I'm saying you're carrying my progeny. That's your
number-one job. And I'm getting nervous. Because you're
not taking your job very seriously. Because I think, and Dr.
Wayne agrees, that you should be putting your babies'
health before your own, and you're not."

She tried to keep her voice from quivering. "I just want
to fill in the holes, that's all."

"Fill in the holes? You're playing games, Joy. Let me ask
you, do you think it makes sense to endanger your health,
your baby's health, so you can remember the color of the
rug in your bedroom when you were twelve?"

"You don't understand," she got out, a whisper.

"Enlighten me. Please." It was his lawyer voice. His trial

voice. His winning voice. She had lost her case. "What do you want me to do?"

"You're a grown woman. I shouldn't have to tell you what you should or shouldn't do. This is making me very nervous."

"Why?"

"Because I'm starting to get the feeling that my children are going to be raised by someone who is still a child herself."

She shot up out of her chair, her voice rising with her. "How dare you call me a child?"

"Listen to yourself," Lanny said calmly. "Don't you see? Even now. You're hysterical." The calm lifted. His anger surged. "And I don't want to wake up in bed in blood again." He regained his composure quickly. "Joy, it's because I love you. You know that."

Slowly she sat back down and bit her trembling lip.

"Are you calmer now?"

She was. She nodded.

"Do you see my point?"

She did. She was too worked up.

"There's another problem," he went on, "with the meeting this morning."

She took a deep breath. "With the radiologist?"

He looked at her, perplexed, like she should know. "With the Catco deal." His voice dropped, as if he was afraid of being overheard. "We hit a snag. A second suitor turned up on our target's doorstep. We have to sweeten the marriage proposal. I have to deliver it in person tomorrow."

He'd switched gears too fast. She couldn't keep up. He moved from behind his desk and sat in the visitor's chair next to her. He brushed a stray hair off her face. "I have to go to San Francisco tonight. Who's going to take care of you?"

A laugh burst out, a nervous laugh, a laugh of relief. "No one has to take care of me. I'll take care of myself."

"You have to stay in bed. Dr. Wayne wants you to stay

in bed for a few days, and you have to promise me, while I'm away, you'll stay in bed."

He was so worried. His forehead was so creased. His lips were pressed so tight. It was sweet to see him this worried. "I'll be fine."

"I've asked your mother to come. I left a message on her machine.

"No," Joy said firmly. "I'll be fine on my own."

Lanny looked pale, unwell. "You're not listening to me. We're talking about the health of your baby here."

"Babies," she said, smiling, trying to loosen him up, lighten the mood. "Babies." She held up two fingers.

His mouth puckered as he stood up and resumed pacing. "I hate to leave you alone now."

"Don't worry." She had never said that to Lanny before. Lanny didn't worry about anything. "I won't go out. I won't even get dressed. I'll work in my bathrobe."

"Goddamn it," he interrupted her. "You're not supposed to work. You're not supposed to go spraying fixative on your paintings, or dousing yourself with mineral spirits or inhaling those paints with the windows closed. Just get the fuck in bed."

"Lanny." He never talked to her like this. It wasn't sweet anymore.

"I'm telling you, this is serious. If you refuse to take care of yourself and those babies now, how the hell am I supposed to believe you're going to be able to take care of them after they're born?"

She felt pummeled, bludgeoned.

"I'm going to be gone for three days. Do you think you can manage to rest for three days?"

Numb, she nodded to appease him.

A knock on the door broke through the stifling mood, and Kelly, Lanny's secretary, let herself in.

"There's a Mr. Seidenberg waiting for you," she announced, "who's been here since three. He's very annoyed."

"Fuck," Lanny said, and he struggled to remember what the meeting was supposed to be about.

"He's a personal friend of Mr. Berger's," Kelly prompted him, "who wants some advice on the entertainment industry."

"Then why the hell doesn't he get himself an entertainment attorney?" Lanny said to the air.

Kelly remained at the door, her face blank.

"Get him," he said finally.

Kelly left the door open. Joy stood up, feeling dismissed.

"I'll call you from the airport," Lanny offered. "Kelly will arrange for a car to take you home."

She felt well enough to take the train, but it wasn't worth arguing. They embraced stiffly.

"This is why you keep me waiting?"

They broke apart, and Lanny offered a hand to the athletic-looking man before him. "Mr. Seidenberg." He grinned easily, all good cheer and easy confidence. "This is my wife, Joy."

"I figured your wife or your mistress. And considering your condition, my dear, I'm glad you're the wife."

Joy managed a dim smile and returned the firm handshake.

"Take care of yourself," Lanny called after her, his voice suddenly warm with concern.

As she continued down the hall to the reception area she heard Seidenberg's voice boom, "You always keep friends of your boss waiting like this?" But she didn't hear Lanny's reply. All she heard, as she waited for the car to arrive, were her husband's harsh accusations echoing endlessly in her head.

CHAPTER
EIGHT

HER KEY WAS in the front door lock when she heard someone walking up the side path from her backyard.

"Hi, there," Molly called out. Cookie ran to Joy's side and licked her hand. "I was out looking for her for over an hour. I just found her, tied up to a tree in your backyard."

"In my backyard? How did she end up there?"

"How do you think?" Molly barked.

Joy had no reserve left to deal with more anger. "I don't know," she responded quietly.

"Oh, Joy. It's not your fault. It's those goddamn, rotten kids. I could kill them, if I were the violent type."

"Why would they tie up Cookie in my backyard?"

"Practical joke. Funny, right?" Molly stared at Joy. "You don't look well."

Joy started to brush off the inquiry, but instead she found herself telling Molly about the staining, the sonogram, the bed rest, Lanny's trip to San Francisco. She told her about everything, except for Lanny's inexplicable anger. She was afraid to tell her about that. Afraid that Molly might agree: Yes. You're not fit to be a mother. It would be better if you gave up the twins.

"I'm going to take care of you," Molly announced. "I'll bring dinner and breakfast over, and make you sandwiches for lunch."

"That's not necessary," Joy protested. "I'm really fine."

44

"Don't be silly," Molly persisted. "When I was pregnant with Trina, I was in bed for six weeks. And believe me, I couldn't have survived without the help of my best girl-friend."

Joy made a mild attempt to fend off the offer, but in the end, she gave in. At seven o'clock when the doorbell rang, she roused herself from a catnap to find Molly standing on the front steps carrying a bowl of piping hot spaghetti and meatballs. Trina, her daughter, held a long Italian bread out in front of her, like a sword.

They all went upstairs, and Trina positioned herself at the edge of the bed, at Joy's feet, studying her while she ate. "She doesn't look sick, Mommy," she finally decided.

"I'm not sick, honey," Joy explained.

"Well, I'm not allowed to eat in bed unless I'm sick."

Quickly changing the subject, Joy let drop that she was an artist who had her own drawing studio stocked with crayons, markers, and paints. Trina held her hands together and looked at Joy expectantly.

"If you want to go up there and draw," Joy said, winking at Molly, "your mother can take you. But you have to promise to put the caps back on all fifty markers."

"Fifty markers!" Trina exclaimed. She clapped her hands and raced after her mother up the stairs.

When Molly came down she climbed into bed beside Joy and propped herself up with pillows. Toes wiggling on top of the thick blanket, relaxed by a glass of Bordeaux, she told Joy the story of her brief marriage to Dick. Handsome and rich, but a drinker, one year after Trina was born he be-came violent, and Molly realized she had to leave him. But before she had gathered the courage to do it, he got sick. The diagnosis: lung cancer. Molly and a crew of health-care workers nursed him through the final days of his illness while his parents footed the steep bill. The cancer took him in three months. She had been prepared to be a struggling divorcée. She ended up a rich widow. She put most of the inheritance into a trust for Trina because the money embar-rassed her. She felt like she'd stolen it.

"How about you?" she asked, swallowing the last of her wine. "What skeletons are hiding in your closet?"

Joy shrugged. There was too much to explain. People never understood.

"Oh," Molly shifted uncomfortably. She got out of bed, embarrassed that she had divulged so much when Joy wasn't giving at all.

"I have a brother," Joy said suddenly, stumbling over the words.

"Well, spit it out. He can't be any weirder than my brother, David. He used to lure all the neighborhood cats to the house by putting out plates of Eskimo Pies. Then he'd lock the cats in closets or in the basement. You never knew where you'd find a dead one. It was very cozy. Can you beat that?"

"No," Joy admitted. "It's just that we were twins. We are twins. We were twins."

Molly looked at her quizzically.

"When we were thirteen he was kidnapped."

Her friend's good-natured smile vanished. "Where? By whom?"

Joy let out a massive sigh. "I don't know."

"Was he walking to school like Etan Patz?" Her eyes grew wider. "Were you with him?"

"I don't know."

"What do you mean you don't know?"

"I can't remember," Joy told her. "I can't even remember if I ever knew. My memory is fairly . . ." she searched for a word, "unreliable."

"So if I say something really dumb, I don't have to worry? You won't remember it anyway?"

Joy's eyes started to crinkle as she smiled. Then her face disintegrated into a mass of lines of worry and despair.

"I'm sorry," Molly apologized. "I was just kidding."

Joy covered her mouth with her hands. "No," she said quietly. "I'm sorry." Molly gently stroked Joy's shoulder as she took several deep breaths. "It's just that no one will let me talk about it." Her voice cracked, and Molly had to lean close to hear. "My mother refuses. It's practically policy with her, not to discuss unpleasant things. And Lanny. He was Buddy's best friend. He won't talk about it at all."

"Was there a ransom note? Was he killed?"

"I don't know anything but that he's dead. And I don't even know why I know that. It's as if it never happened. I didn't think about it for years. Until we moved into this house. It's so much like my old house. Now I can't stop thinking about it."

"Is that why you moved here?" Molly asked, her eyes widening. "To help you remember?"

"No," Joy laughed. "It's a coincidence."

Molly pursed her lips into a whistle that collapsed into a sigh. "Some coincidence."

They sat in silence and private thought.

"Don't you think it's strange?" Joy asked. "To be unable to recall entire years of your life? I can't remember anything about what happened to my brother. Not the police coming or neighbors searching. I remember nothing. No one else seems to think it's strange."

Molly met her eyes. "It's very strange."

Joy felt like weights were being lifted off her shoulders, two at a time.

"Where is your old house?"

Joy moved the pillows and stretched her back. "It's in New Jersey," she said. "I haven't been back since we moved away."

"That's what I'd want to do," Molly offered. "I'd want to go see the house."

Joy felt light-headed. "I do," she got out. "I do want to see it."

"Do you want me to go with you, once you're allowed out of bed?"

As Joy nodded, almost imperceptibly, Trina burst into the room, clutching a pile of drawings. "There are monsters up there, Mommy," she cried. "I want to go home."

Molly couldn't calm her down, so Joy led them to the door. She turned on the porch light. Molly hurried Trina out ahead of her. The October air had turned raw, and neither mother nor daughter were properly dressed.

The little girl's scream pierced the night as she came running back into the house, burrowing her head into her mother's stomach.

"What is that?" came her muffled cries. "Mommy, I stepped on it. What is it?"

While Molly stroked Trina's head, Joy raced to get the flashlight where she stored it, in the refrigerator. But even as she shone the light on the furry carcass stretched out beneath her front steps, she wasn't sure what it was. Trina stopped crying long enough to steal another look and to tell her mother she thought it was a funny cat. To Joy it looked more like a mammoth rat. Molly finally identified it as a dead opossum. Then she pointed to the depressions on the flattened grass, where the animal had dragged itself, or been dragged.

Joy brought up a shovel from the basement and Molly, amidst Trina's screams, dumped the heavy, hairy body in the trash can with the thud of dead weight.

CHAPTER NINE

SHE SHUT THE door to her studio, to shut out the world. With a pillow supporting her back and the wastebasket turned upside down for a hassock, it was almost like resting in bed. As she grabbed an oversize art book to use as a lap desk she chewed on her second peppermint Lifesaver to get rid of the bad taste in her mouth. Then she sat down, stretched out her legs, and studied the black-and-white photographs of the models she was sketching for the book jacket.

The full shot of the wholesome Ivory Snow blonde was the victim. The head shot was Fred, the murderer, who would appear, obscured by a shadow, in a corner of the cover.

Sketching the victim came easily. She floated in the middle of the page, head slung toward her shoulder, her green eyes wide open and glassy, her hair dangling to her waist in long soft waves. The colors would all be muted shades of pale pink and white except for the spot where her neck was slit open. There the black handle of a kitchen knife jutted out from an ugly wound. Trails of blood, now congealed, formed a jagged pattern, a bloody mountain range across the top of her satin nightgown.

Drawing Fred, however, wasn't working out. She started him, erased him, began again, threw him away, started once more. The model they photographed for Fred had been exactly on target, just what the publisher's instructions had asked for. His angry, heavy-lidded eyes and twisted smile had frightened her even in the safe confines of the shoot. But now her hand wouldn't cooperate. His face kept filling out. His eyes insisted on opening wide. His hair refused to stay greasy and slicked back. It was as if she was fighting some urge to make him look normal. But Fred wasn't supposed to look like the boy next door. She crumpled the useless drawing and pushed it off the table. The phone rang, startling her.

"Did I wake you?" Lanny's voice sounded tinny, far away, but the worry came through with clarity.

She cheeked her watch. It was ten o'clock. A reasonable hour to still be awake. "I was just resting."

"Where are you?"

"In bed," Joy lied. "Where are you?"

"On the plane. Miracles of technology, right?"

Joy laughed, to fill the void.

"So is everything okay?"

"Just fine." She didn't tell him about the dead opossum. He didn't need anything else to worry him.

"Listen." His voice was obliterated by a wave of static and then it came back. "I'll try to get home earlier if I can. Make it a one-day and catch the red-eye tomorrow night."

"You don't have to rush." She drew an oval on a piece of paper, then colored it in with the side of a charcoal pencil.

"What's that noise?" Lanny asked.

"Static, I think." She put the pencil down.

"Are you sure you're resting?"

"I'm sure," Joy confirmed, shifting in her chair, feeling suddenly exhausted, overtired.

"Okay. I don't know if I'll be able to reach you tomorrow. I'll be in meetings all day. So promise me, will you stay in bed?"

Joy promised, even as she drew a picture of a hand, with fingers crossed.

She hung up the phone and rolled her head to loosen her neck, then stretched her fingers to avoid cramping. On a fresh page she began again, drawing two figures: boys, Lanny and Buddy, outside a building that was their clubhouse. In front of the closed pine door she added cans, two paint cans and a bucket filled with large brushes. They were painting the clubhouse. Then she remembered.

The piercing buzzer of the square alarm clock she'd tucked between her stuffed bears awoke her, as scheduled, at four. Miraculously, no one else stirred. She pulled the box of shirts out from under the bed. There hadn't been much left of her father's things. Her mother had wanted everything out of the house right away, after he died, so by Joy and Buddy's sixth birthday, there wasn't even an old pill bottle with his name on it in the medicine cabinet. But somehow a box of his shirts delivered by the cleaners a week after his demise escaped the trash heap. For years the box had sat, forgotten, in the back of Dorothy's closet. But the night before, while helping her mother reorganize her summer clothes, Joy had come upon the thin box, hidden beneath a pile of hats. She removed it while her mother was on the toilet, transferring it to her own hiding place, under her bed. Now, in the early dawn light, she pulled out one of the stiff shirts, tore off the paper wrapper and put it on as a smock.

The paint cans were in the basement, just where she'd stashed them, behind the now abandoned workbench. She'd wanted to be done painting by the time Buddy and Lanny were awake, but it went slower than she expected. When they found her she was halfway through turning the ceiling of their clubhouse red.

It surprised her that Buddy was so mad, screaming that she was stupid, that it wasn't her clubhouse, that she had no right. But the louder he shouted, the more she giggled. She had never heard him yell before.

Lanny didn't say a word. He stood, thumbs hooked into his belt loops, surveying the paint job, and then left. Buddy chased after him, his faded flannel shirttail flying behind him as he cried out, "Hey, she's not my sister anymore. Hey, I'm going to get a divorce."

So she finished painting the ceiling alone. Later, while she was cleaning up, her hands still red with paint, Lanny returned. Leading her by the elbow, he walked her to the clubhouse and pressed her damp hands on the front of the door. "You should always sign your work," he said.

Joy stared at the drawing on her makeshift lap desk, at the quickly rendered clubhouse with two handprints sketched on the front door. Her stomach cramped. She stuck the drawing in a folder and lifted herself out of the chair. As she washed up for bed she half expected to see the water running off her hands turn red with the paint that was no longer there.

Sleep came instantly and then was pulled away, just as fast. She was sitting up in bed, breathing hard, thinking about the black car and about Buddy's stony face. Lanny's bedside digital clock read three-fifteen. Then she heard a noise and realized that was what had woken her. She had heard it in her dream, thought it was a car engine revving. Now, as she heard it a third time, she knew, it was laughter. Low, male laughter.

She sent her feet fishing under the bed for her slippers until her right toe found the heel of her sheepskin shoe. Her foot was halfway in when she heard it again, this time more clearly. It was a rumbling sound. A teenage boy's sadistic laugh.

Angry and alert, she raced downstairs to peer out of the living room window but saw nothing. Quietly she opened the front door and stepped out onto the porch. She could see them, two boys in light-colored shirts. Two boys, maybe three, crouching in the middle of the lawn, next to the berry-bearing dogwood tree.

When she switched on the porch light they froze, like deer caught crossing the highway. Then, in a flash, they scattered. The porch door creaked as she opened it. She stepped out into the cool night.

The porch light didn't extend very far, so she made her way slowly across the lawn to where the boys had been sitting. Halfway there her left foot brushed up against a small mound. When she bent down to touch it her hand met furry skin. A low, long groan crept out of her mouth as she ran to retrieve the cold flashlight.

At first she was relieved to discover it was just a dead squirrel, and a small one at that. But then, as she pointed the circle of the flashlight's glare over the lawn, she saw the corpses of nine more. Dead squirrels with teeth gleaming yellow in the light, their mouths stretched back to their ears as if they had died screaming. Their black beady eyes were stuck open, their claws extended and ready to fight. And next to each one the lawn had been dug up. The holes were perfectly spaced, shallow and about a foot long. Finally it came to her. Little graves.

CHAPTER TEN

THE COLLAR OF the detective's leather jacket dug into his thick neck as he sat, dwarfing the small love seat. He concentrated hard as she spoke, waiting politely during her awkward pauses. When she finished, he flipped backward through his pad to the first page of his carefully printed notes and asked her if she would mind telling him all over again.

The second time, the story came out shorter. She didn't think there was a need to repeat the details, how many squirrels there were, how big the opossum had been. Detective Burner seemed relieved by the brevity. When she finished he excused himself and went outside to survey the front lawn, poking his flashlight in the holes, kicking the dead squirrels until they flipped over, picking up several stray pieces of trash. Finally, seeming satisfied, he returned to his position on the love seat. As the early-rising blue jays began their dawn cry, Joy wondered how much longer he would stay.

"Believe me," he said. "This kind of thing doesn't usually happen in our town. And when it does, we don't like it. Do you have any idea why someone would do this? Anyone have a grudge against you?"

Joy felt him eye her, felt him trying to figure out if the dead squirrels were well deserved.

"I think it's the neighborhood boys; the boys on the block, playing pranks."

The detective winced. "You want to give me descriptions? You want to tell me names?"

"It was dark," she explained. "I'd be guessing." She wanted to give him names, but she had no way to know if they were the right names, so she gave him nothing more.

"All right, ma'am. I know the kids. I'll have a word with them."

Joy followed his gaze to her lap, to the tiny bits of tissue she'd been shredding. Embarrassed, she quickly rolled them in a ball that she stuffed up her bathrobe sleeve.

Detective Burner stood up. "I'll be on my way. If you call the animal shelter in White Plains, they'll cart the squirrels away for you. Probably cost you twenty bucks."

He offered his hand, and Joy accepted his cool tight grasp. "Lock up now," he cautioned as he let himself out.

Joy watched him get into his car. The radio crackled through the night silence. She climbed the stairs slowly, the anger gone, washed away by exhaustion. Midway through wondering why Burner hadn't driven away, she drifted to a restless sleep.

The scream that woke her turned into the shrill ring of the telephone. She had the receiver to her ear before she knew she was awake, before she knew that morning had long ago arrived.

"We're having a coffee klatch over at Donna's," Barb's chirpy voice came at her, too loud, through the phone. "You want to join us?"

Joy rolled over and checked the clock. It was ten-thirty.

"I'm supposed to stay off my feet," she said, begging off, thankful for the medical excuse.

"No problem," Barb bounced back. "We'll just pack everything up and bring the coffee over to you. Give us five minutes, okay?"

Before Joy could compose another excuse, Barb had hung up the phone.

She was splashing her face with cold water when the

doorbell rang. In a panic, she grabbed her sweatshirt and then thought better of it, throwing it on the bed. If she was still in her bathrobe, maybe they wouldn't stay long.

From her living room window she could see her neighbors' faces contort with disgust as they completed their hike around the obstacle course of dead squirrels. When Joy swung open the front door Sue was still checking the bottoms of her sneakers. Barb's distressed scowl flowed right into a bright smile.

"Morning," she chimed, as she led the way, carrying a silver tray that held a tall white kettle. Donna followed holding a stack of bone china dessert dishes, a pile of matching cloth napkins resting on top. Sue straggled in last, balancing a narrow platter of tiny pastries with one hand as she stomped on the doormat, to get her soles clean.

They followed Joy into the kitchen, where Barb noticed out loud that there were only two chairs. As if it were her home, she went off to find additional seating, returning moments later with the wing chair from the parlor. She placed the chair beside Joy, and took her seat, across from Sue, at the kitchen table. Donna remained standing, leaning against the counter.

The small talk didn't last long. While Barb poured coffee, Sue pushed up the sleeves of her lavender sweatsuit and leaned over toward the wing chair. "Did you hear?" she asked. "Molly's dog was hit by a car last night."

"Is she all right?" Joy asked, thinking of the furry mass of squirrel she'd stumbled upon the night before.

"It's her own fault," Barb butted in, taking a miniature sticky bun and passing along the platter. "She never kept her tied up on a leash. You'd think she'd have learned."

Using her short nails, Donna worked on dislodging a dried dot of egg yolk from the counter while Joy fought an urge to get out the Fantastik.

"Maybe we should just get to the point." Donna gave up on the egg and turned her attention to Joy, who didn't know there was supposed to be a point. She felt a baby kick, and then her stomach cramped with another Braxton-Hicks contraction that made her short of breath.

"Do you get the Edgebury paper?" Donna went on.

"No," Joy answered cautiously.

"Let her look at mine," Sue suggested, downing the liquid in her cup.

Joy noticed the paper, spread open on the table next to Sue, like a prop.

"See here?" Barb picked up the paper and displayed a page quickly. "It's got a column called Police Blotter." She closed the paper, punching it to get it to fold neatly. "That used to be my favorite part." She handed Joy the folded newspaper and waved another sheet of paper in the air. "May I read you this?"

Joy sat more erect.

Barb cleared her throat. "This is going to be in next Thursday's Police Blotter. I have a friend at the paper who called me this morning to tell me about it. Shall I read it out loud?" She didn't wait for a response. " 'Several juvenile suspects are being investigated in the harassment of an Epsom Court resident, climaxing on Tuesday with the discovery on the resident's front lawn of ten dead squirrels. Detective Bill Burner'—that's Sue's husband—" Barb interrupted herself. " 'Detective Bill Burner is investigating. No suspects have been charged, but several Epsom Court residents are being questioned.' "

Joy looked into her lap. She heard Sue blow smoke into the air, then saw the cloud drift toward her.

"For example, Charlie was interviewed," Sue added. "By his father, the detective, at seven o'clock this morning."

"He was at my house at seven thirty," Donna reported.

"And at mine at a quarter past eight. Dennis was late for school." Barb rolled her eyes and shook her head.

"The thing is," Donna said, "instead of calling the police, you should have called us."

"Because in this pretty little town," Sue added, "it's considered very bad taste to turn someone in to the police, especially if you can't prove they did anything." She stubbed the cigarette out in her half-eaten pastry, for the first time meeting Joy's eyes with an icy stare.

"I called the police because it was the middle of the night and my lawn was covered with dead squirrels. What would you have done?"

"Not that, honey," Donna said, helping herself to a third cream puff.

"You wouldn't call the police, no matter what happened? Whether your lawn was dug up, or your dog was let loose, or your cat was shot dead?"

"See, this is what I don't like," Barb said as she began gathering the china dishes. "How did we get from digging a hole in the lawn to shooting a cat? Who said anything about a gun?" She recaptured her smile. Her gray eyes twinkled with manufactured kindness. "Now I know your pregnancy is not going very well." Joy's face clouded, and Barb quickly added, "Because your adorable husband called to ask me to be sure and stop by to see if you needed anything."

Joy fought an urge to push the tray of neatly stacked plates to the floor.

"My sister-in-law was the same way," Barb went on. "Pregnancy just did not agree with her."

"Little did she know," Sue added, "how right she was to worry." She laughed her gravelly chuckle, but no one joined her.

"But my sister-in-law realized that when you're going to have a baby, or in your case," Barb continued, pointing to Joy's belly, "two babies, you have to expect that when they get bigger, kids do things."

"Absolutely, honey," Donna added. "I hope you didn't think having kids was all making cupcakes and going to the circus. I mean, if you don't like kids," she paused and shook her head, "you shouldn't have gotten pregnant."

"I love kids," Joy blurted out. "This isn't about liking kids."

"Let me explain something," Donna went on, like a schoolteacher with a one-track mind. "When you call the police on our kids you embarrass the whole block. Now it will be in the paper. The kids will look bad. The block will look bad. And you. You will look very bad."

"Maybe she just didn't know," Barb speculated.

"Do yourself a favor, honey. Try and cool out." Donna put her porky nail-bitten hand on Joy's shoulder. "I mean, you're not just pregnant. Barb told me you're supposed to stay in bed. You don't want to be in a situation where you can't call your neighbors and ask for a hand, do you?"

Joy cringed at the threat oiled with false kindness.

"Take her advice," Sue said, standing up, looking down. "The last thing you want is to end up as the wicked witch of the block. Kids love to torment the wicked witch."

"So is there anything you need?" Barb offered. "I told Lanny I'd be delighted to take care of you. Do you have milk in the house?"

"I'm fine," Joy told her, numb.

"Well, if there's anything we can do," she reiterated as she led the other two women on a parade out the front door, "just call. Any of us. Any time. Day or night. That's what neighbors are for."

CHAPTER ELEVEN

THE STUDIO WAS beginning to have the cluttered feel of a garage sale. There was the boxy portable refrigerator Molly had lugged over, stocked with bottles of Evian, club soda, and fruit. She'd also brought up a small black-and-white television, in case Joy wanted to take a break from working without walking downstairs. Several trays filled with empty tea cups, orange peels, and half-eaten crackers littered the floor. Three foil-lined milk boxes, the kind children took to school for lunch, lined the windowsill. It reminded her of her dorm room, without the dirty laundry. Joy took off her white socks and threw them at the milk boxes, pretending her targets were her neighbors. She missed the box that was Barb, but Sue, the middle box, was a direct hit.

"Gotcha," she said when the box tipped over. She was wiping up the milk that had dripped to the floor when a bang broke through the quiet: the front door slamming shut.

"Hello?" she called out, her voice tentative. Lanny wasn't due until tomorrow. Molly was supposed to be at school. Dorothy didn't have a key.

Her eyes flitted everywhere as she crept down the stairs looking for signs of movement that she didn't want to see. Outside of her bedroom she stopped, waiting for shadows, finding none. She noticed the door to the back bedroom was closed. A wave of nausea came and went as she quickly swung it open.

The shades were drawn, the light was dim, but there, next to the window, a figure stood frozen in surprise. Slamming the door behind her she raced out of the room down the hall, to her bedroom phone. But her finger poised to dial for help, she stopped. This time before she called the police she had to be sure.

With her back flat against the wall she crept along the edge of the carpet until she got to the door. She knelt down and peered through the keyhole, not breathing. But it was too dark to see.

Slowly, still holding her breath, she turned the knob until she felt the door unlatch. Carefully, silently, she pushed it open a sliver, then a crack, until she could see. He was still there, at the window. Only he wasn't a burglar. He wasn't a neighborhood boy. He was a navy blue duffel bag, propped up on its end, resting against the wall.

Returning to the hallway she called out in a small voice, "Anybody there?" There was no answer. She wound her way down the stairs and circled through the rooms, then climbed back up to her studio. At the top of the landing she stopped and peered down three flights. The circular rug in the front foyer stared up at her like a giant eye. But nothing moved. Just her own eyes, blinking.

As soon as she was back at her drafting table she shut her eyes and breathed deeply to push air into her tight lungs. Then her eyes popped open, making sure she was really alone.

The model for Fred stared back at her with a menacing sneer. The radiator banged again. She jumped, then reminded herself it was just house noises. Old pipes groaning with the force of hot steam. Creaky floors expanding with the heat. She leaned back in her chair and turned away from her fears to face the wild-eyed stare of the fictional killer before her.

She laid out a sheet of paper and several mechanical pencils. But the hulking figure she drew, with big round eyes, beefy arms, and huge clumsy bear paws for hands, wasn't Fred. She fought the urge to crumple the picture, instead pushing the unwanted visage off the table. She watched the stranger float to the floor.

She began again. Her hand outlined a wide, round face, dark eyes, big with surprise, thick hair cut choppy and short. The neck was wide, the shoulders broad, the chin strong. The big bear hands clutched a small stick, a stick with a circle on top and notches on the side. It was a key. The man held an old skeleton key.

This wasn't from the book. This wasn't anyone she knew. But as she studied the face she thought, what if he was slightly thinner and the hair was longer and the eyes were bright blue? What if the fat was muscle and the grimace a friendlier smile? The shape of the chin was familiar, as were the long, thin lips and the angular nose. It was Lanny, she realized. Lanny fatter, Lanny older, Lanny bigger and meaner. It was Lanny as he could end up looking, fifteen years from now, if his life took an unpleasant turn.

Her hair tickled her shoulders, and her uterus contracted. It was early afternoon but already exhaustion was sweeping over her. She felt drugged, in desperate need of sleep. She got up slowly, turned off the light, and made her way downstairs.

When she got to the bedroom she turned the television on for background sound. Then she kicked off her shoes and rolled down her pull-on maternity pants, running her finger along the red mark the pants had left where her waist used to be. She threw back the quilted duvet cover and climbed into bed.

The slow stilted drama of the soap opera droned on as she rolled onto her side, molding her body into the mattress. Her head settled on her pillow. The nausea came over her fast and full blown. The musty smell she'd noticed when she first walked in the room now seemed thoroughly foul. As if she were playing a game of hot and cold, she got out of bed and followed the stench from one corner of the room to the other. She ended up outside the door of the small closet where her bathrobe and nightgown hung on scented padded hangers Lanny had bought for her for Valentine's Day two years ago.

Vomit rose in her throat as she pulled the door open. Half a dozen decayed squirrel corpses came tumbling out, rolling onto her feet. Frozen in place she stared at them for several minutes. Then the phone rang, releasing her.

At first she was gripped by the irrational idea that it was Barb on the phone, calling to deny that the squirrels were the work of her son. But on the fifth ring, when she forced herself to pick up the receiver, Lanny's anxious voice came on as clear as if he were just next door.

"Hi. We're breaking for lunch. Are you in bed? Are you okay?"

Joy struggled to answer. "Just a minute," she said finally. She put the receiver in her lap while her stifled sobs came out like coughs.

"Are you okay? Hello?" came the voice, sounding small, in her lap. "Joy? Are you there?"

She blew her nose, picked up the receiver, and blurted out what had just happened. Clutching the long phone cord she walked to the window where she stood, breathing the crisp autumn air that burned her tear-stained face.

"You have to call the police," he said matter-of-factly.

"I can't. That's not how things are done here."

"That's ridiculous. You have to call the police."

"When are you coming home?"

"Oh," Lanny said, suddenly remembering why he'd called. "I have to stay at least one more day. Promise me you'll call the police."

"No, I can't," she insisted. She was angry now. Angry that he was away, that he had to stay away, that he had asked Barb to look in on her as if she were a child. "I'll handle it some other way."

"Joy. I'm asking you. Call the police."

Instead, when she got off the phone she called the animal shelter for the second time that day.

CHAPTER TWELVE

IT WAS THE same pest control man who'd joked with her earlier when he'd removed the squirrels from her front lawn. Now he followed her upstairs in silence, eyeing her suspiciously, as if she'd crossed some line.

After swinging open her closet door he whipped out his

heavy flashlight and twirled it around like a cowboy show-ing off his stuff. Then he pointed it, lighting up the dust-free closet floor.

"Were they alive or did you move them?" he asked her.

She pointed to the bare wood. "They were right there."

"And where are they now?" He checked his watch, then readied himself, slipping his hands into a pair of heavy rub-ber gloves that had been bitten half a dozen times, torn by long, gnashing teeth.

"Where could they be? They were dead." She tried to fend off the surging panic that was shutting her down, mak-ing her dizzy, confused.

He shook his head slowly. "I don't have the slightest idea where they are." He took off his gloves. "But if you don't have any squirrels for me to remove, I've got an army of carpenter bees in a house up the block chomping away at the wood, waiting for me."

She brushed past him and pushed aside her satin night-gowns, looking deep in the back of the closet. There was nothing there. She threw open the door to the second closet where Lanny's summer suits were stored, sheathed in plas-tic. His beige suede shoes, tennis sneakers, and Dock-Siders were lined up on the floor in a perfectly arranged row.

"I got to charge you," he called after her as she ran into the adjoining room where she checked the floor underneath the shelves of Lanny's neatly stacked sweaters.

"It's fifty bucks for a house call," he yelled as she disap-peared into her bathroom, checking the sink, behind the toi-let.

"You want me to look and see if they crawled under the bed?" he asked when she returned to face him, pale and be-wildered. "Fifty bucks," he repeated, waiting.

He followed her downstairs, waiting on the porch while she wrote three checks, her hand shaking so badly the first two were illegible. When she finally handed him his due, he stuffed it in his pocket and left without saying good-bye. As he crossed the street a police car pulled up in front of her house. Two uniformed cops got out and sauntered up to her front door.

"I'm Sergeant Brady," the older one said. "And this is Patrolman McShane."

Joy opened the porch door, unintentionally blocking their way, until Sergeant Brady motioned that he'd like to come in. She stepped aside.

"You called and said you found something?" Brady took his pen out of his pocket and waited. McShane shuffled nervously, looking like it was his first day at work, looking like he was too young to drive.

"I didn't call," Joy said. The houses across the street stared back at her, hostile, watching.

Brady looked over her head, through the open door into the hallway, as if he expected to see a prone body lying on the foyer rug. He took out his notebook and checked his writing. "Your husband phoned in that you had an intruder."

"He was mistaken." She was going to handle it differently this time. She was going to take care of this herself.

"He was mistaken," Brady repeated, but his eyebrows raised with interest.

"Yes."

"Is your husband home now?"

"No. He's out of town. He called you from out of town."

Brady rubbed his chin as if he had a beard. "So your husband called from out of town to say there was an intruder, and you're home, and you say there wasn't an intruder."

"I'm sorry. We had an argument on the phone. I told him I thought someone had broken in, but I wasn't serious. Let's just say it's a false alarm." She tried to make it sound light. She wanted the police car away from her house.

Brady took off his cap and scratched his head. "I'll tell you, Mrs. Bard. We don't like false alarms at the police station. We're a lot like firemen that way. We don't like them." He had nothing more to say, so he turned and left, his partner following him back down her front walk to the

stre
they
tion.

Jo
pou
the
she
still.

Sh
her
her
The

Fr
wide
their

On
to he
and

asleep, not awake, while the sounds of th
through her wandering thoughts: the
house crowded with people, Lanny
was half in a dream when a noise
of sleep. Her eyes came unstuc
Slowly she lifted her head
stiff and sore from lying
to her cheek. She peele
stretched her arms t
loud banging nois
From her ch
small door,
of the att
was i
cou

her p ... to disappear into her work. But all that would come were the same two faces. Two teenage faces.

One was thin, with lots of hair, held back in two thick braids with loose pieces flying about, the way she wore it as a young girl, before she cut it off. It was a new thought, that she had sheared it off, held it high above her head, took a pair of scissors and cut so that the top was less than an inch long. But she knew right away, it had happened.

The face next to hers had wide open eyes, fine hair, and a cocky smile. It was Lanny's smile, a teenage Lanny sitting next to her, in a diner, on a train, in a bus or a car. Then she knew, it was a car. A blue 1965 Plymouth Fury. Lanny's father's car.

Her fingers flew to the gum eraser and within seconds Lanny's face was gone, a pile of dust. She blew it away, a thinner face replacing it, with curly hair, a scrawny neck and narrow shoulders. It was Buddy, his mouth wide open, as if singing.

She couldn't draw anymore. Her eyelids were heavy as stones. She lay her head on the table, just for a second, not

e house filtered
abies coming, the
yelling, angrily. She
broke through the cover
k. She was wide awake.
from her desk. Her neck was
visted to one side. A pencil stuck
d it off. As she arched her back and
ward the ceiling she heard it again. A
e from across the hall.
air she could see out of her studio to the
ve feet high, that led to the unfinished portion
c. She didn't have to strain to listen. Someone
there. She heard footsteps, banging, and then, a
h.

Quietly she pushed her chair back and stood up. She carefully tiptoed down the hall, stepping lightly on the floorboards that invariably creaked. When she reached the second floor she raced to her bed where the phone sat in the middle of the blanket. Her fingers quickly pressed the emergency police number she'd reluctantly pasted to the receiver, thinking she'd never use it.

"Edgebury Public Safety," a female voice announced.

"There's an intruder in my house," she whispered.

"Okay now, just stay calm and give me your address."

Her throat was closing. She could barely get out the words. "Nine Epsom Court."

"I'm sending a car," the dispatcher reported after a second. "Will you be able to let us in?"

"Yes," she whispered, as if the intruder were in the room with her.

"Okay then. Open your front door and wait out in the street."

She slammed the receiver down and, taking two steps at a time, raced through the house. When she got outside her teeth were chattering.

The sound of tires on the wet street broke through the silence like rolling thunder. The patrol car screeched to a halt, and Brady walked up to her quickly, his hand perched on his gun handle.

"Is this another false alarm?"

She shook her head, her eyes filling up.

"Where is he?" He seemed kinder now.

"In the crawl space across from my studio," she got out. "Three flights up."

Brady gave McShane directions in a controlled, tight voice. Joy thought the young patrolman's eyes looked unnaturally bright, as if he were scared. She watched the men disappear through her front door.

Rain was falling steadily now, making her hair hang heavy, dripping down her neck. She let herself onto the porch and stood in a corner, waiting.

"Mrs. Bard?"

Brady stood at the porch door, looking for her through the screens.

"Yes?"

He stuck his flashlight back onto the large loop of his belt. McShane walked past him out of the house to the car, without meeting her eyes.

"What time was it when you bolted the door to that crawl space?"

"What do you mean?"

"I'm not saying it wasn't a good idea, if you thought somebody was up there. I'm just trying to get the time frame right here. Do you remember what time it was when you locked that door?"

She didn't understand. She hadn't locked anything. She felt stupid. She hated feeling stupid.

"Ma'am, would you follow me?"

She walked behind his rounded back up the three flights of stairs where he pointed to the door to the unfinished part of the attic. Three-quarters of the way up the door frame was a dead bolt. It was engaged.

"What time was it when you locked the door?"

"I didn't," she insisted. It wasn't locked, she was sure. In fact, she thought it had been open a crack. She remembered it open, just a crack.

"It wasn't locked. It was open. I didn't lock it."

"Well, ma'am, you can't lock a dead bolt from the inside, can you?"

"No," she answered softly. She thought a moment and said, "So someone else locked it. Someone is in the house somewhere."

"We checked the house, ma'am. You're well secured. Is your husband going to be home tonight?"

The question took her by surprise. "No."

"This is your first time alone in the house?"

"Why?"

"Don't get edgy," he cautioned, speaking to her pregnant belly. "It's just we get about ten of these calls a week. Ladies who aren't used to sleeping alone in old houses that creak, where things go bang in the night. Nine times out of ten that's all it is. Noisy pipes.

"And the tenth time?"

Brady broke into a wide smile. "This isn't the tenth time, because we checked your house, and there's no one here but us."

"I heard someone," Joy said. "I'm sure of it. Did you check everywhere? Can you check everywhere again?"

Brady played with his nose for a minute as if he were making sure it wasn't loose. Then he made up his mind and trotted down the stairs, taking one last look over his shoulder at the locked attic door.

Joy followed him to the street but hung back while he exchanged quiet words with McShane. They walked briskly past her into the house, leaving her to watch, through the rain, as their flashlights danced in the windows, lights flicking on and off. They were moving fast.

"You're safe," Brady said, when he rejoined her minutes later. "All you need is a good night's sleep. In the morning everything will look normal again. Now let's get you back inside."

"Lock the doors," McShane's voice rung out, surprising

her with its deep register. She engaged the locks and sat on the living room couch, studying the shadows, listening to her own quick breathing. After a while, when she caught herself drifting to sleep, she hoisted herself off the couch, closed all the windows, ran the dishwasher, checked the doors, and went to bed.

CHAPTER THIRTEEN

SHE WOKE UP so groggy she didn't notice she'd left the milk out on the counter all night. It was only after spitting out the first sip of curdled coffee that she stuck her nose in the carton and discovered it was warm and had gone bad. The day didn't improve.

When the drugstore truck pulled up to deliver her refill of maternity vitamins, she opened her wallet and found no money. The credit cards were lined up where they belonged, across from her driver's license and calling card, but the cash was gone, the coin purse flat and empty. Eventually she located a crumpled ten-dollar bill in the pocket of her raincoat and paid the man.

She was standing in the shower, the hot water pounding her back, when she noticed there was no shampoo. But she never threw an empty shampoo bottle away without placing a new one on the shelf. It was a habit Dorothy had ingrained in her. She did it automatically, without thinking.

Then it occurred to her—she was sure she had put the milk away before she went to sleep. She remembered closing the kitchen window, turning on the dishwasher, putting away the milk, noticing the bottom of the carton was damp, being too tired to do anything about it.

She turned off the water and stepped, dripping, out of the shower. Her hair wet but unwashed, she wrapped it in a towel, grabbed her robe, and ran downstairs. There, at the front of the top shelf of the refrigerator was a cloudy square, the half-dried remains of last night's leaky milk.

Next to the refrigerator her wallet still lay on the counter, open and empty. But she was sure her change purse had been full. If nothing else she was always flush with nickels, pennies, and dimes.

She stood, listening to the stove clock tick weakly. The radiator blew steam. Then she heard running water. It was the shower. But she had just turned it off. Slowly she walked up the stairs, doubting everything.

"I'm turning the faucet off," she announced out loud, as if to set the record straight. Then she inspected the house, room by room, checking to be sure all the windows were locked, that the doors were all secured. Finally she forced herself to climb the stairs and face the crawl space entryway. The dead bolt was still engaged.

When she returned downstairs, the towel slipped off her head in the foyer. In a daze she noticed but left it there, lying in the center of the rug.

As her hair dried, uncombed and matted, she wandered the first floor nervously. When the mail came she waited for the postman to walk out of sight before running to the porch to retrieve it. She ripped open the first envelope she grabbed, cutting her fingertip as she did. Using a long strand of paper towel, hastily torn off, she fashioned a bandage to stop the bleeding. Then she pulled out the photograph stuck snugly inside. Her mother had remembered after all.

There was no note, just an Instamatic photograph already fading with time. But it wasn't of the outside of the house. It was of Lanny and Buddy in Buddy's room, their faces pure annoyance at having been caught by the click of the camera. They sat on the floor atop a mound of clothes built out of crisp cotton, fresh flannel, and stiff denim. She remembered now how Buddy used to assemble it, a nest made of the new clothes that Dorothy bought and he refused to wear. Every week she would scoop them off the floor, wash them as if they'd been worn, and return them, neatly folded, to his drawers. But Buddy remained faithful to his blue and green flannel shirt and his white-kneed dungarees, wearing them week after week, day and night. Eventually the new clothes, freshly laundered, found their way back to the floor so Buddy could have something soft to lie on, a new nest to sleep in.

She wanted to drink up the picture, absorb every detail. But the doorbell rang. It was Irene, an old friend of Lanny's, come to pay a visit.

"Hi, there," Irene sang out, attempting to be cheerful. It didn't work. Irene wasn't a cheerful person. Hard-working and fiercely loyal, she was a prosecutor for the department of human resources, who was occasionally mistaken for one of her own defendants, due to her aversion to shopping and makeup. She had met Lanny in law school where they shared the notoriety of being at the top of their class. Even though she was an unlikely friend for him, a driven, hard-edged woman who complained constantly, they became close companions. Spared the distractions of romance by a total lack of sexual chemistry, they formed instead an exclusive study group that they both made clear welcomed no other members.

Irene's mind was a perfect match for Lanny's. Like him, she was obsessive about detail, could memorize volumes of facts, and was meticulous in her construction of brilliant and intimidating arguments. They both thrilled in facing each other off in mock trials. Their voices, screaming from behind closed doors, became legendary during their tenure as students at the University of Chicago Law School.

But Irene had no interest in the lures of corporate law. Instead, she dedicated herself to public service, spending long days prosecuting child abuse and neglect cases, doing her part to save the world.

"Much as I hate it, I have to go to Yonkers to take a deposition," Irene explained. "But I remembered Lanny mentioned you were under the weather, so I thought, I'm in the neighborhood—I'll just drop by."

Joy felt Irene assessing her. The messy hair. The towel lying on the rug. "I just got out of the shower," she explained, forcing a small laugh. She fingered her hair. "I haven't even had a chance to comb it yet." The blood-stained paper towel bandage came off her finger and dropped to Irene's feet. "A paper cut," she added, smiling weakly.

Irene stooped down and picked up the paper and the towel. "I'm totally parched. Can we have a cup of tea and talk?"

"Sure," Joy said, sounding too eager. "Just let me get dressed."

Alone in her room, while she slipped into maternity leggings and one of Lanny's sweatshirts, she tried to convince herself that this was just a social call. But it was hard to believe. On the rare occasion they got together, she and Irene visibly strained to be friendly. They all acknowledged the awkwardness, so Lanny kept this friendship to himself.

"How do you feel?" Irene asked Joy when she returned to discover her guest had made herself at home in the kitchen, looking through the cabinets until she'd found the tea.

"I'm fine." The less said the better.

"You know," Irene went on, as she filled the tea kettle, "don't worry about bothering me. I'm busy, it's true. But if you need anything, you really should let me know. I mean, people owe me. I can pull a few strings and arrange a nurse to come in. After all, now that you're pregnant, you're kind of in my department. Do you think you might want to talk to someone? A social worker maybe? Just to talk?"

"What exactly did Lanny tell you?" Joy asked, her eyes narrowing.

Clinging to the guise of sociability, they sat at the table facing each other.

"Nothing. Really. Just that you're on bed rest for a few days. And you had some staining. Just that." She was a bad liar. "You know Joy," she went on, "sometimes it's so depressing. I see such horror stories in my work."

Joy stared, stony-faced.

"And the thing is, a lot of these child abuse cases could have been averted if the mothers had gotten help before they gave birth. In fact, there's a movement now to try to convince the state we should be allowed to intervene prenatally. Of course, you can imagine how the women's groups are reacting to that."

The electric teakettle clicked off. Joy poured while Irene rattled on. "But all those women from all those groups should spend one week with me, and they'd change their tune. The things people do to their babies." She shook her head, then seemed to remember why she'd come. "Look, I'll be straight with you. I hope you don't mind my asking, but, as a friend, I have to. Are you okay about having these babies? I mean, are you . . ." she struggled to find the right word. "Are you well enough?"

"What are you asking, Irene? Are you asking if I might drown them or drop them out a window?"

Irene put down her teacup. "No," she said, stunned. "I wasn't asking that at all. I was just wondering if you needed a name of a good baby nurse. I see a lot of bad stuff, that's all. I wanted to know if you wanted a referral for a good baby nurse."

"Oh," Joy said.

"But I can see this isn't a good time to talk." Irene got up and poured her tea down the drain. "I guess I should have called first."

"No. It's fine. I'm glad you came. I just haven't been sleeping well." Joy needed to save things. She didn't want Irene leaving with the wrong impression. "Please, stay awhile."

"I wish I could," she answered, returning to the parlor

where she'd left her coat and briefcase. "But I have that deposition in Yonkers."

"You know I didn't mean that about drowning the babies," Joy explained, desperately. "It was a joke. Sarcasm. I'm just not myself."

"I can see that," Irene said quietly.

"I've been up for a couple of nights in a row, and I'm exhausted."

"Get used to it. You're probably going to be up for more than a couple of nights after the babies come. You're probably going to be up for months."

"Yes, but that's different," Joy defended herself.

"Look," Irene said, putting on her coat. "I didn't come here to give you a hard time. Really, I didn't."

"Why did you come then?" Joy found herself asking.

"I'm late. I have to go," Irene begged off. "I hope you feel better soon." Then she was gone.

Joy was still feeling shaken when she planted herself at her drafting table and pushed the unpleasant visit out of her mind. Working steadily, furiously, she finished two sketches for the book cover and then let her mind wander as she drew several more sketches, for herself. When Molly arrived, she realized she'd lost all sense of time.

Grateful for the company, she eagerly accepted the plate of chicken salad and crusty bread, gobbling it up hungrily. When she finished, she put the tray on the floor, but before Molly could take it away, she gently touched her arm. "Can I show you something?"

"Sure," Molly said, sitting down on a box of books she dragged next to the table.

"Look at these."

Molly leaned closer to the pile of drawings.

"This is my brother Buddy," she said in a hushed voice, pointing to the first drawing, Joy and Buddy in the Plymouth Fury.

"He looks like he's screaming," Molly observed quietly.

Joy handed her the next one. "This was Lanny and Buddy's clubhouse." She passed over a third picture. "I just finished this one. They're playing a game called 'Trust Me.' "

Molly lifted the busy, detailed sketch and studied it. Train tracks marched across the center of the page, alongside thick woods. Buddy and Lanny stood next to the tracks, a rope tied around each of their waists, several yards of slack between them. Lanny held up a box of mangled coins that had been crushed by the weight of passing trains.

"They'd go up there to the tracks," Joy explained, "where we weren't allowed. Buddy would wear a blindfold and put cotton in his ears. Then he'd crawl, feeling his way on the ground, until he got to the first rail. He'd sit on the rail while Lanny stood several feet away. Then they'd wait. I used to watch them. They wouldn't move. Until a train came. They'd let the train get close. Buddy told me once it got so close he could feel its heat. But he never moved. Not until Lanny yanked the rope with all his might, pulling him away."

Molly shuddered and put the sketch down. "Did Buddy ever get hit by a train?"

"No." Joy shook her head stiffly. "He probably would have. We all would have. But the train company sent down a guard. He appeared, walking the tracks, the day I was going to try it. I wanted to join their club, too."

"I guess all kids do dumb things."

"Buddy and Lanny did crazy things all the time. I've been remembering—pranks I haven't thought about in years. Lanny sneaking into our house naked, then sneaking out in my mother's nightgown. Buddy climbing out of the bedroom window, letting himself to the ground with a rope made of tied-together sheets. Snuffing out candles with their palms, stamping out cigarette butts with their bare feet. Once they dared each other to drink an entire bottle of maple syrup. They took turns making up dares. And I wanted so badly to join in."

She took the sketch back from Molly and stared at it. "Something happened to Buddy."

"He was kidnapped, right?"

"But why?" she whispered, as if she was afraid to speak out loud.

"I don't know. Why is anyone kidnapped?" Molly stared at the sketch over Joy's shoulder, then pointed to a figure she hadn't seen at first. A man half-hidden in a cluster of trees. A big man, with a thick neck, thick arms. A man in the woods, watching. "Who's he?"

"I don't know," Joy admitted.

"You've got to show this to someone," Molly said. "Someone who can tell you what happened to Buddy."

Joy stuck the sketch in the middle of a pile of drawings and then slipped them under the bottom of the bookcase. "I'm showing it to no one," she announced.

"You've got to get someone to tell you what happened," Molly insisted. "If you think they know."

"Lanny knows," Joy replied. But Molly didn't hear her. She was busy gathering the dinner dishes onto the tray, getting ready to take it downstairs and return home to her daughter. So Joy repeated it for herself. "Lanny knows."

CHAPTER FOURTEEN

SHE WOKE THINKING about calling Dr. Wayne to ask him why she was walking around in a daze. There was no reason she should have forgotten where she left her slippers. Yet it was as if they had disappeared. It wasn't like her to neglect turning off the faucet in the bathroom sink. But the night before she had left it on just enough so that now the bathroom floor was covered with an inch of water. Something was wrong. Despite sleeping deeply, she woke exhausted. Something was wrong, and she had to call Dr. Wayne to find out what it was.

She finished drying the floor and forced herself to stand up. She stepped out of her nightgown, now damp with the morning flood. As she hung it on a hook to dry she caught a glimpse of her body in the shower-door mirror. She looked away quickly. Her shape had changed. She had to call Dr. Wayne.

As the bathroom steamed up, her reflection clouded over. She stuck her hand in the shower. The water was hot, very hot. She stepped into the tub and let it rain down on her face, her hair, her back, her arms, her stomach. Her foot came up against a sliver of soap. She bent down to pick it up, but it flew out of her grasp. She squatted, holding on to the wall for support, but the steam was too thick for her to see. She didn't want to slip on the soap like the lawyer in Lanny's office who'd broken her hip because of a half-moon of Dove she hadn't seen on her shower stall floor.

Joy turned off the water and waited for the steam to dissipate. When she knelt again she saw it, a tiny head, a mouse head, sliding up to her, sliding away toward the drain.

Groaning she leapt from the shower and ran to the hallway, dripping wet and naked. Forcing herself to go back, she grabbed her robe from the hook on the back of the door and wrapped herself in it. Then she pushed the curtain aside to look again. One little mouse head with unblinking eyes lay on top of the drain like a muddy rock.

Grabbing yesterday's clothes off the chair next to the bed, she raced to the kitchen and vomited in the sink. Then she saw the baseball cap on the dining room table. It was forest green with a red insignia she didn't recognize. But underneath, in small letters, easy to read, she saw the words: Edgebury High.

Gingerly, she picked it up and placed it on her head. It

fell to her eyes. She threw it on the table, as if it were dis-
eased, then dialed Donna's number.

"Shut up," she heard Donna say to a noisy group of kids.
"Sure, come on over and bring it with you. Just give me a
few minutes to get everybody out the door."

Joy gave her more than a few minutes. She didn't want
to talk to Donna in front of her brood. Besides, she needed
time to think this through, to think about what she was going to say.

In the end she didn't get very far with a plan. She just
stood, watching the clock tick off minutes that passed like
hours, while her anger mutated to fear and then to awkwardness and embarrassment.

Even though she walked slowly, stalling before ringing
the bell, when she arrived in the Thomas kitchen it was still
in the midst of the tornado created by five kids trying to
delay getting ready for school.

"Get Seth," Donna told Jimmy, her ten-year-old, who
was crushing Fruit Loops on the counter with the palm of
his hand.

"What did he do?" the boy asked, his eyes bright.

"Get him down here now," Donna said as she clapped
together a salt and pepper set shaped like two bronzed baby
shoes.

Jimmy dragged his feet as he left the room. Donna continued setting up cereal bowls and boxes on the long
yellow-speckled linoleum counter. Joy sat on a white plastic
chair, nervously fingering the baseball cap that lay in her
lap, heavy as lead.

"Mom." One of Donna's teenage daughters stomped into
the kitchen, her jeans skin tight, her sweater pushed off one
shoulder, exposing the thin pink strap of her bra. She
walked past Joy without a glance, as if strangers sat rigid
on their kitchen chairs every morning.

"Could you please get Louise out of the bathroom? I
can't go to school like this." She grabbed her tangled hair
with her fingers, flashing the neon green of her painted
nails.

Donna handed her two full cereal bowls. "Deal with it. In the den. Mrs. Bard and I have to talk to Seth. In private."

"What did he do now?" Melissa asked with growing interest, as if she'd only just noticed Joy.

"Out of here."

"I hate this place," she grumbled. She stomped out of the room, studying Joy as she passed her.

"If you want a cup, help yourself." Donna pointed to the Mr. Coffee at the far end of the counter, but her tone was uninviting so Joy didn't move.

"What now, Ma?"

Joy recognized Seth's whiny voice as he straggled into the room, looking as if he'd just rolled out of his bed, his shirts and pants wrinkled, slept in.

"I couldn't have done anything. I'm not even awake yet."

"Well, get awake."

The front door slammed, and a voice rang out, "Hello," as Charlie bounced into the room. He looked fresh and crisp. His just-washed hair was damp, the comb marks still visible. His scrubbed cheeks were rosy and shining. His pack was slung over his athletic shoulders as if it were filled with air.

"Good morning, Mrs. Thomas," he said smiling brightly. "Good morning, Mrs. Bard. Hope I'm not interrupting anything."

Joy saw his chocolate eyes stop at the baseball cap she'd placed on the table, and a film passed over them making him look older, and mean.

"Sit down, Charlie. Mrs. Bard has something to say to both of you."

Unsure of himself, Seth remained standing. Charlie turned his chair around and sat down, legs spread, straddling the back. Donna sat across from him, her dimpled hands resting on the tabletop, one cupped atop the other as if she was hiding something underneath.

"All right," she said. "We're all listening."

Joy took a shaky breath and began. "I want to come to an understanding."

"Oh?" Charlie's smile broadened, and his eyes twinkled. "About what?"

Donna reached over and slapped his hand. "Behave," she said.

Joy took another breath. "Someone has been playing pranks on us. Not very nice pranks."

"Like what?" Seth asked, his mouth hanging open in anticipation.

Donna's lips and hands pressed together hard, her fingertips turning white.

"Dead squirrels on my front lawn."

Donna loosened her grasp, and her fingers turned back to pink. "Haven't we already discussed that?"

"Dead squirrels in my closet."

"That's not what the exterminator said when he came to do my bees," Donna muttered. Joy ignored the comment and pushed on.

"A mouse head in my shower."

"You're kidding." Charlie's eyes glistened. "A mouse head?" He sounded like he thought it was a great idea, an idea to be proud of.

Joy's shoulders sagged. She hadn't thought this through. She should have thought it through. "Someone broke into my house last night." But she wasn't sure it was last night. She'd been so absentminded lately she couldn't be sure how long the cap had been sitting there.

Donna, Seth, and Charlie stared at her, waiting for her to go on. She pushed the cap to the center of the table. Donna folded her arms across her wide chest, protectively. Joy met her hard gaze and said, "They left this hat."

"They weren't too bright," Seth said, snorting a laugh.

"Seth." Donna picked up the hat. "The woman wants to know whose hat this is."

"I don't know," he mumbled. "They gave them out last year to everyone in school. So I guess it's someone from school." He turned to Charlie and winked, proud of himself. He couldn't stop himself from smirking with satisfaction at his smug answer.

"Try on the hat, Seth," his mother ordered, her voice flat.

"Come on, Ma. What will that prove?"

Donna held it out to him. "She wants to see you put it on. Let's get it over with. Put it on."

"I'll try it on, Mrs. Thomas," Charlie said, taking the hat and balancing it on the tip of his finger. "But it won't prove nothing."

"Why is that?" Joy asked. She could barely talk. Her chest was tight and her throat was closing up.

"Because." Charlie twirled the hat faster and faster until it spun off his hand. Then he scooped it off the floor and held it up in front of his face like a catcher's mask. "These caps?" He looked at her through the wide mesh weave. "They only come in one size. See?" And to show her, he ripped open the adjustable back strap so that now it was a cap that fit anyone, or no one at all.

CHAPTER FIFTEEN

SHE HURRIED DOWN Donna's front walk, with little time to make the train. The old man in the run-down gray house next to Molly's sat, bundled up, on his front porch rocker. She didn't even realize he'd said hello until she was on the next block.

The wind blew a pile of dried leaves against her legs. The sun broke through the thick clouds, trying to warm the

air. As she raced to the station, she undid the big buttons of
her oversize swing coat, took off her black leather gloves,
and massaged her belly, where the slow steady pressure of
contractions persisted. By the time she reached the train station, she was out of breath and sweating.

"Joy. Joy Bard. Right?"

She swung around quickly to face the unfamiliar stranger, tall, with a long, narrow face and big ears that stuck
straight out like wings.

"Art. Art Thomas."

She returned his handshake but still didn't know who he
was.

"Donna's husband. You were just over to my house. Surprised you didn't hear me follow you here. You know my
son, Sethy, right?"

Joy felt her shoulders rise as if ready for a blow.

"You've been having a lot of problems over at your
place. Break-ins and whatnot. That right?"

"Yes," she said quietly.

"You need an alarm, that's what you need. My brother-
in-law sells alarms."

She hadn't thought of it, but it struck her now as a good
idea. Except not Art's brother-in-law. Not if he was like
Art. Art was standing too close. Talking too loud. She
could smell a morning whiskey on his breath.

The screech of the approaching train gave her a chance
to look away.

"Don't let those old bats intimidate you," he went on,
standing even closer, talking right into her ear. "They're
just a bunch of frustrated tomatoes."

The train eased to a stop directly before her. She hoisted
herself up the steep metal steps, ignoring Art's helpful hand
on her elbow.

"They're always jealous of a pretty new face," he said,
following her as she turned into the car on her right.

She pretended she didn't hear him and slid into a seat by
the window, holding her breath, hoping he wouldn't slide in

beside her. When he didn't, she unclasped her knotted hands. Then she felt him again, too close.

"Jealous tomatoes," he said from the seat behind. "That's all they are."

A piece of paper appeared over her head and fell onto her lap. She unfolded it and read, "Whittaker Fire and Security, No Job Too Small." She slipped the note into her purse and shut her eyes, resting her head on the dirty glass window.

When the conductor tapped her shoulder for her fare, she jumped up in her seat.

"Bad dream?" he asked, laughing heartily.

Her mouth turned up in a smile as she tried to ride the wave of his good humor. She handed him a five-dollar bill, damp from being squashed in her tight fist.

His smile vanished. "What did you do with this? Give it a bath?" He returned her change, then wiped his hand on his shiny blue pants. She leaned back in her seat and shut her eyes.

From Grand Central Terminal it was twenty blocks to the doctor's office, but when she saw Art standing at the corner, waving for a taxi, she decided to walk. Still, she couldn't shake the feeling that she was being followed, that Art was hovering behind, waiting to see which way she turned, staying at a distance, never letting her get too far out of his sight.

Finally she twisted her neck to look behind her, to see if she could spot him, to put her fear to rest. But the light had just turned green and the dense crowd behind her surged forward, carrying her along with it. She picked up her pace, half running to the ivy-covered brownstone where Dr. Wayne's crowded reception room awaited her.

The nurse had already brought out several folding chairs to accommodate the patients who were stacking up, lined against the wall, massaging their growing bellies. It was a bad sign.

"Sorry, sorry, sorry," Dr. Wayne said when he finally

joined Joy in the small exam room. "I think it's a full moon. I always get backed up when it's a full moon."

He pressed his big hands on her belly and felt around, pushing everywhere. Too hard, Joy thought.

"My shape has changed," she said as he continued his methodical manual search.

"Now, now, now," he said, still pressing.

"And I'm distracted. I forget things. I'm exhausted all the time."

He took a small flashlight out of a drawer and aimed the sharp light into her eyes. "Well, you're pregnant." He switched off the light. "That comes with the territory."

"What about my breath?" she went on. "I have this bad taste in my mouth all the time. Is that normal?"

"I must admit," he said after scribbling on her chart. "I'm worried."

"Why is that?" she asked quickly.

"All these questions of yours. What's behind them?"

"What do you mean?"

"You're distracted. All right. Every pregnant woman gets distracted. But then you don't like your shape. You don't like your breath. I'm hearing 'depressed.' "

She jumped off the table and lifted her dress. "Is this a normal shape, Doctor?"

"Normal? There's no such thing as normal. What exactly are your expectations? If you're thinking you might qualify for the *Sport's Illustrated* swim suit issue, well, no, that's true. You won't."

"I don't look right," Joy insisted.

He scribbled some more on her chart, and when she stretched over to read it he snapped the covers closed.

"Joy," he said slowly, his eyebrows lowering. "I'd like to recommend you see a psychiatrist. It's nothing to be ashamed of. Given your history, it's to be expected."

"What history?"

He cleared his throat, annoyed that this wasn't going to be easy. "Well, for starters, growing up as an identical twin. Then having your twin disappear."

Joy couldn't stop a tired smile from spreading on her face. It suddenly seemed so laughable. Dr. Wayne talking about Buddy disappearing, like he was an old pair of shoes that someone had misplaced. But he wasn't misplaced. He was gone.

She slipped her feet into a pair of too tight suede shoes. "He didn't disappear, Dr. Wayne." She picked her purse off the white counter and brushed her hair out of her eyes.

"What do you mean, dear?"

"We all know Buddy was kidnapped. And it was no accident that they took him. There was a reason. Do you know what it was?"

"No. What?" He was cheerful, polite, humoring her.

"I'll be sure to let you know as soon as I find out," she snapped back.

"Joy?" Dr. Wayne called as she hustled out of his office and raced through the waiting room. "Will you wait for Madeleine to give you the phone number of that doctor I'd like you to talk to?"

The slamming door was his answer.

CHAPTER SIXTEEN

"YOU JUST HAVE to do it, don't you?" Dorothy dug the shrimp out of her puff pastry and lined them up on her plate, two by two, like schoolgirls in line for a fire drill. "You really enjoy humiliating me."

Joy knew it was coming. She'd called the restaurant to

say she'd be late as soon as she saw Dr. Wayne's crowded waiting room. But she knew even as she did it, it wouldn't help. The Russian Tea Room always put Dorothy in a vile mood. She hated waiting behind the velvet ropes while one woman after another, with big hair and bigger jewelry, walked in, escorted by men in open shirts and perfect roasted-marshmallow tans. She hated watching the maître d' kiss their cheeks and glide them past the holding pen to one of the many vacant, spacious banquettes. She had been coming here before most of those women had been born. Why didn't that count, she wanted to know. Why didn't loyalty get her any special treatment?

Yet year after year she insisted on coming back to sip her tea and eat small spoonfuls of jam while waiting for the famous to pay their bills. At least then she could drop a name or two—tell an easily impressed client that she had eaten lunch across the room from Sean Connery and how he was even more handsome in person.

Never mind that she misidentified people all the time. A loud-talking publicist with black hair, cut spikey, became, for future reference, Liza Minelli. A salt-and-pepper haired banker with sky blue eyes turned into Paul Newman. She was shameless in her errors and surly when corrected.

But today, Joy didn't care. She didn't care that her mother was in a foul mood, snapping at everything she said, banging her fork on her plate, complaining of bad service and small portions and of the wait, the very long wait she suffered through while Joy dawdled at the doctor. Today Joy let it all wash over her like white noise. She let herself drift in and out, only dimly aware of her mother's harsh red-lipsticked scowl.

The busboy cleared the table and the waiter arrived with two cups of tea, a small dish of raspberry jam, and a stubby rectangle of baklavah that Dorothy had ordered when she first sat down. Soothed by the tea, her eyes resumed their dance, checking out the room for stars. She looked around and sighed.

"There's no one here today. It's not like it used to be."

She motioned brusquely for the waiter to bring the check and then opened her compact to repair her faded lips with fresh paint. When she snapped the case shut, she noticed Joy drawing faces on the inside of a matchbook cover.

"I wish you wouldn't do that. It's rude." She blotted her lips on her white napkin, pulled a small envelope out of her crocodile purse, and waved it in front of Joy as if she were perfuming the air. "I brought something for you," she announced. "But now I don't know if you deserve to see it."

"What is it?"

"Another picture that I'll give to you as soon as you stop being such a pill."

Dorothy slid the envelope across the red tablecloth but didn't let go. "Now would you please try treating your mother with some respect?" She waited for a response, let out a disgusted sigh, and removed her hand.

Joy grabbed the envelope and lifted the unsealed flap, pulling out a small black-and-white photograph. She held on to the bottom scalloped edge. The date was stamped on top. October 1965.

It was a house she hadn't seen before, slightly smaller than hers, with a narrow patch of front lawn. Seated in front, on the sidewalk, were three children. Joy looked more closely and recognized herself, her perfect braids tied with matching rubber bands. Then she saw Buddy, his curly hair cropped short, his tongue stuck out at the camera. Behind them, with one hand held over their heads, his pinky and thumb spread out in the sign of a hex, stood a teenage Lanny.

"Does this make you feel better now? Are you human now?"

But Joy couldn't stop staring. For there, in the open doorway of the house, was another figure. The same man she'd drawn in the shadows of the woods, next to the train tracks. The same man she'd drawn holding the skeleton key.

"Who is this?" She passed the picture back to her mother and pointed to the large head, the beefy body.

"Please. Stop it. You know who that is."

"I don't. Really."

"Henry," she let out, from pursed lips. "Your father-in-law, Henry. I suppose you expect me to believe your memory is too delicate to remember Henry?"

"Was something wrong with him?"

"Are you serious?"

"I don't remember."

Dorothy sighed and rolled her eyes. "Poor, big Henry. He shook the floor when he walked. He spoke too loud. He was deaf in one ear. You children were terrified of him."

"Why?"

"I have no idea why. You know, Henry and I had some lovely times. We might have ended up together had circumstances been different."

"What do you mean?"

"I told you. You children acted like he was a monster."

"And what else?"

"I knew I shouldn't be showing you these pictures. You're so fragile. You look positively chipped."

"What happened to him?"

Dorothy pressed her lips together and her eyelids fluttered briefly. "Poor Henry went into the garage one day, put a gun to his head, and pulled the trigger," she explained with disgust. "As if you didn't know."

Joy's teacup clattered as she dropped it. The people at the next table stared. A waiter appeared to wipe the spill. She grabbed the bunch of linen napkins from him and began patting her lap where she could feel the warm tea soaking through.

"She's pregnant with twins," Dorothy told the waiter apologetically.

"I see," he replied, with no interest. Joy passed him the bunch of wet napkins, and he disappeared into the noisy room.

"What is wrong with you?" Dorothy dabbed the damp tablecloth with a tissue she pulled out of her sleeve.

"Nothing. I'm fine. Let's go." She slipped the photograph in her bag while her mother signed the check.

"Do you have any more pictures?" Joy asked, squinting as she stepped from the dark restaurant into the blustery day.

Her mother tied a scarf around her hair to protect it from the wind. "If I did I'd throw them away," she said, putting on her sunglasses. She started walking down Fifty-seventh Street, her heels clicking. "You take one look and your memory snaps off. Then you get hysterical. Why would I show you more pictures?"

"I'm not hysterical," Joy insisted. "I want to see more, if there are any."

"Oh, you do."

"Yes. I do. I have some things to figure out before the babies come."

"What now?" Dorothy's eyes stared straight ahead as she paved a path through the throng of mid-day walkers. "There is absolutely nothing to figure out. This is an exercise in self-torture. Lanny will be furious with me if he finds out I've upset you with all this talk about poor Henry. Obviously you two don't talk about him. We shouldn't either."

"Don't worry. I won't tell him," Joy offered, which seemed to make Dorothy relax.

They continued east toward the furniture showroom where Dorothy was taking Joy to see an elegant chameleonic glass table she swore was the latest thing. Joy nodded occasionally as her mother redirected the conversation to the beauty of a table that could change color. But she wasn't listening. She was adding another piece to the puzzle. Lanny never talked about why he went to live with his grandmother although she knew, from the few stories he told, usually following several shots of Absolut with a twist, it had been an unpleasant arrangement from the start. She knew he and three cats shared a room that had once been a large closet. That on some nights he was forced to camp out in the hallway because his grandmother had decided her super was a Nazi who was planning to get her. On good days she had him scrub down the blinds and wash the woodwork before inviting him to her room in the evening to brush her thin hair. There he'd run her brush, covered with more greasy strands than were on her head, over her ancient scalp one hundred times, while she applied Wesson oil to her cheeks and then to his, to keep them soft. And once a week he was called to the bathroom to rinse out her shampoo while she soaked, her wrinkled accordion skin barely covered by several inches of sweet oily bath water.

She knew his mother had been ill and sent away when he was young, just before he moved to Toney's Brook. But after Joy and Dorothy moved into their West side apartment they never heard anything more about Lanny's father. It was as if he had vanished. Even as they planned their wedding Lanny avoided answering questions about him, or about anyone else in his absent family.

"He's dead, and there's no one else," he'd shouted at her one night, one of the few times he'd ever lost his temper. "How many different ways do you want me to say it? The man is dead. Stop stabbing me with your questions."

She stopped asking and then forgot Henry completely.

Dorothy rambled on about indirect lighting as they waited for the traffic light to change at the corner of Fifth and Fifty-seventh, so she didn't notice Joy stiffen. Nor did she know that Joy had suddenly lost all sense of sound around her and was staring, frozen, across the street.

It was hard to get a clear look. The lunchtime crowd was sizable and in constant motion. Women leaning together, dissecting the subtext of their lunch meetings, men clutching briefcases, hailing cabs as they checked their watches. Everyone angling for the best spot to get a jump on the light, bunching up three deep, then spreading out in one long line. But across the street, through the rippling crowd, she saw a pair of familiar shoulders and the angle of a familiar nose and then a glimpse of Lanny's eyes.

She glanced over to see if Dorothy had noticed him, too,

but her mother was deep into a monologue about a painter she knew, an artist when it came to marbling walls. When Joy looked back she couldn't find Lanny at all.

Then she saw him, standing directly across the street, his eyes drilling into the crowd, not seeing her.

She forced herself to smile and wave, but Lanny's face betrayed no hint of recognition. His mouth remained flat, his hand didn't rise to wave back. He stared straight ahead. But his bright blue eyes pulled her to him.

"Lanny," she called out.

Dorothy stopped talking and watched the light turn yellow as Joy began to cross the street. A smoke-belching truck sounded its blaring horn, but Joy didn't seem to hear. The crowd watched in horror as the driver hit the brakes, but the truck couldn't stop its forward slide. Dorothy pushed her way past a messenger and yanked her daughter out of the way.

"Are you trying to kill yourself?" she shrieked. "Didn't you see that truck?"

But Joy didn't answer. The truck jerked down the street as she scanned the crowd that was fast approaching. Her head swinging from side to side, she studied the people who pushed their way past where she stood still as a lamp post, blocking them. But he was gone.

"I saw Lanny," Joy said, dazed.

"You are out of your mind. Lanny's out of town."

Despite her silence, Joy knew what her mother was thinking. That her suspicions about the marriage were right all along. That it really was too good to be true.

"We'll call him," Dorothy announced, as she regained control, ran her fingers around her lacquered hair, straightened her suit, and checked her lipstick in her compact as she walked. "That's all. We'll call him."

The first three pay phones they passed were broken. At the fourth, a woman balanced an open briefcase on the tiny shelf inside and ignored them completely while she made her mid-day sales calls, one after another, without glancing back to see the growing line.

Dorothy sighed loudly at twenty second intervals, but Joy was relieved by the wait. It gave her time to rehearse what she was going to say. She didn't want to make a fool of herself, to get pegged as a suspicious wife.

"Has he called in yet this afternoon?" she asked Kelly when the saleswoman finished her day's work and passed the warm, damp receiver on to Joy.

There was silence on the other end of the line, and Joy felt compelled to fill it in. "I was expecting to hear from him this morning to tell me what flight he's catching tomorrow, but I haven't been home all day."

"I'm sorry, Mrs. Bard, but I didn't make his reservations. It all got done from Mr. Berger's office this time. Do you want me to call up there and ask them? Is everything all right?"

"Everything is fine. Don't bother anyone," Joy said, trying to sound cheerful. "Just tell him I called."

"Will do, Mrs. Bard," Kelly said.

"So?" Dorothy asked when Joy hung up.

"So he's still out of town."

"So. Now you're imagining things."

Joy didn't argue. There was nothing to be gained by arguing. She knew what she saw.

"Well, let's get this expedition over with. Dr. Wayne told me you've been cooped up in that old house for too many days. You need some fresh air." Dorothy ran to the corner and beat out a young man to a taxi.

Joy sank back into the torn seat of the cab. She could vaguely hear her mother talking about crushed velvet and antique silk, but there was no need to respond. She let the sound flow over her as she set about figuring out how she could explain that she was in danger, when she didn't know herself what the danger was. Silently she went through the names of everyone she knew, trying to figure out whom she could turn to, whom she could absolutely trust. But in the end, she knew, there was no one but herself.

CHAPTER
SEVENTEEN

SHE'D LEFT MESSAGES for four alarm companies. John O'Brien, from O'Brien Security, was the first to return her call.

"Six o'clock all right for you?" he asked, and the appointment was set.

The ruddy-cheeked salesman walked in moments after Molly arrived with a roast chicken big enough to feed a family of four. He took a sniff with his bulbous nose, then rolled his watery eyes.

"I sell security systems to protect the home. And this," he said as his arm swept the room, "smells like a real home."

The women exchanged amused glances that O'Brien graciously pretended he didn't see.

"Two minutes late." He pointed to his digital watch, getting down to business. "Sorry about that. Hate to be late." He put his heavy black case down in the living room and rubbed his hands together, expectantly, his eyes already taking in the house, sizing up the windows, the doorways, the lighting, and the overgrown rhododendron bushes that were just beginning to obscure the living room window view.

"Old house," he said, nodding to himself. His face said, I've seen this before. I know this setup. I see the problem.

"Nice part of town here." He crept up the first flight of

stairs, looking down, around, turning, measuring with his eyes, counting windows on his fingers.

"Thanks," Joy said, standing at Molly's side at the foot of the stairs.

"Burglar's dream," he went on, disappearing into the rooms above.

"Get references," Molly whispered as O'Brien quickly descended the stairs, holding his body angled sideways, as if he was afraid of falling.

Joy followed him to the kitchen. "Have you installed a lot of systems in Edgebury?"

"Did a house last month, right around the block. Robinson family. Know them?"

Joy didn't.

"Nice people," he said as he lifted and lowered her kitchen windows, nodding his head whenever one of them stuck. "Guy wanted every window and door, three flights up and the attic." He made several notations on his clipboard. "Tried to talk him out of doing the third floor and the attic, but he wanted it—we did it." He put down the clipboard and turned to Joy and Molly. "Used the system twice. Called a couple of days later complaining it was broken. Said the alarm kept going off for no reason. Sent a serviceman over. No answer. Pete, my best man, can't get in the house. Calls the cops. Found the whole family tied up in the basement. House cleaned out. Thank God, no one was hurt."

"What happened?" Molly asked.

Joy answered for him. "Someone must have been hiding in the house, waiting for them." O'Brien pointed his finger at her like a gun and clicked his tongue to say, Bingo, you got it.

He opened the heavy painted wood door next to the kitchen pantry.

"Basement?"

Joy nodded and followed him down the rough wood steps.

"Need to replace these," he said, the stairs creaking under his heavy feet. "Fire hazard."

He weaved through the dark rooms of the unfinished cellar, nodding every time he opened and closed a web-covered window.

"No problem getting in here." He counted aloud, nine windows, then added some figures to his proposal.

"Amazing thing," he said turning to Joy, putting his pen back into his shirt pocket. "Month before last. Woman wanted all her windows and doors covered, then decided not to bother with the basement. 'Nothing to take down there,' she told me. They took her washer and dryer. Nice woman. Three kids. Told me later, the thing about coin Laundromats is you never know what went in the machine before you got there. Ended up wiring her basement after all. And her garage."

He opened a door to the outside. "Backyard?" he asked and Joy nodded. "Need lights," he said. "Good security system always includes lights." He took a thin flashlight out of his back pocket and stepped into the night.

Joy returned to the kitchen where she and Molly watched from the window. The flashlight moved about the yard, stopping in a far corner as O'Brien looked for something. When he returned to the kitchen his pink hands clutched a white dish.

"Dead raccoon out there," he announced. "This yours?" He held up the dish. It was a dog's dish.

"That's Cookie's," Molly said. "We kept a water dish for her in the backyard."

He put the dish under Joy's nose. "No water in here." The smell made her gag.

"Know what it is?"

She shook her head.

"Sure you do." He put the dish on the counter, and Joy covered her mouth with her hand, hoping she wouldn't get sick.

"Peanut butter," he said. "To start with, peanut butter."

He lifted the bowl again. "Green and white specks mixed in, see?"

The wave of nausea deepened, and Joy averted her eyes, hoping that would help.

"Ever clean toilets?"

"Pardon me?" Molly said.

"Ever clean toilets?"

"It's Drano," Joy said quietly and O'Brien looked at her like she was smarter than he'd first thought.

"The crystals," he expounded. "Mixed in like sugar."

Joy pushed the bowl farther down the counter, and Molly picked it up and dumped the whole thing in the garbage can.

"You leave it out there? To catch raccoons?"

"No," Joy said.

"Your husband?"

"He's away."

"Then, Mrs. Bard, I'd say you need a system in this house fast."

Joy wondered if he'd had time to get the dish out of his car to plant it in the back, but he didn't have time, and besides, Molly had said it was Cookie's dish.

They followed him to the living room where he took out two sample keypads and explained how they worked.

"You need to cover your basement, your first and second floors. Shock detectors, motion detectors, spots in back, side and front. Everything gets hooked up to the monitoring service. Alarm goes off, they call you. You're not home, you don't say the password, they call the police."

He leaned back in the chair, sighed heavily, and let his manicured fingers move quickly over the tiny keys of his credit card–sized calculator to tally the figures he'd scrawled in the margins.

"Thirty-five hundred. You'll sleep like a baby. Husband travel a lot?"

"Some," Joy said, shivering as she thought about Lanny for the first time all night, wondering where he was.

"Look it over," he said, passing her the clipboard, "while I make sure I didn't miss anything."

While O'Brien walked around the first floor, and up to the second, Joy tried to decipher his squashed handwriting. When she heard him reach the third floor, she put the clipboard down and went up to join him.

"Me," he explained, surveying the third-floor landing, poking his head into her studio, "I don't believe in alarming attics." He stared across the hall at the little attic door. "Guy wants to get in all the way up here, he'll get in. Know what I mean?"

"Does that look like a new lock to you?" she asked, pointing to the dead bolt. Then she noticed. The bar wasn't in the thin metal sheath. The crawl space door was open a paper thin crack.

"Can't tell you that," he said, shaking his head. "Good lock, though. Good lock to have up here. Anyone breaks in, they're pretty well stuck there. Unless of course you got a kitchen inside stocked with food and beer. People do all kinds of things." He stared at the door. "Won't work unless you keep it locked, right?"

Joy nodded and wondered if a lock like that could come undone, slowly, all by itself, from the small stresses of an old house.

O'Brien swung open the small door and ducked inside, returning a moment later. He shot the bolt into the casement. "You're safe here," he announced, clapping his hands. "Now what about in the rest of the house?"

"How soon can you install the system?" she asked, surprising herself. Thirty-five hundred dollars was a lot of money. This wasn't the kind of decision she'd ever made before, on her own.

They walked in silence to the living room where he took out his large calendar, the small squares of dates covered with his squashed, indecipherable scrawl. He sighed again, heavily. "Don't want you to wait. Love to do it for you tomorrow." He shook his head, wearily. "Has to be next week. Can't fit you in before next week. Meantime I can rent you some portables. Motion detectors, I mean. For the interim. Provided I've got a set in my car."

By the time Joy went up to bed, the small black boxes were sitting at attention in the living room, dining room, foyer, and right outside the basement door, watching the dust fall, waiting to protect her.

Exhausted, she picked up the bedside shoe phone, vowed again to replace it, and called Lanny.

"Mr. Bard is not here right now," the hotel receptionist's sunny California voice rang out. "But don't worry," she went on, talking through her nose. "When he calls in for messages, he'll get all of yours."

She hung up the phone and crawled under the covers, rotating in regular intervals, like a chicken on a spit. But her heavy body felt off-balance. She couldn't find a comfortable position. And her mind wouldn't turn off. The house, her work, the babies. Lanny, the teenagers, the babies. The babies.

Her breathing steadied. The black door slammed. Buddy pressed his face up against the car window, his nose squashed by the glass. She pulled at the handle, but the door wouldn't budge. When she let go she started to fall, Alice down the rabbit hole, down, down, down.

Her body jerked as she tried to stop her descent. her eyes popped open. Her feet were tangled in the sheets. She rolled over to her other side to get a look at the digital clock on Lanny's night table. A body blocked her view. She was staring at the back of a body lying next to her in bed.

She shot up, raced to the bathroom, slammed the door, and locked it. All was quiet. She waited. Silence enveloped her. She waited longer. Still, no sound, no sign of life came from beyond her hiding place. She unlocked the door. She pushed it open slowly and peered out. The bedclothes were in a jumble, and next to where she had lain two pillows stared back at her. But this time she was sure it wasn't her imagination. She had felt the warmth of a body beside her.

"Damn," she muttered as she pushed the pillows and

comforter to the floor. Then, wrapping herself in her robe, she trudged up to her studio. Too wired to sleep, she'd try instead to disappear into her work.

She picked up her mechanical pencil, ready to tackle drawing Fred, the murderer on her cover. At first her hand fought her. She kept erasing his cheeks to flatten them out, erasing the eyes so she could resketch them hooded with heavy lids. Then, in a rush, her pencil cooperated and the murderer came to life.

When he was done his cheeks were sunken, the skin slightly pockmarked. His hair, which she would paint a purplish black, was slicked back like it was coated with corn oil. His nose was thin, as were his uneven lips, the bottom one half-withered away. She slipped Fred into her portfolio and zipped it closed. She was calmer now. She was tired. Once again she was very tired.

She left a trail of lights behind her, climbed down the stairs and crawled into bed, her robe still on, an extra layer of protection.

Her thoughts wandered. Where was Lanny? How could she have forgotten his father's suicide? What was wrong with the pregnancy? She turned and looked at the phone beside her as several high-pitched electronic beeps rang out of the small amplifier. Lanny was making a call from the kitchen phone. Then she remembered, Lanny wasn't home. Someone was in the house.

For several moments she lay, paralyzed. Someone was in the kitchen making a call. Then she struggled to lift herself up, her arms half-asleep and uncooperative. Ignoring the sting of pins and needles, she grabbed the phone and placed the toe to her ear. The dial tone rang out loud as church bells.

And she remembered—there couldn't be anyone in the kitchen. The black boxes were there, watching. They were watching the house, waiting to tell her of the slightest movement. There was no way to climb around the electric eye and disconnect them. The man had said so.

She wondered if it had been a dream. She didn't think

so, but she couldn't be sure. She tried to think of what she could be sure of, as she lifted the blanket over her head, but before she could complete the thought, she'd given herself up to the warm cover of sleep.

CHAPTER EIGHTEEN

THE BLACK DOOR slammed. A siren blared. Buddy stared at her through the rear window, his mouth open, screaming. She struggled to hear him, but the siren was too loud. She fought to open her eyes, but they resisted as if they were sealed shut with glue.

She sat up in bed, wide awake, still engulfed by the blaring noise. Drowsy and thick, she tried to turn it off, tried the radio, the television, the alarm clock. But they weren't on. The siren continued. When she picked up the phone, the noise stopped, the silence shocking her. Then it started again, and she realized it was the alarm. The alarm downstairs was going off at two-minute intervals.

Plugging one ear with her hand she lifted the phone and dialed the police, her voice trembling with confusion as she gave her name and address. She fought the overwhelming urge to hide and forced herself up and outside, racing through the noise as if she was running through flames. In the cold night air she paced in front of the house in what she suddenly realized were her bare feet.

Shivering, she rubbed her arms and ran in place until she saw a set of headlights round the corner. She walked to the edge of the curb to meet the car. But it was Donna's car, turning into Donna's driveway. As she listened to their car doors slam shut, she realized the police came slower each time she called.

"Are you all right?" Donna asked as she crossed the street. She held her heavy fur coat closed tight against her chest. Her black shoes and stockings made her legs invisible, as if she was floating through the night. Joy wished she could disappear, vanish like Donna's feet. But she couldn't be missed, a figure in a white hooded robe, bobbing up and down against the cold.

"Did you lock yourself out?" Donna challenged her.

Against Joy's will her voice cracked. "There's someone in my house."

"Art," Donna called to the figure slowly making his way to their front door. "Art, come here."

He moved slowly, like a man unaccustomed to wearing a cummerbund and patent leather shoes, like a man who'd had a lot to drink.

The alarm broke through the silence, screaming.

"Oh. You took my advice," Art shouted over the noise.

"Art, there's someone in her house."

"What? Does she thinks it's Sethy again?"

"I don't think it's Seth," Joy interrupted.

"Where's your husband?" he reeked of Scotch and cigars.

"Out of town," Joy got out.

"Art, there's someone in her house." The scream of the alarm abruptly stopped, leaving Donna's voice too loud in the dead night.

Art looked at the house, at Joy, at Donna, weighing his civic duty.

"I called the police," Joy interjected. "They're on their way." She could see Art relax and Donna stiffen.

"Great," Donna said as she turned to Art. "They'll be over at our place in an hour, guaranteed."

Joy saw a flash of understanding pass between them as Art placed a proprietary hand on Donna's back.

"If the police are coming, you're all taken care of," he said to Joy, avoiding looking at her bare feet. "Anyway, it's probably just squirrels. We've all had squirrels."

He guided his wife toward their house, and they disappeared in the darkness. Moments later Joy saw their bedroom light up. Then the lights went on in Sue's house, first in the living room, then the hallway, then the bedroom in the front where two silhouettes came to the window, rippling the narrow blinds as they peered out.

She thought she saw more lights go on at Barb's, but her house was discreetly hidden behind the cover of several fir trees, so it was hard to tell.

She collapsed, hunched and cold, onto her front steps, the blaring siren paralyzing her, until the patrol car finally swung down the block. Sergeant Brady and Patrolman McShane climbed out of the car.

"Hello," McShane said, but he didn't look at her. His eyes went directly to the house, to the sound of the alarm, and his hand went to his gun.

"See anyone?" he asked, and after Joy shook her head the two men trotted through the front door. Within moments the siren went dead. The only sound was of her deep, quick breathing.

They returned carrying her winter coat and the slippers she'd mislaid days ago.

"Mrs. Bard," Sergeant Brady said, watching her fumble as she tried to get her arms through the sleeves of her coat, "we've checked everywhere. Your house is secure. But those portable alarms are a pain in the neck. They pick up flys, clumps of dust. I never recommend them."

"I know there's someone in there," she said.

"And how do you know that?" McShane asked.

But Joy was at a loss. How could she explain about the phone that beeped when someone dialed on another unit? Or the feeling she had of being watched, of things being moved out of place? She couldn't explain it without sounding like what she feared she was becoming. Insane. Thoroughly insane.

"Why don't you get yourself a mousetrap," Sergeant Brady suggested, with a smile. "I bet you anything you'll find your little guest that way."

"I don't need a mousetrap," she said calmly. "They arrive at my house dead and beheaded already."

The two men shifted uncomfortably.

"Besides. It's not mice. And it's not squirrels. Unless you know of rodents that can open and close doors."

"Ma'am?"

"My attic door," she went on. "Yesterday it was locked. Today it's open."

Brady nodded to McShane and they jogged back in the house while Joy waited. But before they returned, she realized what they would find: the door was locked. O'Brien had locked it.

While McShane ran off to search the backyard, Brady returned to Joy.

"I know someone is in there," she said before he had a chance to speak.

"Okay. Who do you think it is?" he asked, beleaguered. "Someone you know?"

She considered her words carefully. "I'm not sure. Neighborhood boys. Maybe my husband?" She hadn't meant to say it. She hadn't even acknowledged thinking it.

Brady's firm voice broke through the air like a hatchet. "Doesn't he live here?"

"Yes. But he's supposed to be out of town," she whispered.

Brady took a deep breath. "Mrs. Bard, did you call us here because you think your husband came home earlier than you expected?"

She was so confused. "I'm saying I don't know who it is. But someone has broken into my house. I'm saying," she forced herself to continue although somewhere she knew she should stop, "that someone is trying to frighten me."

He stifled a cough. "If you have a problem with your husband, you should call your attorney. Or a counselor.

Have you tried counseling? This is something for the family court system, not for the police department."

"Surely it's a police matter if someone's broken into my house?"

"But no one has broken into your house." He said it as if he were speaking to a child—simply, without room for discussion. "You have anywhere you can stay tonight?" he asked. McShane joined them, shaking his head. There was nothing in the backyard.

"Any family, or a neighbor who would put you up?"

"Why?" Joy asked quietly. "Do you believe me?"

"There's nothing to believe, ma'am. We've checked everywhere twice. There is no one, not even your husband, in your house." He ignored McShane's questioning glance.

Joy stared ahead blankly. The cops were wrong. They were totally wrong.

"I'm happy to walk you through the room," the sergeant went on. "And if you like, my partner and I can stick around outside for a while, until you fall asleep. But trust me. All you've got is an irritable alarm system and an overactive imagination. Throw the damn alarm out. It's not good for anything but giving you a case of the willies."

"A big dog would be a better idea," McShane offered. "If I were you, I'd get myself a nice big dog."

"Does your husband have a key?" Brady asked.

Joy nodded.

"Then we can eliminate the need for him to break into your house, right?"

She nodded again, weakly. "You don't have to stay," she told him. She didn't want them standing in front of her house, trading jokes at her expense. "I'll be fine."

"You sure?"

She nodded.

"Well, then," the sergeant said, "good night." Wordlessly, they returned to their car and drove off.

She sat for a while on the front steps as if she was waiting for someone to pick her up and take her away. Then one of the babies kicked hard, reminding her it was cold and late.

The only other place to go was her mother's. But she didn't have the energy to listen to Dorothy's patronizing questions. Then she thought of Molly.

"I know it's late," she said as Molly ushered her inside.

Molly pulled her red flannel robe tighter and stifled a yawn, trying to look like she hadn't been roused from a dead sleep. "Come on in. It's fine." She switched on a lamp in the living room. "Just give me a second. I have to get Trina back to sleep. She had a bad dream."

Joy settled in a corner of the couch with her legs tucked under her. She could hear the comforting rhythm of Molly's voice reassuring Trina back to sleep, and it calmed her, too. She ran her fingertips in circles over her belly, and opened her robe to watch as a wave of movement rolled across her middle.

"I remember that," Molly said from the archway to the room. "Watching my stomach move."

Joy closed her robe and smiled. With Molly everything was easy. She had no agenda of her own, no expectations so she couldn't be disappointed. Joy couldn't help but wonder how different her life would have been if she had made a friend like Molly years ago. Someone with whom she could have shared secrets, instead of burying them. Someone who would have been like a sister.

She thought of Buddy, about how twins could be such close friends. But they never had a chance. It would have been different now, she thought. Then she realized Molly was watching her, waiting to hear why she'd come over in the middle of the night.

"There's someone in my house," she said quietly as she let the thoughts of Buddy drift away. "The police don't believe me."

"Did they come and look?"

"Yes. But they couldn't find anyone."

Molly sighed loudly and sat down across from her. Joy

wondered if she might be beginning to doubt her now, too. And why not, she thought, when she was beginning to doubt herself.

"When is Lanny coming home?"

"Tomorrow, I think." She had to be careful what she said. She couldn't risk Molly turning her out, thinking she was insane. She couldn't take a chance by telling her how she'd seen Lanny in the city. How her mother accused her of having hallucinations. She wasn't going to make the same mistake she'd made with Brady—admit she feared that someone was in the house, stalking her.

The silence deepened, and Molly excused herself to put up water for tea. When she returned, Joy was fast asleep.

Molly got a blanket from the upstairs linen closet and took one of the pillows off her bed. As she draped the blanket over her friend's legs, Joy's eyes opened, tiny slits.

"In the car," Joy said, still asleep. Then she drifted deeper under, leaving Molly to double-lock her doors before tiptoeing up to bed.

Joy woke to the smell of coffee and toast, and the sound of "Sesame Street" on low.

"Did I just pass out?" she asked, stumbling into the brightly lit kitchen where Trina was stirring her Cheerios and watching, on a counter-top television, Cookie Monster noisily devour a plate.

Molly was dressed to go out, in a long green skirt and matching wool sweater that made her eyes look emerald, almost artificial.

"You must really have needed to sleep," she said as she broke two eggs and let the innards drip into a small blue bowl. "Scrambled?"

"I'm all done," Trina announced.

"Then go get ready. I laid your clothes out."

Trina's short arms just reached the TV controls. She turned off the set proudly and skipped out of the kitchen.

Molly stood at the stove, beating the eggs with hard rhythmic strokes. "You're in trouble, Joy," she said. "You look like shit."

Joy's eyes welled up with tears, and she pressed her lips together. "I heard someone in my attic," she said quietly. "It wasn't my imagination."

"So why couldn't the police find anyone? Ghosts?"

Joy laughed. She wished she believed in ghosts. She wished it was as simple as ghosts. Buddy haunting her. Trying to tell her his secret. But she didn't believe in ghosts, and she didn't believe it was simple.

"Maybe it's those awful boys," Molly suggested. "Why don't you have another talk with their mothers?"

"If it were the boys, the cops would have found them."

"So we're back to ghosts."

Joy sighed. It wasn't ghosts.

"I'm all mixed up," she admitted, poking her fork in the eggs Molly placed before her. "Things aren't right with Lanny. Or with the pregnancy. Or with the house." She returned a fork full of uneaten eggs to her plate. "I know what I have to do. I have to go back to my old house in Toney's Brook. To see it for myself. To see what's there."

"What do you think is there?"

"My childhood," Joy reflected, after a moment.

Trina's shriek broke through their silence. She came running into the room, her pajama top half off.

"There's a monster in the closet, Mommy," she said, burrowing into her mother's chest.

Molly smiled at Joy as she lifted Trina into her arms, ready to repeat the newest routine, checking the closets for monsters that weren't there.

"I'm done with my classes today at two," she said to Joy as she carried Trina to their monster hunt. "I can go with you then. You can wait here if you're afraid to go home alone. We can stop off at your house on the way."

"Where are you going, Mommy?" Trina asked, the monster temporarily forgotten, an adventure in the offing.

"It's a date," Joy replied. She smiled gently as Molly struggled to explain their upcoming expedition to her monster-fearing daughter.

CHAPTER NINETEEN

EVEN THOUGH IT wasn't necessary for Kelly to proofread Lanny's entire call sheet since all she'd done was add one more message to the last page, she did it anyway. It was important that Lanny didn't come back to sloppy errors. He was a perfectionist, which was why he appreciated her. She was a perfectionist, too.

That's why she'd greeted Mr. Seidenberg with the same pleasant voice each of the four times he phoned. She laughed, on cue, when he kidded her about how Lanny had kept him waiting just so he could make out with his pregnant-as-a-cow wife. She never let it annoy her when he suggested Lanny wasn't out of town, that he was sitting in his office, ducking calls. She let the threats and insults slide right off her back.

Even Lanny didn't know she'd overheard his explosive argument with Seidenberg—that his outburst of profanity had been audible all the way at her small work station.

"You fucking arrogant" something or other, she'd heard, and then a loud bang. She didn't tell anyone she saw Seidenberg storm out clutching his hand as if it had been run over by a train. That was what made her the best. No idle gossip trading for Kelly Graham. Loyalty was all, and Lanny deserved hers. He never missed a birthday, and when raises were frozen, he had supplemented her salary right out of his pocket. But what she'd never forget was how he tracked down the best surgeon in New York for her mother's bypass, insisted she take that week off, and then never reported it to personnel.

She had rearranged the folders on his blotter three times and dusted twice. If she had been able to find out exactly when his plane was due in, she would have had a mug of black coffee waiting on a coaster on his desk.

Suddenly the room went black as a pair of warm hands fell over her eyes. As the hands dropped away she swiveled around in her chair until she saw the rest of a man, his face obscured by a large white box bedecked with pastel-colored ribbons. Then she saw the shoes. The expensive black leather shoes, perfectly shined, bows evenly tied.

"Mr. Bard," she said as Lanny lay the box on her desk, revealing himself.

"How did you know it was me?"

Kelly shrugged. There was no point in letting him know everything. After all, she knew he found modesty attractive.

"Aren't you going to open it?"

She looked around to be sure her friends were watching. Pauline was watering her philodendron, and Roz was spell checking on her word processor, but she could tell they both had one ear pointed toward her desk, one eye on the box.

She lifted off the paper carefully. She liked to keep wrapping paper in the office in case she needed to give an emergency gift, a coffee mug, a pencil cup, a dancing flower. She took her time untying the ribbons so she wouldn't have to cut them with scissors. They were too beautiful to throw away.

Lanny didn't seem to mind at all. In fact he was enjoying it, everyone watching him be a model boss. Half of the lawyers in the firm didn't even say good morning to their secretary, let alone come back from trips with a gift. When they were away, it was worse. They would overload the phone lines with anxious calls all day long, from the car, from the plane, from the hotel, from the client. Not that Lanny didn't occasionally overdo checking in. But this time he had been incredibly well behaved. This time he hadn't called once. She'd trained him well.

She was just about to lift the top off the gift when Ray sidled up to the desk. "Hey, Lanny. Welcome back."

She saw the look Lanny flashed Ray but ignored it and continued opening the box. When she shot a smile at Lanny, she didn't miss noticing Ray was biting his lip, holding back whatever it was he had wanted to say. She paid no mind.

The belt made her gasp, just loud enough so that Marilee stopped, on her way to the Xerox machine, to watch her wrap it around her tiny waist.

"Does it fit? I had them make extra holes."

"It's perfect," Kelly said, inserting the buckle through the soft leather.

"If you don't like it, they said the New York store will exchange it for you."

She threaded the leather through three loops. "I love it. It's beautiful. You did't have to." She came around her desk and planted a respectful dry kiss on Lanny's cheek. He smelled good. He always smelled good. It's what set him apart from someone like Ray, who smelled of deodorant or wine, depending on the time of day.

"There's something else in there," Lanny said.

She dug around in the red tissue paper and pulled out a small bottle of silver polish. She hadn't realized the buckle was real silver.

"Sorry, but it needs some upkeep. They said to be sure to tell you to keep the polish away from the turquoise."

"Oh, I'll be careful," she said, stroking the belt with newfound respect.

"So, Ray," Lanny said, grabbing him by the elbow, "you free for lunch?" He pulled Ray in to his office and closed the door.

"Sorry I had to shut you up out there," he explained as he scanned his mail folder and picked up his call sheet. "I was afraid you'd forgotten she thinks I was in San Francisco."

"Not to worry. When Berger gave me your tickets and it-inerary, I just left. I told everyone there you had the flu. I didn't tell anyone here anything at all."

"Hell, Ray. It happened so fast. Kelly thought I was already on my way to the airport when I was still sitting like a dunce in Berger's office. What was I going to do? Admit to my secretary I was ordered home for a couple of days to cool out? Tell my wife? Top lawyers don't get sent home to cool out. I'm telling you, Ray. I think I'm out of here. Berger's on my ass too close."

The intercom interrupted. Lanny picked up and listened. "Berger," he mouthed, then motioned for Ray to sit down.

"Hello," he said into the phone, sounding relaxed. "Yes. Yes, it was restful. No, I understand, absolutely. I know. You're right. I needed to take the time off. I went too far with Seidenberg. You were right. We all need a break, and I wouldn't have taken one if you hadn't insisted. I'm thankful, actually." He listened, grimacing, rubbing his forehead, forgetting Ray was there. "Sure. Yes. All right, sir." He hung up the phone and pressed his sweaty hands on his black wood desk, leaving large prints behind. He looked up, noticing Ray. "You know what he said?"

Ray's eyebrows lifted and he waited.

"He said he sent me home because I'm too industrious for my own good. You know what I should have said?"

Ray shook his head and stifled a sigh.

"Like hell, sir," I should have said. "Like fucking hell."

Ray wasn't sure what to say so he just sat there as Lanny continued to flip through the pages on his desk.

"You free for lunch?" Lanny asked again, without looking up.

"Sure," Ray answered, feeling on edge.

"Good. On your way out, ask Kelly to make us a reservation at the Russian Tea Room. A friend of mine went there the other day, and now I've got a craving for blintzes."

Ray laughed. This was the Lanny he liked to work with. The one who loved to go out to lunch and eat well. The one who liked to order appetizers and dessert, and who skipped the Pelegrino to indulge in a bottle of good wine. Ray chuckled as he strode over to Kelly's desk, until he remembered. Kelly thought Lanny had been in San Francisco. And so did Joy. His cheerful smile faded so quickly that even buttoned-up Kelly commented on the deep creases that suddenly ran across his wide, sweaty forehead.

CHAPTER TWENTY

RAY WATCHED IN well-concealed awe as Lanny lifted another spoonful of borscht to his mouth without spilling a drop of the magenta soup on his starched white shirt. Then he realized he wasn't listening; he had drifted off again.

It wasn't that he wasn't interested in what Lanny was saying. It was just too much. Too much coming at him. Lanny hadn't paused for a breath from the second they sat down at the table. Now Ray was having a hell of a hard time keeping up with him, and he was nervous that Lanny was going to notice. No matter what, he couldn't let Lanny notice. Lanny was his ticket to partnership in the firm. Everything was riding on him. Ray had worked hard to get himself assigned to the golden boy. He'd put a lot of time into getting Lanny to trust him and rely on him. Now was not the time to get sloppy. Now was not the time to blow it.

"Out of the office only three days," Lanny rambled on. "And already I can tell that O'Connell and Shapiro are weaseling their way into the Catco deal, which is not to say, Ray, that I expected you to protect the turf while you were in San Francisco, but I think that they've gotten signals, from the top, that I'm chopped meat, headed for one last trip through the grinder."

"Get out. O'Connell is tied up in that antitrust thing, and Shapiro's been out of town for two weeks."

Lanny put his spoon down and waited for the waiter to clear his bowl and put down the steaming lunch plates. Then he leaned close to his companion.

"Hey, guy, you can be straight with me. How many people in the office know I wasn't in San Francisco?"

Ray stared at the butter dripping out of his chicken Kiev. How the hell did he know how many people knew? The client knew. Berger knew. How the hell did he know who else Berger had told?

"Ray. No bullshit here. Did you leave the reservations in my name like I asked you to?"

"No leak there," Ray said, catching on. Lanny was worrying about a leak. He'd been speculating about it for days. Catco had received that second offer because there was a leak in the firm. That's what this was all about. Closing the hole. He should have realized. He should have realized that Lanny was one step ahead of him all the time. When he looked up from his plate, Lanny was staring at him, staring hard, like he was trying to see into his soul.

"Sorry, guy," Lanny said. "I know. I'm bearing down hard on you. But I haven't slept. I haven't slept in three nights. For three nights I've been creeping around, trying to be quiet. You know what would have happened if Joy found out that I got sent home, like a ten-year-old sent home from school? You think she would have any fucking respect for me then? Hell, I know about disappointing people. You do it once, and they never look at you the same. You make one mistake and you're fucking marked for life." He put down his fork, stared off into space, then squinted at Ray, trying to read his expression. "I ever tell you about my father?"

Ray shook his head no, and shoveled in another spoonful of cream-and-butter-soaked rice.

"My father was exactly like Berger. Never took any shit from anyone. You learn, with people like that. You learn never to fuck up. You learn to keep them happy."

Ray was lost again, thinking about their upcoming meeting with Berger. It wasn't supposed to last more than an hour, just long enough for him to brief Berger and Lanny on precisely what had transpired in San Francisco. Ray looked around and shifted in his chair. If the service was any slower and if Lanny kept going on like this, they were going to be late for the meeting.

"I mean a tornado temper," Lanny was saying, "that I got damn good at sniffing out. That's how I learned to creep around. That's what got me through the last three days."

Ray was confused. He made himself listen harder, figuring he'd missed something along the way.

"Do you know how to smell a rotten mood? I do. When I used to smell it on him I'd crawl on my belly right past his feet so he didn't even know I was there. You ever have to do that Ray? Crawl right past someone and not even breathe, so they didn't even know you were there? I'll tell you I would have made one hell of a Marine. You ever have to do shit like that?"

"Not really," Ray said. His palms were sweating. Something was off. He finished his chicken, gathered his courage, and asked, "Where've you been staying Lanny, these past few days?"

"Home, Ray. In my attic. You ever have to do that Ray? Sneak into your own house so no one knows you're there. So you have time to think things through? Really think things through. You ever want to do that?"

"I live alone. I don't have anything to think through." He didn't want to ask, but he needed to know. "Why not stay at a hotel?"

"Because, Ray, I needed to know." He ran his fork across the tablecloth, the prongs leaving indentations like tracks. "And now I do." He pressed the prongs, leaving tiny marks on his fingertips. "She's out of it, Ray. She's out of her mind. Joy's not fit to mother an ant. Can you keep a secret?"

He could but he didn't want to. "Yes," he said.

"Me, too. I'm a warehouse of secrets and you know what? There's no one better at keeping them. Did I ever tell you about my grandmother, Ray?"

Ray started to say no, but Lanny didn't wait for an answer.

"I moved in with her when I was fifteen years old. I was her pet, another one of her pets. Three cats and me. She fed us together and sent us to bed together, and if we did something she didn't like, she punished us all. The fucking cats. If they scratched the couch, it was my fault. I'd get locked in their room for a week."

Ray put his knife and fork down gently, not wanting to interrupt. But he was thinking, I'm screwed. I'm really screwed.

"You know what punishment she saved just for me?"

This time Ray didn't bother answering. He just lifted his lids wearily, his shoulders sagging.

"A fork. She wanted things from me Ray. She wanted me to be someone special. And so I wouldn't forget it she'd poke me with a fork. You ever get poked with a fork?"

Ray frowned and shrugged his shoulders.

"She'd take a fucking fork, Ray." Lanny lowered his voice. "And she'd stick it in me. And I don't mean lightly. She'd stick it in me until she drew blood."

But Ray was barely listening. He was staring at Lanny's hand, where Lanny was pressing his fork, the dulled tips of the stainless steel prongs denting his skin. He was watching Lanny grit his teeth and press harder and harder until all at once, like tears, four drops of bright red blood appeared.

Lanny dropped the fork.

"Shit," he said, pressing his palm to his mouth and sucking. "Shit." He looked up at Ray's puffy white face. "Look what I did Ray. Can you fucking believe it? Look what I did."

CHAPTER
TWENTY-ONE

AT FIRST SHE thought her mother had left the receiver lying on the table. Left it lying on its side while she walked right out of the apartment. Then she heard the click-clack of sensible heels. Dorothy's tired voice came back on the line. "I have it."

"Okay. What is it?"

A sigh rang through the phone, so loud that Molly, sitting at Joy's side, heard it, too, and smiled, sadly.

"I don't know why you insist on doing this."

"I'm just going for a drive. That's all."

"Eighteen Dowling Place. If it's even still there."

"Thanks, Mother," Joy said. "I'll let you know."

"Don't bother. I don't want to know."

Joy hung up and made a quick stop at her house, Molly waiting at the door while she ran in to check the machine for messages.

"Well?" Molly asked when they got back to the car.

"No call from Lanny yet," Joy said as she buckled in. "Just from the Weird Sisters."

"All three of them?" Molly started the engine.

Joy nodded, looking straight ahead. "They wanted to let me know that their angelic children were home in bed last night when the police car pulled up in front of my house. Someone must have written a script. They each said the same thing, word for word."

Molly shook her head as she put the car in gear and drove up the winding street. Trina sat in the back, singing nursery rhymes to herself.

Joy thought about the message she hadn't mentioned, from Ray.

"Please call me as soon as you have a moment alone," he'd said. It was clear he meant for her to call when Lanny wasn't home. She could hear it in his voice, a hushed, secretive tone. She tried to think of what Ray would want to tell her, but before long her eyes closed, and her mind went blank.

In less than an hour the car was cruising down the main street of Toney's Brook. They pulled in at the first gas station in town, where the grubby attendant drew a primitive map on the back of a grease-stained envelope.

"You girls are lucky you stopped here," he said as he waved and made faces at Trina, just rousing from a nap. "It's just one block, Dowling Place, and not everyone knows it. You're lucky you found me." He stood up straight. "Nice houses up that part. You visiting?" He walked around to see their license plate. "Came all the way from New York, huh? You from New York City?"

"Let's get out of here," Joy said under her breath.

"Thanks for the directions," Molly shouted out the window as she drove away. She held the rough map above the steering wheel as they passed a Grand Union, a bicycle shop, and a pharmacy sign announcing DRUGS, LIQUOR, AND CANDY. "Anything clicking?"

"No," Joy answered. Nothing felt familiar. She couldn't help but wonder if this was all a big mistake. If maybe there wasn't anything important to remember. Still, she strained her eyes looking for signs of something that might jog her memory. But the town flashed by like cardboard scenery, the park, the flower store, the bakery. Until her spine stiffened, alerting her. "Turn right at that light."

Molly slowed down and looked at the map. "We're not supposed to turn yet. See?" She passed the map over to Joy, who put it down on her lap without looking at it.

"Make a right at that light," she directed.

"Right turn, Mommy," Trina called from the back.

"Okay," Molly said as she pulled up behind a school bus at the red light. "But Mr. Texaco doesn't agree."

"This is the way," Joy said. "I'm sure of it."

"What do you remember?" Molly asked quietly.

"I remember how to walk home from school."

They waited behind the flashing red lights of the school bus while several young passengers were discharged.

"It's not the most direct route," Joy said quietly as she watched a young boy shrug off his mother's attempt to hold his hand. "But it's how I used to go."

The bus belched smoke as it pulled out, and Molly turned right.

"What now?" she asked. The car cruised down a wide boulevard with grand houses perched high up on leaf-covered hills.

"Keep going," Joy directed, not sure what to do next. Molly cruised slowly.

"Pull over," Joy said suddenly. "We missed the turn." She pointed to a small street sign half a block behind them that said Lily Lane. "It's back there."

Molly made a wide U-turn, and turned right onto Lily Lane. The houses were smaller and older but still well kept.

"Up ahead is my street."

The street sign was blocked by a huge oak tree, but as they passed under the heavy branches they could see the small black-and-white sign for Dowling Place.

Molly stuffed the envelope in the ashtray. "So much for Mr. Texaco," she said.

"Mommy, are we lost?" Trina asked from the back.

"No, precious," Joy said, without turning. "I think we're found."

She didn't need to tell Molly where to pull over. The car came to a halt in front of the familiar-looking house.

Molly lifted Trina out of her car seat. "Stay by Mommy," she said.

They stood at the bottom of the walk. "Will you come?" Joy asked. She felt unsteady, her knees wobbly.

"Come with us, Trina." Molly held her hand on Trina's head and guided her up the brick path. Joy's steps got smaller and slower as she approached the house, so Molly and Trina waited for her at the door. When she reached them, Joy took a breath and rang the bell.

The door opened immediately, and a short, dark-haired woman stood before them.

Joy was speechless. She hadn't thought of what to say.

"Hello," Molly jumped in. "My name is Molly Fischel, and this is my friend Joy Bard. She used to live here when she was a child. We decided to come by on a lark, and we were wondering if we could come in and have a look around."

The woman smiled back at them, flashing a gold tooth. "Me no speaky Englis," she said. "Missy no home."

Joy peered over the diminutive woman's head into the foyer. "When will she be back?"

The woman's face darkened. She closed the door slightly, trying to block the open space with her small frame. "Missy no home."

"What is the name of the family that lives here?" Joy asked, her voice tight.

"Okay?" the woman smiled, nodding her head. "Thank you. Okay?" She began closing the door.

"What is the name of the family?" Joy asked, louder, enunciating carefully.

"Mommy, what's happening?" Feeling left out, Trina sat down on the front steps and squashed an ant.

"Joy's just trying to explain that she used to live here when she was a little girl like you."

The woman smiled. "Thank you very much," she said as she closed the door, engaging several locks.

"Okay, Trina, back in the car." Molly took Trina's hand and started down the walk. When she turned she saw Joy staring across the expanse of lawn to the house next door.

"Wait here," Molly said to Trina. "Don't move. Play with the leaves."

Trina watched her mother run over to where Joy stood. When she got there Joy was hunched over, her hand hovering near her mouth.

"What is it?" she asked, holding Joy's arm and trying to get her to look in her eyes. "What do you see?"

A woman opened the door of the house, shook out a small rag rug, and went back inside, slamming the door shut behind her. Joy's hands flew to her ears. Her eyes snapped shut. Quickly she squatted, to avoid fainting.

"Tell me what's wrong," Molly said, kneeling beside her. "Do you want me to go next door?"

Joy opened her eyes and stared at the house. It was starting to spin. She could feel her face hot as fire.

"What is it?" Molly persevered. "What do you see?"

The door to the house across the way opened again and the woman stepped out. "Hello?" she called over. "Can I help you?"

"Do you want to talk to her?" Molly asked quietly. "Would it help?"

"Is everything all right?" the woman called out again.

Joy lifted herself up, ran down the path to the car, and locked herself in.

"What's wrong, Mommy?" Trina called out.

"Nothing, honey," she answered, helping Trina back into her car seat. "Joy's just a little upset. That's all."

"Why, Mommy?"

"I don't know, honey," she said as she closed the door and got into the front seat, trying hard to avoid meeting the quizzical gaze of the woman staring at them from her front steps.

"Please, just drive," Joy said quietly, and Molly did, back through the quiet streets, down the boulevard of expensive homes, and through the commercial district. Once they were on the highway Molly stole a look and saw that Joy was staring straight ahead, rigid.

"It's got to help to talk about it," she said.

Joy covered her mouth with her hand, as if she was afraid to say.

"What is it? What's wrong?"

Joy took several deep breaths and let her hand drop. "Something awful happened there," she said slowly, in a whisper. "Everybody knows it, and no one will say. I know it, but I can't see it. I can't see what it is."

"It's going to come," Molly said gently, handing her a tissue. "When the time is right, it's all going to come."

CHAPTER TWENTY-TWO

THE FRONT DOOR slammed. The house was still. Joy padded down the stairs. In the foyer Lanny stood looking at her through two dozen red roses crammed between bunches of ferns. Through the creases of the clear plastic wrapping she could see his face, tight, tense, worried.

"I missed you so much," he said, holding out the flowers. She took them but couldn't think of what to say. The pause was too long. His forehead creased further.

"Me, too," she got out finally. He squinted at her, trying to figure out what that meant.

Then his face relaxed, as if he'd come to some decision. He watched Joy lay the flowers on the hall table. "Don't I get a hug?"

She walked toward him, into his open arms. But on contact they both stiffened. The hug was awkward, sad.

"I'm so glad to be home," he whispered into her ear. He pressed her tighter. She wanted to believe everything would be okay. He sounded sincere. Her body unwound a notch.

"You all right? You feel all right?"

At the sound of the panic in his voice, her muscles knotted up again. She nodded but didn't meet his eyes.

"Then why don't you get changed? I want to take you out to dinner."

Feeling like she was moving underwater, she made her way upstairs. There were a hundred questions lined up in her head, waiting to be asked, but she wasn't ready. She swung around. Lanny was right behind her, following her. He trailed after her into the bedroom and splayed himself across the bed, his hands folded behind his neck, watching her with cold, calculating eyes. The hairs on the back of her neck stood erect.

She disappeared into the walk-in closet and took down a dress, then sat down against the wall, clutching it to her. She wasn't sure she could go through with this, sitting through dinner, saying nothing. She took a deep breath. She had to hang on. It was better not to start what she wasn't yet prepared to finish. It was better to wait. She would go to dinner. She would get through the night. Tomorrow she'd have time to figure things out, and she found herself thinking: prepare your escape.

"Honey?" Lanny called. "Everything okay?"

She pushed herself off the floor and put on her dress without taking of her pants. If he came in, she didn't want him to find her naked. She didn't want to be exposed.

"I'm fine," she called back.

He walked in as she was stepping out of her pants. "That looks great," he said, looking her over, moving her hair off her neck, kissing her.

"It's too tight here," she said, brushing her hand over her chest. Lanny caught her hand and held it there, pressing it hard against her full breast. Then he pulled her closer.

"Oh," she called out, and Lanny stepped back. "A kick," she said, rubbing her stomach.

Lanny grinned, then pulled off her dress and knelt on the floor, kissing her stomach, stroking her thigh, licking his way down her leg. Joy closed her eyes, stifling a scream, hoping Lanny didn't see the tears gathering on her lashes.

He didn't notice. Not when he drew her down onto her side on the cool oak floor. Not when he entered her from behind, his arms wrapped around her hard belly, his head burrowed into her hair, nibbling her neck, his breath hot on her head.

Joy lay immobile, staring straight ahead into a pair of black patent-leather sling-back shoes that had fallen on their sides. As he pounded himself into her, her eyes remained locked on the dark impression her heel had made where the shoe's label was half worn away. It was someone else lying on the floor, she told herself. Someone else's stifled sobs bursting out like staccato moans that Lanny mistook for pleasure.

"Mmm," he moaned, rolling onto his back, finished. "I forgot how good that was."

A noise came out of her mouth that Lanny took as a laugh.

"I was beginning to wonder if we'd ever do it again."

Joy pushed herself up with her elbows, straightening her sling-back shoes before she stood.

"Where you going?"

"I want to shower before dinner," she said quickly. She disappeared into the bathroom before Lanny could protest.

"Honey," he yelled through the closed door, trying to be heard over the sound of the pulsating water. "I'll meet you downstairs.

"Okay," she called back. She put the lid down on the toilet and sat on it as the bathroom steamed up. Then, hugging her legs, she let loose, her body heaving with sobs.

It seemed only seconds had passed when Lanny knocked on the door again, turning the knob, finding it locked. "Hey. Are you almost done? I'm starving."

"I'll be down in a minute," she called back. She shut off the shower and splashed cold water on her face in an effort to get her red eyes to look less puffy. When she rejoined Lanny, he was standing at the dining room table, leafing through the mail.

"What's this?" he asked, holding up a letter from Dorothy. "How come you haven't opened the mail yet? What have you been doing all day?"

"I just didn't get around to it," she said, brushing by him. She took the oversize square envelope out of his hand and slid her finger under the flap. They both watched as a photograph slipped out and floated to the floor.

Lanny picked up the picture while Joy read the note.

"What does it say?"

"Nothing."

"What do you mean, nothing?"

She gave the note to Lanny and took the photograph out of his hand.

For a moment he just held the note, lamely, like a used tissue. Then he remembered it and read it aloud. "Here's another one I found."

He walked behind her and took another look at the picture over her shoulder. It was his clubhouse. His private boyhood clubhouse. Buddy's head was sticking out the window on one side. His head was sticking out the door. Joy was standing in front, just waiting to be asked in. That was the mistake, he thought. If he had never asked her in, it never would have happened. He wouldn't have had to up the stakes if she hadn't been so goddamn bent on getting in.

The picture started vibrating in Joy's hand. She doesn't need to look at old photographs, he thought. Her memory is squirting out enough images on its own. She doesn't need anyone helping it along.

It was coming undone. He'd been so careful, arranging their lives. The courtship, the marriage, all carefully planned. Building her trust, winning her love, getting her pregnant. All carefully orchestrated, just to avoid this: she was figuring it out after all. After all this time, she was starting to remember.

He sighed loudly, and Joy put the picture down. When he circled round to get a look at her face, it was blank.

"What made Dorothy send you this old picture?" he asked as he put on his suit jacket and opened the front door.

Joy stuck the picture in her purse and shrugged her shoulders. "I guess she thought I'd like to keep it. As a memento."

Lanny put his hand on her back and guided her outside. "She send you any others?" He tried to keep his voice casual, curious. He pasted a friendly smile on his face and didn't take it off, even when his jacket sleeve caught on the door knob, even when he saw from Joy's stony expression that there was nothing casual about her tonight. Something was heavy on her mind.

He shut the door behind them.

CHAPTER TWENTY-THREE

"TO A WORRY-FREE pregnancy." The glasses clicked without resonance. Lanny lifted hers out of her hand and motioned for the waiter.

"You can take this now," he explained unnecessarily. "We just wanted it for the toast."

Joy looked away. She wanted to keep the glass and drink her wine. But she let it go. It wasn't worth the fight. It was time to pick and choose her battles.

She gazed around the room. It was the only restaurant in Edgebury, which was the only reason anybody ate there.

"Come back," Lanny said. "Come back to me."

She looked at him and tried to think if this was new, his hating her silence. "Just thinking about the restaurants around here," she said, shaking her head as if to signal: it's not important, let it go.

"You're still stuck on that guy you saw, aren't you? The guy who reminded you of me."

"He looked exactly like you," she repeated, slowly. "Exactly."

Lanny laughed. "The apple doesn't fall far from the tree, does it? Who did your mother think he looked like, Henry Fonda?" He laughed again, heartily. But under the table he pressed his fork into his palm. He had hoped she hadn't recognized him in that crowd.

"I could have sworn it was you," she muttered, but her resolve was faltering.

"Okay, it was me. I was walking down Fifth Avenue while at the same time sitting in a smoky conference room on Montgomery Street in San Francisco, saving a deal. That's a neat trick. How did I do it?"

She pushed the thick orange dressing off the cucumbers in her salad.

"Listen, you think I wasn't in San Francisco? You call Kelly. Berger. Ray. Your choice."

"I believe you," she said as she pierced a wad of sprouts that had escaped the glutinous coating.

"You know what I think?" He pushed his salad to the side.

"What?" She scraped clean a cherry tomato with her fork.

"I think you can't tell your fantasy life from the real thing anymore. I think you were missing me. You saw someone who looked like me. You wanted it to be me. It became me."

She put down her fork. He was so far from the truth it was laughable. But she didn't laugh. Because she knew she was in trouble. If Lanny was telling the truth, if he really had been in San Francisco, she was losing her mind. But if

Lanny was lying—before she could finish the thought she felt a kick, followed by a cramp. She speared a fork full of lettuce and devoured it, but it didn't get rid of the terrible taste in her mouth.

"Do you want me to get you a salad with no dressing?"

"No," she said. "I'm fine."

Their teenage waiter appeared in his sauce-streaked apron and scooped the wooden bowls away, setting down in their place two small cutting boards, a dripping sirloin lying on top of each.

Joy cut into hers quickly. Her hunger had arrived full-blown. Bypassing the huge pile of French-cut beans and the enormous baked potato, she speared piece after piece of well-done meat, thankful for an activity other than conversation. When the meat was gone she put down her fork and knife and glanced over at Lanny who was still carefully grinding his first piece of bloody steak. Their eyes met, and Joy looked away.

"Cat got your tongue?" he asked.

"I'm not a lot of fun when I'm hungry," she said. "You'd think I hadn't eaten all week."

"Feel better now?" He sliced himself his second piece.

"Yes," she said. But she didn't feel better. Her stomach felt bloated and crampy, and she was sitting on the edge of her seat, at the threshold of fear.

"Well then, talk to me while I eat. Tell me about your visit with Dr. Wayne."

She took a deep breath and let it out quietly. He knew something was on her mind. But even if she told him the truth, that nothing had happened at Dr. Wayne's, he'd just keep probing. He couldn't help himself from probing until he got what he wanted. Only she wasn't going to tell him. Not about her trip to Toney's Brook with Molly. Not now.

"Hello," he said, waving his serrated knife in front of her face. "I'm over here."

"Sorry. I was thinking about those teenagers." She ducked away from more dangerous thoughts.

"I'm going to take care of them," he said, pausing while

he chewed carefully. He didn't like to speak with his mouth full. She used to think it was good manners, but now it seemed an affectation.

"I'm going to call Barb. I'll have a talk with her to-night." He cut into his meat again, slicing off a wide strip and putting it on Joy's board.

The blood oozed a path across the wood. "I'm full, thanks," she said.

"Come on. We have to keep you healthy."

She smiled weakly.

Lanny slammed his silverware down on the laminated wood table. The people sitting on either side of them looked over and then away. "What's with this silent treatment?" he asked, trying to speak quietly and failing. "If something is upsetting you, tell me. Get it out in the open. Stop walking around like you're filled up with secrets all the time."

His gaze was strong and burning. His jaw was clenched, and his shoulders were drawn up to his neck. She forced herself to eat the potato she had just scooped onto her fork, but her mouth had filled up with an acrid juice. Her appetite was gone.

"I don't have secrets. I have holes." She felt her throat closing up. She held on to her hands tightly to steady them. "And I'm going to try to fill them up."

Lanny stretched his damp hand across the table and placed it over hers. "You can't force it," he said. "It's nothing terrible, not remembering. It's just a handicap. You've done a great job learning to live with it so far."

She put her hand to her mouth. She was nauseous and overheating. "I don't want to live with it anymore." She hung her head, hiding from the couples who were sitting next to them, coughing too much, struggling to keep up their own conversations. She stared at her board, filled with the dark red blood of the steak and a thousand cracks where other people's knives had dug into the wood.

Lanny raised his handkerchief like a white flag, then passed it to her across the table. She pressed it to her dry eyes without thinking. The people next to them had stopped talking altogether.

"I'll help you," Lanny said quietly, leaning across the table so only she would hear him. He squeezed her hand, and she looked at him with full sad eyes.

"I'll help you after the babies are born," he went on, not noticing how his words had made her draw back. "You have to think of the babies now. We can't take any more chances. Dr. Wayne agrees with me. What's most important is that you stay calm."

She pulled her hand away. "What happened to my brother?"

"He was kidnapped."

"What else happened?"

Lanny wiped his mouth and sat up straighter. "Listen to me, Joy. You're endangering the lives of your babies by pursuing this. Is that what you want? Don't you care about the health of your babies?"

"Why did Irene come to see me?" she shot back. "What did you tell her?"

"Irene is a good friend of mine. And right now, I'd say she's more concerned about your pregnancy than you are."

She concentrated on her breathing until her heart stopped pounding.

"I promise I'll help you with this crazy mission of yours once the babies are born. But you'll have to wait. Can't you see that? Can't you leave it alone until then?"

She dipped her fingertips into her glass of ice water and pressed them to her temples. Her eyelids hung heavy as she stared into Lanny's tense bright eyes. He looked like a desperate man. She wished she could oblige.

"No," she said softly, shaking her head. "I can't leave it till then. If you want to help me, it's got to be now." She watched a rivulet of blood run off her steak board and drop onto the edge of the table. When she looked up again, Lanny was at the front of the restaurant paying the bill.

CHAPTER
TWENTY-FOUR

"I'LL STRAIGHTEN THIS thing out with Barb," Lanny said as he opened the door to the house. "Do you think you can manage to go lie down and rest?"

When she looked at him with defeated eyes, he realized how far things had gone. She wasn't going to give it up. Things wouldn't go back to how they were. He'd planned for years to avoid this. Now it was unavoidable.

"I'll be in my studio working," she said. "I'll hardly move at all. Just my wrist."

Her sarcasm grated on him, but he caught himself and smiled. No need to make her more upset.

"Don't work too hard," he advised as she walked into the house. For a while he stared at the closed door. It was too bad, what he was going to have to do. He'd give anything to change things, to go back to how they had been before. But there was no going back.

He brushed his hair out of his eyes, rolled his shoulders, took a deep breath, and walked across the street. Even as he rang the small brass bell he could smell Barb's perfume leaking out between the cracks around the mail slot. When she swung open the door, he could tell that in the short time since he'd called from the restaurant, she'd changed and put on fresh makeup. But he didn't want distractions. He ignored the unspoken invitation and followed her into her living room, to her white couch, her white carpet, her white pillows, her white walls, where she stuck out like an exclamation mark, in black.

"I'm sorry to come over so late," he said, settling himself on a chair, a safe distance from where Barb sat on the couch, her legs aligned neatly together, covered with black stockings that glittered faintly.

"It's no problem," Barb said, crossing and recrossing her legs. She slipped her feet out of her black pumps and rubbed her toes on the white carpet, nestling them into the deep nap.

"But my wife is pretty upset."

"She gets upset a lot, doesn't she?" As Barb leaned across the table to pour Lanny a glass of wine her loose blouse fell open slightly, giving him a long free look at her black lace bra and the freckles in her cleavage.

He loosened his tie, took the glass, and smiled without letting her know that he'd seen and that it looked good. He didn't have time right now. He needed to take care of business and get home. He needed to get moving with Joy.

"She's going through a rough time," he explained gently. "She's got a bit of an overactive imagination."

"You mean she's paranoid?" Barb offered.

"She's not well."

"Listen, don't feel bad. You're not telling me anything we all don't already know."

Lanny forced his smile into a serious frown. "What do you mean?"

"Nothing." She'd caught herself sounding catty and backed off quickly. "Just that we can tell your wife is very delicate."

She topped off Lanny's glass and then cursed when the doorbell rang. "Poor man," she said under her breath, just loud enough so Lanny could hear her, as she squeezed between his legs and the coffee table, going the long way around to answer the door.

"Lanny Bard, Sue Burner," Barb said when she returned, introducing her guests with a bored look that told Lanny she wasn't happy with the interruption. "Sue's just stopped by for a minute. She's Charlie's mother."

He stood up, shook her hand, and returned to his seat. Sitting side by side on the couch, the two women made quite a pair. Barb was tiny, all curves and places to grab on to. Sue was tall and lamp post thin, with hardly any ass at all. But her jeans were wrapped tight around a pair of long muscular legs that looked to him just made for locking around thighs.

"Because we're not unreasonable people," Sue was saying when Lanny tuned back in. She was staring at him hard. She'd been watching his eyes travel over her body, stopping for too long on her thin T-shirt where her nipples had risen, her long thick nipples on her small upturned breasts. Risen, he thought, to meet his eyes.

"Is she under a doctor's care?" Barb asked, leaning toward him.

"There's only so much a doctor can do," Lanny said, looking from one set of eyes to the other. They were both sending off the musky odor of sex, but he bit his tongue to keep himself from getting aroused. He couldn't do this now. Not until everything was settled. Not until everything was over. He put his glass down on the table.

"I don't want you feeling sorry for me," he said, standing up. "I love Joy, and when I married her I made a commitment to her that I intend to keep. Taking care of her the best way I know how."

"It's not the life I would have chosen for myself," Sue said, picking up Lanny's full wineglass and downing it.

Barb stood up and linked her arm through his. "Is there anything we can do?"

Lanny ignored the gentle pressure of her fingers on his wrist. "Just be patient with her. She's going through a bad time. When the pregnancy is over, all this confusion will settle down. And if it doesn't, then I'll deal with it. Can you manage to forgive her until then?"

"Sure thing, Lancelot," Sue said, putting down the empty

glass. "But if you're ever lonely in the meantime, feel free to give me a call."

"Sue," Barb barked. "He's a devoted husband. Leave him alone."

Barb walked him to the door and kissed his cheek, her breasts pressing into him. Then her pelvis, almost imperceptibly, drove into his groin. When Sue approached, Barb stepped away and wiggled her fingers in a girlish wave.

He skipped across the street like a cat, without a sound. Ducking inside the house, he removed his shoes and climbed the stairs to the third floor, ignoring the squeal of Joy's chair as she swiveled around behind the closed door of her studio.

He stepped inside the attic and quickly gathered up the clothes that lay in a pile, crumpled by the weight of his body where he'd slept. The clothes were old, soft, worn— Buddy's clothes that Dorothy had given him years ago. He chuckled as he thought of how Joy had never looked in the large box he'd marked PERSONAL years ago and carted from apartment to house. If she ever had a carton marked PERSONAL he would have torn it apart trying to get inside it. But then he couldn't compare himself to her. He walked around with all senses on crisis alert. She was in a daze, half-asleep. That's why it had worked for so long. But now she was waking up. And he couldn't let her. It was as simple as that. He couldn't let her.

He looked at the small gray sweatshirt in his hands, at the balled up white T-shirt, at the stretched-out socks. Buddy was like that, half-asleep. In those days Joy was a bundle of fire, unstoppable, into everything. But not Buddy. Buddy was his little slave.

"Close your eyes and let yourself fall," Lanny would tell him. "I'll catch you. Trust me. I'll catch you."

Buddy wouldn't hesitate. His eyes would snap shut, and he'd let everything go. Even if Lanny didn't catch him the first two times, Buddy was still good for a third try.

Lanny shoved the old clothes in a garbage bag except for the small pile that remained at his feet. Out of that he lifted

Buddy's faded jeans and jammed the legs with newspapers until they stood up by themselves. Then he worked on stuffing the blue and green flannel shirt.

When he was done he licked his fingers, unscrewed the hot, naked bulb next to the door, and replaced it with a dim red one. In the nightmarish glow, he could hardly tell. Hardly tell it was a scarecrow. Hardly tell it wasn't Buddy standing in the middle of the attic, waving hello.

Leaving the attic door open, he crept across the carpet, stopping outside the studio. "Joy," he called out in a loud high voice. "Joy. Help me. Joy."

He disappeared down the stairs just as she opened her door and stepped out, into the hall. The floor above him creaked as Joy made her way into the dim red glow of the attic.

CHAPTER TWENTY-FIVE

THE SMELL HIT her before she opened her eyes. Lysol mixed with chicken broth. Lunchtime at the hospital.

"Thank God," her mother said, as Joy turned to see Dorothy sitting stiffly in an orange molded chair pulled close to the bed.

"What am I doing here?" She was afraid to move. She didn't know how she was supposed to feel. She didn't know what had happened.

Her mother's eyes fluttered as she studied her. "Lanny was here all morning. He left ten minutes ago for the office." She pulled a tissue out of her sleeve and began spinning it into a long snake.

The rustle of thick plastic broke the silence as a tall man walked into the room carrying a large arrangement of blue flowers and Mylar "It's a Boy" helium-filled balloons.

"Excuse me," he said, as he made his way past the opaque beige curtain to the roommate Joy hadn't yet known she had. "Maria," he cooed to his friend, "I knew it was going to be a boy. Didn't I tell you it would be a boy?"

"Lanny tried to get them to put you on another floor," Dorothy said quietly, pulling Joy's attention back to her. "But they say you have to be in maternity."

Joy's hands flew to her belly. Her shoulders relaxed as she felt the familiar mound. She pushed her fingers in and her belly resisted, still hard as stone. Then her hand found the cable that ran from between her legs to the nearby monitor. "What's happened to the babies?" she whispered as her eyes closed.

"Calm down. Dr. Wayne was leaving when I came in. He told me there's nothing to worry about at all."

Joy's eyes flew open, angry. "What does that mean?"

Dorothy leaned back as if she'd been struck. "You know, some people who lose consciousness are just happy to be alive. You don't have to scream at me."

Joy pulled her arm out of the covers to check the date on her wristwatch but her watch was gone. She pulled her other arm out from under the sheet, nearly disconnecting the cloudy tube of the IV that was stuck in her wrist.

"How long have I been here?"

"I'm not sure of the exact time you were brought in," Dorothy explained, relieved to be talking about something concrete. "It was either midnight or two. Lanny said it was two, but then I thought he called to tell me at midnight, so how could it have been two?"

"Two when?" Joy asked too loud.

Dorothy stared a moment before she spoke. "Do you want me to see if Dr. Wayne can give you something to help you calm down?"

The edge in her mother's voice was a warning. "No. I'm fine." She strained to sit up. "I just want to know how long I've been here."

"Oh." Dorothy's mouth turned into a smile for a moment, then flattened out. "You've been here almost a day. Well, since last night." She pulled the chair across the gray streaked linoleum floor, closer to the bed. Then she leaned back as if she dreaded the answer to the question she was about to ask. "What happened?"

It was the question Joy was about to ask, too. She lay her head back on the thin, flat pillow and looked up at the press board ceiling squares, trying to remember. Then she turned to Dorothy, to the anxious stare that came back at her. Her mother was sitting stiffly erect, ankles crossed, hands cupped in her lap. Her paisley dress in muted shades of beige and brown blended in perfectly with the hospital decor.

"Don't you remember what happened?" she asked as she forced her twisted mouth to relax.

"No," Joy answered. "As usual."

Dorothy sat up even straighter in her chair, looking relieved. "Then I suppose we'll never know."

But Joy wasn't ready to accept that yet. She probed her stingy memory, looking for anything, the smallest glimmer of a recollection.

"Lanny tried to figure out what happened, but he couldn't. I'm sure it's not easy finding your wife fainted dead away on the attic floor."

It rushed back to her in a whirl, Buddy staring at her in the attic, and she began to retch. From far away she heard her mother's desperate voice calling for a nurse.

A black hand holding a white kidney shaped bowl descended in front of her face.

"Here you go," the voice said.

Joy dropped her face into the dish and vomited while the hand lifted her hair away from her mouth, out of her eyes.

"It's all right child," the voice said in a Jamaican lilt, as the fleshy hand stroked her forehead.

She was done. Her mouth tasted of bile, and she was

shivering. The fat nurse with the soft voice stood over her, drawing the sheets up to her neck. She left the room with the dirty bowl and returned a moment later with a thermometer sheathed in plastic.

Dorothy looked on, terrified. "Shall I call her husband? Is she all right?"

The nurse ignored the question and went on with her routine. She held the thermometer in Joy's mouth for seconds, then pressed a button that ejected the protective sheath, which landed in the wastebasket next to the bed. "She'll be fine," she said as she read the thermometer.

"You're fine," she said to Joy in a gentler voice. "You just lie still and rest." She turned to Dorothy and flashed the whites of her eyes. "Five minutes and visiting hours is over."

"I didn't make her vomit," Dorothy said defensively.

The nurse left the room, and Dorothy turned back to Joy.

"I saw Buddy last night," Joy blurted out before her mother could begin her tirade about the quality of nursing care in America.

Dorothy's veiny eyes filled with water, and she pursed her lips, her face drawing tight. "Do you say these things just to hurt me?" Tears began to spill out of her eyes, paving a path through her Elizabeth Arden foundation to reveal her pale, liver-spotted skin.

Joy turned her head to the bars that hung down the side of the bed and tried to imagine how it would feel if they went up to the ceiling, if she were locked in, if everyone else was locked out. Then she rolled over on her side giving her mother her back.

When she awoke she was alone listening to the weak cries of the baby in her roommate's arms and then the soft sound of a Spanish lullaby.

"Hello, hello," Dr. Wayne said loudly as he walked into the room, pulling the curtain around Joy's bed, enclosing them in a hot tent. He dropped her chart on the end of the bed and rubbed his eyes.

She studied his shoulders, which sloped down sharply, looking as if nothing could rest there, not even dust.

"I need to know exactly what's wrong with me," she said.

He stopped rubbing his eyes and dropped his hands, looking out from beneath his furry eyebrows as if he wanted to disappear behind them. "You lost consciousness for a little while there, but everything seems to be all right now. However, given the close calls of the last few weeks, we don't want to take any chances."

"When can I go home?"

"Tomorrow."

"Do I have to stay in bed?"

"Lanny and I discussed it, and we both feel you need your rest. It's not so much that you have to stay in bed. But bed is the best place to get rest."

"Why are you talking to Lanny? I'm the patient. Talk to me."

"Well, he is your husband, after all. He does have your best interest at heart and that of the . . ." He wiggled his hands while he searched for the word.

"The babies," she finished for him.

"Yes. He's worried. It's natural. He's a first-time father to be. He wants everything to be perfect."

"Does he?"

"Joy. Do you remember that doctor I mentioned to you? The one I said you might want to talk to."

"The shrink?"

"He's a psychiatrist, yes." He scribbled a name on a piece of paper, avoiding her eyes. "You do remember when we talked about this, don't you?"

"Yes, of course," she said, accepting the paper, not reading it. She needed to be careful about what she said. If Dr. Wayne found out she'd fainted because she saw an apparition of her brother, he would lock her away in a padded room, taking the babies away first. "How can I see this psychiatrist if I have to stay in bed?"

He twirled the gray and white hairs above his right eye.

"Well, now, you've had some trauma, and you're under some strain, but you're not an invalid. You just have to use common sense."

"Can you be specific?"

He scratched his eyebrows wearily. "Stay calm. Stay calm. Stay calm."

"That's it?"

"And see Dr. Friedman. This is supposed to be a happy time for you." He rested a hand on her shoulder. "You have to take care of yourself. Your mother and your husband will be very cross with me if you don't."

"I'm your patient, Dr. Wayne," she said, dipping her shoulder so his hand fell off. "They're not."

"I want you to promise me you'll call Dr. Friedman," he said, pulling at his eyebrows again.

"I'll think about it." She pushed the button on her bed and rose to a seated position.

Dr. Wayne pressed his hands around the mound that was the babies, feeling their position through her skin. Then he checked the tape coming out of the fetal monitor. "All right. I'm keeping you here overnight, and then I want to see you in three days. With cheeks blushing and in good health."

As soon as he left the room, she lifted herself out of bed and grabbed on to the IV pole, wheeling it out of the room ahead of her to get away from the sound of the newborn in the bed beside hers. Dr. Wayne was standing right outside her door, in hushed conversation with a short, bearded man.

"Here she is," Dr. Wayne said too loudly, opening his arms as if he was waiting to embrace her. "Joy. This is Dr. Friedman."

"Hello," she said quietly.

Dr. Friedman smiled, but his stern eyes scanned her face, evaluating her condition. "I hope I'll be hearing from you soon." He extended his hand like a vulture's claw, poised to pick her apart.

She smiled weakly as she shook his bony hand. He returned the smile, warm but watchful.

As she wheeled the IV back into her room she saw Lanny's leather briefcase on her visitor's chair. She ducked her head around the opaque curtain, to where her roommate lay, propped up with extra pillows she'd brought from home.

"Did you hear my husband come in?" She tried to sound casual, light, easy.

"Sorry," her roommate replied, shaking her head.

"Hey. You. What are you doing out of bed?"

She turned to see Lanny standing in the doorway. His voice was breezy, his mouth a perfect smile, but the mood in his eyes was black night.

CHAPTER
TWENTY-SIX

EVEN IN THE morning the library felt like night to him, dim and hushed and dead. He found a chair at the end of a long table, vacant but for an old man sleeping with his head hidden in his arms, smelling his own mold. Lanny moved his chair to the farthest edge of the table and opened the book. He only had an hour. Joy would be discharged at noon. He wasted the first ten minutes thinking back.

The librarian who ran the children's room had hands like a child's and a little head on top of a huge chest that stuck out like a shelf of books. He walked straight over to where she stood at the main desk, checking index cards against a thick catalogue.

"Excuse me?"

She looked up over her half glasses and raised an eyebrow, waiting.

"I'm writing a story for my school paper, and I need some help."

She nodded wordlessly, but her eyes said, all right, go on, hurry up, spit it out.

"It's about potential poisons in the home—like if you take too many aspirin, or what happens if you swallow bleach, or inhale carbon monoxide—things like that. Where should I look?"

Her face lit up. What a great idea for a young boy, her eyes seemed to say. Writing an article on home safety. She marched over to her dusty black filing cabinet and yanked out the top drawer. "Let's see what we have in the vertical file." Her hands flew over the old folders until she found the one she wanted.

"Here," she said as she licked her fingers and started pulling out government pamphlets and skinny booklets, piling a dozen of them on the small wooden work table. Then she limped back to her desk and continued flipping through her cards.

They were poorly Xeroxed pamphlets with titles like *Protecting Your Family from Poisons*, *Ten Quiet Killers* and *Is Your House Safe?*, but none of them told him what Joy insisted he find out. How long does carbon monoxide take before it kills you?

At another table Buddy sat with the *World Book Encyclopedia* in his lap. What he read made him nervous. "It says you get stomach pains," he complained, as if the pains had already begun.

"You won't be there that long," Lanny told hm.

"How long do you have to be there before you get stomach pains?" Buddy peered over Lanny's shoulders at the large book open in Lanny's hands.

Lanny snapped shut *Fishbein's Illustrated Medical and Health Encyclopedia* before Buddy got any more ideas. "You have at least an hour before the poison gets in your system, because first your body breathes in all the good air and then it starts letting in the bad stuff. At least that's what it says in this." He waved *Carey's Common Sense Safety Tips* in front of him, but before Buddy could grab it, Lanny walked over to the librarian and handed all the pamphlets back to her.

Joy and her mother were waiting for them in the car. As soon as the boys got in, Joy turned around and mouthed the question, What did you find?

Lanny winked and gave her the thumbs up sign, and Buddy did the same. Later, in the clubhouse, Lanny told her how they had at least an hour before the symptoms would begin, and that he'd let them out before the hour was up. They had at least an hour, he reiterated, and by then he forgot he'd made it up.

He explained again how the Trust Club worked. If Joy wanted to be a member, she'd have to give him her total trust, just like Buddy had. She'd have to trust a hundred percent that he'd come when he said he would. And if she stayed with Buddy until he let them out, if she stayed the whole time, then he and Buddy would vote on whether to let her in as a charter member. As for Buddy, this was his final test.

Lanny smiled as he thought of Buddy, eager as a puppy to do whatever was asked of him. Then the smile vanished abruptly. The memory of the smell in the garage the day Buddy died hit him with a force that made him gag.

Fishbein's Illustrated Medical Encyclopedia had been right, he thought. Buddy had vomited profusely. Even after Lanny cleaned it up and doused the concrete with Chlorox bleach the smell lingered, breezing into the kitchen every time his father opened the door to the garage.

His father never said anything about the smell. But he did get the car washed every other day, and he did take it to the shop at least twice a week, complaining about noises. He must have known.

Dorothy didn't. She spent the whole summer sitting in

her driveway on a green and white aluminum folding chair, parked like a car, waiting for Buddy to be returned.

He didn't have to die there, Lanny told himself yet again. That wasn't the idea.

The first time Lanny went into the garage after it happened, he had to hold his breath. He squatted and looked around and thought about what he would have done if he were stuck inside by himself, breathing poisoned air that smelled fine but could kill him.

But Buddy hadn't worried about that. He trusted that Lanny would come and get them out in time.

The walls of his garage were crowded with pesticides and fertilizers and rusty coffee tins that had belonged to the people who lived there before. There were hoses that were too tangled to use, bicycles Lanny had outgrown, a sled that had become a shelf for storing paint, and rakes and shovels hanging from hooks stuck in the concrete.

There were no windows, and the light was dim. But still Lanny could see the ax hanging from the back wall. And the rusty pitchfork leaning next to it. And the saw, dangling from its rough wood handle. The saw wouldn't cut through concrete, but it would have cut through the automatic door. Buddy could have gotten out. He could have saved himself. He didn't have to wait.

The man next to him started coughing so hard he couldn't catch his breath. The librarian walked over, his scrawny neck peeking out of the collar of his shortsleeved shirt, and whispered softly in the man's ear. When the man stood up, he nearly toppled over, muttering and glowering at Lanny like it was somehow all his fault.

Lanny turned back to the open book before him and finished making the diagram of what he needed to do. It was the last thing on his list.

CHAPTER
TWENTY-SEVEN

"I WAS GOING to get a nurse, then I decided you'd be more comfortable without one." He stepped aside to let her into the back bedroom where a surgical bed stared at her from the middle of the floor. A hospital tray stood next to it, with a yellow juice jug, a stack of paper cone cups, a pile of magazines, and a box of tissues carefully arranged on top.

"What is this?" she asked.

His voice was gentle. "I rented it." He gestured to the bed, proudly. "You can make it go up and down, just like in the hospital."

"Why?" she asked, keeping her anger in check.

"You're going to have to spend a lot of time in bed now. I want to make sure you'll be comfortable." He picked up the control panel and made the bed go higher, then lower. "See? It's great." His smile was broad, but she could see the tendons in his neck flexing. He was nervous showing her the bed. He didn't know she was relieved that now she could sleep alone.

"That's very thoughtful," she said vaguely.

"And furthermore, I've made a thorough investigation in the attic. Everything is absolutely fine up there. There's nothing to be afraid of. Your mind was playing tricks. You just have to put it out of your head."

But she wasn't worried about that. She'd accepted that

she'd had another hallucination. She'd accepted that she was unraveling, slowly. She just didn't want Lanny to know.

"It's as good as forgotten," she said, stepping out of her shoes and climbing into bed.

He stood in the doorway, watching. Then he hoisted himself up and sat down at her feet.

"I hate to treat you like a child, Joy, but you've been acting like one lately."

She stared back blankly.

"Let me make something clear for you," he went on. "I can't take those babies away from you now, and I don't want to. But if you don't show me that you can take care of yourself, I'll make damn sure a social worker is standing at your bedside the minute they're born."

"Lanny. Everything is fine. I'm taking care of myself. Don't worry."

"This is okay? You don't mind sleeping in here?"

"It's for the babies," she said, closing him out as she closed her eyes. She lay perfectly still, waiting for him to leave. She didn't mean to fall asleep, but sleep was there, waiting for her.

When she woke, with the dawn, her lips were parched and stuck together. Her legs ached as if she had the flu. Her nightgown was twisted around her like a straitjacket. As she slowly unwrapped her legs and let herself out of the high bed, she tried to remember when she'd changed out of her clothes, but she couldn't.

Quietly, she padded downstairs and into the kitchen, her feet sticking to the cold tiles. She filled a tall glass with the icy water that came out of the tap first thing in the morning and let it slide down her throat in one long swallow. She was awake and alert.

Wandering through the rooms she reviewed her choices. She could leave now, while he slept. Pack a bag and go. Go to Dorothy's. Live there with the babies, until she got back on her feet. Raise them in her mother's dark apartment, with her mother at her side, telling her the way things are supposed to be done. Her stomach reeled.

She could ask Lanny to leave, but he wouldn't go. Not without the babies. Not without a fight. Her stomach protruded like a badly made medicine ball. As she walked, hidden muscles stretched and strained, aching. She wasn't ready for the fight.

She looked out the window, looking for another choice, and there he was, walking on the sidewalk in his bathrobe lugging an overstuffed garbage bag to the curb. He's throwing out something he didn't want me to see, she thought as she went up the stairs to her new bedroom, two steps at a time, her robe billowing behind her.

She disappeared into the hard bed, pulled the sheet above her eyes, and tried to quiet her rapid breathing. The front door closed quietly. Lanny crept up the stairs to their bedroom.

For a second the house was silent, as if they were both asleep. Then, convinced that his stealthy trip outside hadn't disturbed her, came a thud. Now he wanted her up. He hopped out of bed. The bathroom door slammed. The pipes whined as he flushed. And from beneath the sheet she felt the light change. He was standing in the doorway, watching her. Keeping her breathing steady she lay motionless. The light changed again. She heard him walk back down the hall.

Seconds later the volume on the television set in their bedroom shot up high. She felt like Bryant Gumbel was sitting in bed with her, asking her how it felt to sail around the world with her ten kids. She pushed herself up and found the button that made the bed rise to a sitting position. She grabbed a magazine from the bed tray and leafed through it briskly, not seeing the words. Then Lanny walked in.

He looked surprised to see her awake. He moved closer to the bed, and his robe fell open, showing his naked thigh. He hasn't taken a shower, she thought. He hasn't gotten dressed. She wondered if he'd come because he wanted sex. She would, she thought, if he wanted her to. She would open her legs and let him in, if he asked. She wasn't ready for the fight.

"Hey sleepyhead," he said. His hair stood out in a hundred directions. He looked like he hadn't slept.

"Is the bed okay?" His tone was soft and solicitous. It unnerved her. It wasn't what she'd expected. He pushed her hair away from her eyes. She tried not to flinch, but she knew he had felt her recoil.

"I slept fine," she admitted, relaxing as he removed his hand.

He leaned against the bed and hung his head for a moment, thinking. Then his foot began to tap the floor. It was a warning. His mood was getting blacker. She practiced ignoring it and felt a tiny thrill.

His leg went next, jiggling up and down like a jackhammer shaking the mattress. She picked up the magazine again and stared at a perfume advertisement until the images began to blur. The bed stopped shaking suddenly.

"I'm going to get dressed," he said after a moment.

She nodded slightly, still staring at the perfume ad as if she was only half-aware he was there.

"I said, I'm going to get dressed." He waited, his brow creasing.

"Go right ahead," she said, closing the magazine. "I'm not stopping you." Her voice remained steady, but she found herself wondering, if I scream, who will hear me, who will come?

He stomped out of the room. She could hear him moving clumsily, with anger. Snap, the drawers opened. Snap, the drawers closed. Snap, the wooden suit hanger was thrown to the floor. Snap, a pair of shoes were dropped. Snap, he pounded one foot into his shoe. Snap, he pounded in the other. Snap, the bathroom door slammed shut. Snap, the toilet seat went up. Snap, he dropped it down. Snap, his feet stomped down the stairs. Snap, the door flung open. Bang, it closed behind him.

She dialed her mother to see if she could come and stay

for a few days, but when she heard her mother's brittle voice she hung up the phone, thinking maybe there was a way to fix things. Maybe if she just tried a little bit harder, she could make it work. She thought it, but she knew it wasn't true.

CHAPTER TWENTY-EIGHT

HE EXPECTED SOME kind of reaction. He was never home from work before five. He expected surprise, even thanks. At least he expected she'd notice.

"I'll see you tomorrow," she said into the phone as he rested his briefcase against the staircase and took off his suit jacket.

She hung up and smiled like nothing was wrong. Then he noticed she was dressed. He didn't want her dressed. He wanted her in bed. He bit the inside of his cheek and asked, "Who was that?"

Her smile vanished. "I have to drop off my sketch with Anna-Marie tomorrow. I called Dr. Wayne, and he said it's not a problem so long as I take a taxi from the train."

Lanny's fingernails curled into his palm, digging in. He forced his fist to uncurl. "I thought we agreed you'd take it easy."

"This is my last job," she said calmly. "I have to finish it."

She stood at the window staring out at the black sky. She looks so beautiful, he thought. I wish I could keep her.

They wandered into the odorless kitchen. Lanny offered to make eggs. Joy nodded and followed him to the stove. They cooked together, a silent dance punctuated by the occasional bang of a pot, sliding shut of a drawer; even the cracking of the eggs seemed too loud.

Lanny opened the refrigerator and the door bumped Joy's belly. They collided as they set the table. The morning newspaper still lay on the kitchen counter in its pale yellow wrapper, as if neither could remember whose job it was to take the wrapper off. They smiled self-consciously and pushed their chairs back at the same time to get up and get the salt and pepper.

Is this it, Lanny thought? Does the silence mean she's put it together? Does it have to be now?

He stared at her as she gazed out the side door. Her eyes looked tired, the lids puffy. She looked worn down, her color pale. He sighed deeply and continued to stare. It didn't matter. She couldn't see him. She wasn't looking out.

And she looked so vulnerable today. Like a painting that wasn't quite finished. He could see through her translucent skin to the faded blue lines of her veins. And he tried to think, was she always this pale?

"Did you go to Toney's Brook today?" he tried.

"Wasn't that yesterday?" She looked at him blankly.

He clenched his teeth and smiled. "Was it?"

She laughed, a tired laugh. "I don't remember."

He smiled as gently as he knew how. He had no idea what was in her head. "I'm going out to work on the car."

She glanced at the clock. "Now?"

"You told me the locks are sticking. You want them fixed, don't you?"

She didn't remember the locks sticking, but she nodded anyway.

As he left for the garage, Lanny clenched his teeth to press out his fear. Then he noticed her watching him, so he waved and widened his smile.

When the phone rang Joy answered distractedly.

"Joy, it's Ray."

"Lanny," she called out. He was already on his way to the phone when Ray quickly added, "No, I wanted to talk to you." But there was nothing she could do.

"Hey guy," Lanny said when Joy handed over the receiver. "What's tonight's disaster?"

Slowly Joy made her way up the stairs to bed.

CHAPTER TWENTY-NINE

"THIS PLACE IS a zoo." Anna-Marie slammed shut her office door and pressed her body up against it like *The Fly*. "Can I come live in your house? You can have my job."

Joy's face lit up for the first time all day.

"Really. It's easy. All you have to do is to talk a dozen brilliant editors out of their terrible cover ideas. Then, when that doesn't work, you have to convince a really talented illustrator that the bad idea isn't all that bad. After that, you have to get the editor to call the cranky author and reassure him that, in the end, you can't tell a book by its cover. You'd be great."

Joy fixed her dress so it fell smoothly over her large belly.

"It's not a good time for a career change, right?"

"Right," Joy answered, nearly laughing. As always, Anna-Marie was in constant motion. Even as she spoke to Joy she was glancing at covers, half reading plot summaries, rearranging piles of phone messages, sticking notes on her lamp, on her desk, on her hand.

"What have you got for me?"

Joy reached into her portfolio and pulled out the sketch. "I'm sorry it took so long."

Anna-Marie sat down behind her desk and cleared a space for Joy's artwork. "You know me. I don't mind waiting so long as it's good."

She handed Anna-Marie the drawing. This was the part she hated. The first look told everything. Afterward the reaction could be faked, prettied up with politeness. But the first glance spoke the truth.

There was no politeness on Anna-Marie's face. Her eyes widened, and she blinked hard, to focus. Then she lay the paper down on the desk. "This is a joke, right? Now you'll show me the real one, right?"

Joy snatched back the drawing and stared at it. It was Lanny's father, with red scribbles covering his face. She never put this in her portfolio. She never covered his face with red marker.

"Sorry," she said, her hand shaking slightly. "This must have gotten in by mistake." She felt inside her portfolio and pulled out another sheet of paper. She turned it over. It was the drawing of Buddy, with his mouth open, screaming.

"This isn't the drawing I did for you."

"Oh. Well. That's a relief." Anna-Marie stood up and began pulling colored markers out of the lazy Susan on her credenza.

"Look. I'm sorry. I put the right sketch in my portfolio last night. It must still be at home."

"I see. It flew out while you were sleeping. And someone else's flew in."

"I'm sorry." Joy glanced around, checking to see that they were alone. "I've got a problem."

Anna-Marie listened begrudgingly. She didn't have time for this.

Joy whispered, "I think Lanny switched the pictures. Something's happening. I don't trust him." She didn't know why she was telling this to Anna-Marie, who'd only met Lanny once, for a drink after a design awards ceremony.

"I don't generally give advice," Anna-Marie replied matter-of-factly, "but if your husband is a drag, if he's messing with your work, dump him."

Then she noticed how Joy's face had fallen. She liked Joy.

"We've both got problems," she said. "If I don't have a cover, I'm out of a job. You, on the other hand, sound like you're about to be out of a husband." She lowered her voice. "I hear things get pretty ugly when people are getting divorced. But messing around with your work isn't playing fair. Do you have a good lawyer?"

Before Joy could begin to explain herself, a harried woman came racing down the hall. "Anna-Marie—we've got a crisis on the dates for the DeRossi book. Susan wants everyone in her office now."

"I'll send the sketch by Federal Express," Joy yelled after her friend as Anna-Marie disappeared down the long corridor. "You'll have it by tomorrow."

"Great," Anna-Marie yelled back, then vanished around the bend.

Lost in thought, Joy made her way to the elevator. She could see herself putting the sketch in the portfolio. The right sketch. She could see herself zipping it up, leaning the portfolio against the wall.

"You going down?" A messenger was holding open the door.

"Yes," Joy answered. She could see herself putting the sketch in. Then Lanny must have taken it out. "Bastard," she said out loud.

The messenger dropped his two shopping bags of books and looked at her, menacingly. "You call me a bastard?"

"No," she answered quickly.

"Someone else in here with us, I don't see?" he asked.

"Just talking to myself," she explained. "Just myself."

CHAPTER
THIRTY

STANDING IN THE doorway, he watched the blanket rise and fall gently over her large belly. With the sheet pulled up high above her chin, she looked like she was in the morgue. As she shifted to her side, he retreated to the bedroom, dressed quietly, and left. He didn't want to be there when she woke up.

The train was on schedule, but he couldn't get a cab so he took a bus uptown. By the time he got to Dorothy's, it was already after nine.

"My appointment is around the corner in half an hour," he told her from the lobby phone. "Can I come up?"

"Of course," came her delighted answer.

From down the hall he could see her door was halfway open. He could see her standing in the shadows, waiting for him. When he got there she offered her cheek, and he kissed it like a dutiful son.

"You're looking lovely this morning," he said.

Dorothy shook off the compliment, pushing him playfully away, into the dining room, where she'd hastily put out a plate of buttered rolls on her good china.

He let her ramble on, like always. He knew how people who lived alone could babble. But now her son-in-law was with her. Soon I'll be all she has, Lanny found himself thinking, and wondered, will she call me 'son'? Will she

153

ever, even once, accidentally call me Buddy? He leaned forward slightly, looking interested, and kept his smile warm.

She blathered on about how strange it was, the idea of being a grandmother at the age of sixty-one, when she'd just about given up hope. He let her talk, nodding sympathetically where appropriate. He knew no matter how she got there, she'd end up where he wanted her, on the subject of Joy.

"Did I tell you I'm doing a little job for an Arab prince?" She poured milk into his coffee and stirred.

He shook his head, pretending she hadn't already told him. He listened again to how small the prince's rooms were, how high the ceilings, and how dark.

"At least he makes decisions. I can't get your wife to decide on a single roll of wallpaper."

He let her complain about how indecisive Joy was, how remote, how unappreciative, how cold. Then he heaved a sigh, like he just couldn't take it anymore.

"I have to explain something to you, Ma," Lanny interrupted, finally. "There's something you don't understand. Something you don't know. Something I shouldn't be telling you."

"We've never had any secrets from each other, Lanford. We've always been able to talk." Her back was pressed against the spindles of the chair.

"I just hate to upset you."

She looked down into her cup, into the patterns of the Irish lace tablecloth, anywhere to keep away from his eyes. "I'm stronger than you give me credit for. Go ahead. Say what's on your mind."

"Your daughter is obsessed with death."

She looked like her mouth had been squirted with lemon, her lips pinched together. She wanted Lanny to go away, but he wouldn't.

"She's obsessed with death and with Buddy. She's been dreaming about him every night. She keeps asking me why he was kidnapped. Why he was taken instead of her."

Dorothy closed her eyes, but he didn't stop. He wanted to go deeper. He wanted to go all the way.

"She thinks it should have been her. She's got this

twisted idea that if she had been the one who'd been taken, we'd all be happier."

Dorothy shook her head, wanting him to stop, but she didn't say a word so he went on.

"He's the last thing she talks about before she goes to sleep and the first thing she thinks about when she wakes up."

Her veiny eyes were wide and filling up fast.

"Everything she sees is in relation to him. This guy eats like Buddy used to eat. That one has the same color eyes. Everyone is better or worse than Buddy. Nicer or meaner than Buddy."

"I thought she barely remembered him," Dorothy said in a little girl voice Lanny found repulsive.

"That's what she'd like you to believe so you'll keep feeding her more and more stuff about him. I think she's got a plan. I think she wants to join him."

Her cup hit the saucer with a bang. "What do you mean?"

Lanny didn't answer. He wanted to give her time to figure it out for herself. And she did. The color drained from her face as if all the blood had been sucked out.

"It's horrible to even talk about it," he said running the tip of his finger along the thin top of the teacup. "But I am truly afraid for her life."

But not as afraid as Dorothy was. He watched her wrap her arms around herself like it was the middle of the winter and she was out without a coat. She sat shivering in the overheated apartment while Lanny wiped his sweaty forehead with his napkin every time she glanced away.

"I'm very worried," he said.

Her head was drawn into her neck like a turtle. "What can we do?"

"There's nothing more to be done. I've spoken to the doctor, and he's having her see a psychiatrist. I've talked to her people at work and told them to leave her alone for a while. I've even had a word with some of the neighbors. I've removed every stress I could find. But in the end, it's going to be up to her."

"This is just ridiculous," she said finally, sitting up straighter.

She's tougher than I gave her credit for, Lanny thought. Already she's back in control.

"She's got to forget about Buddy," she pronounced. "It's way past time."

"That's exactly what I keep telling her," he said. He sighed with relief as if to let her know she'd spoken his mind. "But it's so hard for her," he went on while she re-filled his cup. "There are reminders everywhere."

"Well, remove them."

She's proud of herself, he thought. She's solved my problem. It's me she's concerned about. Not her daughter. Her daughter is one big headache, same as always. It's her son she needs to protect now. Me.

"Just take away all the reminders and tell her you won't discuss it anymore and I'm quite sure, after a while, she'll put it behind her, just as I have." But even as she said it her resolve wavered. She'd remembered she was the one feed-ing Joy photographs. He saw it on her face. Her thin mouth turned down into a frown, her shoulders fell, her chin dropped toward the top button of her blouse.

"If you don't mind, I think I'd like to give you back that picture you sent her," Lanny said, helping her out of it a lit-tle. "The one of me and Buddy and Joy and the clubhouse."

Her cheeks flushed. She was just like Joy that way, he thought. She couldn't hide a flea in her hair.

"I should never have given it to her." She rubbed the tips of her fingers together, as if she was trying to start a fire. "I should have thought."

"You didn't know." He reached across the table with an open palm. She took his hand and squeezed back hard with her bony fingers.

"How could you know?" he asked her.

She smiled, and her eyes filled up again, but Lanny wasn't in the mood for slop. He freed his hand to push the crumbs on the table into one long line.

"I wish I could stay," he said, brushing the crumbs into

his palm. "But I can't. Are you going to be okay? I hate leaving you like this. It's not your fault she's falling apart. It's not anyone's fault."

"Oh, don't worry about me." She stood up and pulled her sleeves down to her wrist, drew her collar closed, straightened her skirt.

"It's all going to be fine," he said, letting the crumbs drop to the floor, soundlessly. "She's got two tough cookies looking after her. We won't let her do anything stupid."

He didn't have to say what stupid thing she might do. Dorothy's eyes told him she'd already figured that out.

"Promise you won't worry?" He gave her a tight hug.

She squeezed back hard. "I promise."

"About that picture," Lanny said with the door open, his voice sounding hollow from the echo in the hall. "Don't worry about it. I'm sure one picture of the clubhouse isn't going to cause her to do anything horrible."

She looked at him with a frozen face. And he wondered, is she going to tell me she sent two?

"You're an angel for coming by," Dorothy whispered as she kissed him on both cheeks.

He walked to the elevator. She watched him hit the button, change his mind, and come back.

"There's something else," he said in a half whisper. "If I'm going to be honest with you I have to tell you something else."

This time she didn't say a word. She just stared at him and waited.

"There's been a problem with the pregnancy."

She mouthed the words, Oh, God, but all that came out was a soft click when the tip of her tongue hit the top of her mouth.

"Joy doesn't know. She's lost one of the twins. There's only one alive. She doesn't know. The other one is dead."

He caught her before she fell down and walked her inside. The door slammed behind him, and with the sound of it she almost fell again.

"How did it happen? How are you going to tell her?"

"I don't know. But I have to tell her soon." He held her tight, and she clung to him. "As soon as I think she can handle it. Dr. Wayne says if I wait until she delivers the baby, it could interfere with the bonding. But I'm afraid." He forced a quiver into his voice. "Because if she gets upset it could happen again. She could lose the other one, too."

She looked at him with watery eyes. "Poor dear," she said holding back her tears. "Poor Lanny dear."

CHAPTER THIRTY-ONE

"STAY ON THE phone. I'll be right back."

Joy heard Molly's footsteps and then a shriek. When Molly came back on the phone, Trina was crying in the background.

"Sorry. Trina just spilled half a bottle of perfume on the dress I've been ironing for the last half hour for the date that I know you won't believe I actually have. But you didn't catch me at a bad time. It's a great time. We're having a ball over here. What's up with you?"

"Who's the date with?" Joy stalled, unsure of exactly what she intended to say, of how to begin.

"I don't know. I mean I know what his name is and what he does and all, but that's it."

"Well?"

"Dick. Dick Zwick. I'm crazy right? No one should go out on a blind date with a guy named Dick Zwick."

"It depends where you found him."

"He found me. Trina, stop playing with Mommy's stockings—play with this necklace instead."

"He called out of the blue," she went on. "He's in my Thursday class, but I have no idea who he is, although I know who I hope he is. I'm crazy to go, right?"

"No," Joy said quietly. She didn't think Molly was crazy at all. She thought Molly was lucky.

"Uh oh. Something's wrong. I can hear it in your voice."

"We'll talk about it tomorrow."

"Tell me."

"It's too complicated to go into over the phone."

There was silence until Molly broke it in. "How about if I get dressed at your house? In something other than my perfumed dress. My mother is already here, and it'll be better all around if I just leave. Unless . . . Is Lanny home? If Lanny's home I'll feel funny."

"No. He's working late tonight."

"I'm on my way."

When the doorbell rang, Joy opened it to find Molly in her bathrobe and winter coat, her hair squashed under a red felt hat, a shopping bag hanging from the crook of each arm.

"I didn't have time to decide what to wear," she said as she breezed into the house, "so I brought everything. I hope you have a hair dryer." She shook her head to loosen the wet hair that her hat had flattened.

"I have a hair dryer," Joy said, laughing. She took one of the shopping bags and led the way upstairs.

"What in the world is this?" Molly asked as she spied the surgical bed through the open doorway. "Is someone's mother moving in? That's it, isn't it? Someone's mother's moving in."

"No one's moving in. Don't even ask," Joy replied.

"Oh, please. I came all this way. You'll have to do better than that." She tested the equipment, raising and lowering the bed, wheeling around the tray, looking inside the plastic pitcher, listening while Joy explained about her hospital visit.

"I need you to help me," Joy said finally.

"Sure," Molly offered. "You name it."

"I want to go back to Lanny's old house, and I want you to come with me."

"Sure. Then what are we going to do?"

"That depends on what I find. I might just end up putting myself away."

"Come on."

"I might not have a choice." Joy tried to keep her voice steady. "I'm close to losing it, Molly."

Molly didn't argue the point, and Joy took notice. "Why don't we go tomorrow afternoon? Unless you need to go now, tonight."

"Tomorrow's fine."

"Great. We'll go, just the two of us. I'll ask my mother to watch Trina." She looked at her watch. "Shit, I'm supposed to meet this guy in twenty minutes."

"Come and get dressed in the bedroom. There's a mirror there."

She led Molly into the bedroom, the first time she'd been there in two days, and it was a wreck. The bedclothes were tossed in a heap in the middle of the floor. Lanny's underwear, socks, and pajamas were dropped like bread crumbs, marking the paths he'd taken from work to bed to work. She shook out the heavy down blanket and lay on top of it on the bed with the pillows piled up behind her.

"Too sexy?" Molly asked, holding up a fitted black dress with a wide scoop neck. "I don't know yet if I want to turn this guy on."

"Then don't wear that dress."

Molly nodded in agreement and pulled out another one, a simple straight blue silk. Joy approved, so Molly fished out a pair of panty hose to match.

"It's going to be fine," she said as she pulled on the sheer black tights. "We'll drive to Toney's Brook and we'll ring doorbells, ask questions—whatever it is you need to do to find out whatever it is you need to find out."

"I hope so," Joy said, drifting off, imagining how it would feel to tell Lanny she was leaving him.

Molly put on her dress and handed Joy her jewelry pouch.

"Give yourself a break from worrying. Pick out some earrings."

Joy laid out the assortment of hoops and studs and long beaded earrings on the bed, and with shaky hands picked a pair of dangling gold bars.

"Perfect," Molly said as she grabbed them and struggled to find the hole in her right ear while checking her watch for the third time in five minutes. "I hope he doesn't have a thing about women who are late." She combed out her tangled hair. "Hair dryer?" She threw the reject jewelry pouch back in the shopping bag.

"Hanging behind the closet door," Joy directed.

Molly plugged in the dryer and bent over so her hair hung toward the floor. Then she gave a quick blow with the old shotgun machine. The noisy motor blocked out the sound of the front door slamming.

Molly stood up and shook her hair to see how it lay. Then she bent over again. She pointed the nozzle at her head as if she were shooting herself and blew her hair into a tangle. Joy watched and missed the sound of footsteps on the stairs.

Resting the hair dryer on the bureau top, Molly put the final touches of rose lipstick on her full lips. She stuck the lipstick in her small black purse and snapped it shut.

"You know what else we should do tomorrow?" she said, slipping her feet into black pumps that added two inches to her height. "Do I look too tall? Should I wear flats?"

"Flats," Joy said.

"After we get back," Molly went on as she stepped into her patent leather flats, "we should go up into your attic."

Joy felt the babies move. Her belly rearranged itself, slowly, in a wave.

"Why?" she asked when the motion stopped.

"Because you don't really believe in ghosts. So we have to go explore the shadows."

"There are no shadows. If we go up there now, we won't see anything at all."

"So we'll go up and see nothing at all."

"I don't know," Joy said, handing Molly the rest of her

clothes, which she stuffed into the shopping bags like dirty laundry.

"Why not? Just get a good night's sleep tonight—because tomorrow we've got a lot to do. I don't want to go to Toney's Brook unless you're well rested." Molly picked up the dryer for one last blow, then turned it off and put it back in the closet.

When Joy opened the front door to let Molly out, she found Lanny standing on the steps, his key in front of him, as if he'd only just arrived.

CHAPTER THIRTY-TWO

LUCK WAS WITH him. He was on a roll. She'd already eaten and gone straight to bed. It didn't take long before her breathing steadied, with that little catch that told him she was fast asleep. Not that it mattered anymore. She was avoiding him like he had some disease.

But the friend. He hadn't counted on her drawing in a friend. So now things changed again.

He picked up his tools in the basement and crept out to the garage. But the work went slowly. Remembering slowed him down.

Breathless, she raced up to him as he stood on the swing in her backyard.

"You have to let him out," she demanded, her face bright red.

"If he wants to leave he can leave."

"The door is locked. Your father saw me come out, and he locked the door."

"Buddy can get out if he wants."

"The door is locked, and besides, he won't come out until you get him."

He hopped off the swing and kicked a pile of leaves in her face. "Some sister you turned out to be," he said as he walked away. "You just left him there."

"I was getting sick," she snapped back as she spit the leaves out of her mouth. "He's getting sick, too. You have to let him out."

"You know you've blown it. You'll never get in the club now."

"Get him out."

Her scream ricocheted in his head.

The locks were harder to do than the tail pipe. The book he had wasn't doing him much good. But it didn't matter. He disassembled the lock again and started all over. It paid off, taking apart all those egg timers and vacuum cleaners. This was no problem. Except it was taking too long. Because he kept going back.

He lay on the torn-up clubhouse couch while Joy sat crouched outside, refusing to come in, refusing to speak. Because of several days of heavy rain the ground was so soft it cushioned the noise of Henry's heavy steps.

"Lanny," his father bellowed. "Lanny, come out of there."

He raced outside so they wouldn't come in. The sun was low behind them. He couldn't see their faces—just two silhouettes in a line that he recognized from their shapes.

"What's wrong?" he asked. He couldn't see Joy's eyes. He couldn't be sure what she'd say.

"Tell us where the boy is," Henry shouted.

"Buddy," Dorothy butted in. "Where's Buddy?"

He shrugged his shoulders. "I already told you I don't know." He pointed to Joy. "Ask her."

"Where's your brother?" Dorothy barked.

In the silence he could hear cicadas singing, crickets rubbing their legs together, sparrows landing on the leafy trees above them.

"Stand up," Dorothy ordered.

Joy obeyed but wouldn't meet her mother's eyes.

"She was the last one with him," Lanny piped up, "but she says she doesn't remember what happened. I tried to get her to talk, but look at her. She's been like this all day long."

Joy lifted her tearstained face. "He got in the car." Her voice cracked. "He couldn't get out."

"My God, he was kidnapped," Dorothy said, stunned. "My Buddy was kidnapped," she shouted. "My God, my God." She ran across the lawn, back to the house, Henry lumbering behind her. "My God," they heard her shout, until the wind carried her words away.

"Great going," Lanny cheered, once they were alone. "Brilliant. That's it, you're in. You're a member. You're a lifetime member, now. Come on inside here. I want to show you something."

She wouldn't walk through the door. She stood like a statue.

"He was kidnapped," Lanny said again, smiling. "You are brilliant. He was kidnapped." He pushed away the couch, rolled up the rug and heaved several planks off the floor where he hadn't yet put the nails back.

She stood at the threshold, staring at the freshly dug earth.

"There's room for two people down there," he said as he dropped the planks back and picked up the hammer to return the nails to their little holes. "So if you ever tell anyone, remember, there's room down there for you, too."

With the first bang her eyes snapped shut, and she puked, right there, in front of the clubhouse door. Then she ran off into the woods behind the house.

He had to get a pile of leaves to wipe up her vomit. Later he put the leaves in a bucket and took them out into the woods where he mushed them in the ground and peed on them to cut the stench.

The cops came that night. He told them he hadn't seen Buddy all day, but that Joy said Buddy got in a car, a black car, that drove off before she could get help. He told them he'd been back in the woods all afternoon, catching bugs. To prove it there were three big jars standing on his dresser—dog ticks, dying crickets, and a field mouse—just in case they looked.

In the morning he found Joy sitting outside the clubhouse, waiting for him.

"Who kidnapped him?" she demanded, as if she'd been waiting all night to find out.

That's when he knew she believed it. She believed her own lie.

"He was kidnapped," Lanny whispered to the lock, to no one. What else would they think, he reminded himself. After all, there wasn't a body. Not that they found.

CHAPTER THIRTY-THREE

THE BLACK DOOR slammed. She pulled at the handle, but it popped right off. She tried to stick it back on the car, but suddenly it turned into a doorknob and wouldn't fit.

"Get out," Buddy screamed.

Helplessly she stared at the metal knob, watched it drop

to the floor and roll away. Crawling on her knees she looked for it, grabbing anything she could find: sticks, pieces of concrete, crushed cans. She pushed the pile of magazines off her bed tray. They fell to the floor with a thud. She sat up, sleep slipping away quickly, and tried to remember her dream. It was gone.

She dressed in a rush, trying to calm herself. She had woken in a cloud of anxiety. The day had barely begun, she was already unnerved.

Dorothy called at eight-thirty, pleading to come by for a visit, but she put her off until the next day. Then she called Dr. Wayne to reschedule her afternoon appointment.

"Have you been in touch with Dr. Friedman yet?" he asked casually.

"He's next on my list to call," she stalled. But she meant it. If things didn't get settled today, she was going to give the psychiatrist a call. She had to. She was too close to the edge.

Five minutes before Molly was due to arrive the phone rang, and Ray's loud voice came on. Joy was embarrassed. He had left several messages on the machine over the past few days, but she kept putting off calling him back.

"Do you have a second?" he whispered when she picked up the phone, as if they were illicit lovers.

"Yes."

"Okay. I'll talk fast. Here's the thing. Something's wrong with Lanny. He thinks everyone at work is out to get him. He thinks you're out to get him. The thing is, I want to help him. Because if he goes off the deep end, I'm out of here, too. I'm his boy. So I want to help." He blew his nose and went on. "The thing is, it's a pressure cooker here. Plus he's terrified of something happening to his kids. You can't ever let him know I called. But if he explodes, he won't be the only thing to blow up. Do you get my point?"

"What do you want me to do?"

He rambled on, short of breath. "Something. Take him away for a week. Ease up on him at home. He's worried sick about you. If you ease up on him, maybe that's enough. You see, it's the pressure of this Catco deal going through, and the pressure of the babies. All together it's too much. So if you could," he cleared his throat, "just ease up. He says you're into this Sherlock Holmes thing. Digging up your roots or something. Maybe if you let up on that. Maybe that will do the trick."

Suddenly Joy wondered if Ray called out of concern, or whether Larry was standing at his side, holding a script.

"I'm going to Toney's Brook today," she told him, speaking clearly, loudly, in case anyone else was listening on the line. "To see Lanny's old house. After that the mystery will be solved. Then Sherlock Holmes can get on with her life."

She slammed the receiver down and went out to meet Molly, who was waiting in the driveway, huddled with Barb and Sue.

"Well," Barb chirped. "Look who's here. We haven't seen you around for a while."

Joy was about to explain why, but Molly jumped in. "Joy and I were just saying the same thing about you."

Barb cocked her head. "I never know with you, Molly. Are you making fun of us?"

"She's not," Sue said cupping a hand over her cigarette as she flicked her lighter. She took several deep drags, blew out a heavy cloud of smoke, and watched it disappear into the air. "So. Did you catch your crooks? You're not in the Police Blotter this week."

"I guess your kids must all be out of town," was Molly's dry retort.

"Excuse me," Sue said, dropping her cigarette to the ground and stomping it out with her tennis shoe. She took another out of a hard box. "I thought it was Joy here who had the problem."

"Besides," Barb interrupted her friend. "I take offense at your suggesting our kids have done anything wrong. Dennis just spent the summer at Exeter. He's a good kid."

"They're all decent enough," Sue added as she walked up close to Joy. "So?" She stood inches from Joy's face so that Joy could smell her tobacco breath and see the tiny lines around her darting eyes. "We're dying to know. Did you get rid of your little intruders? It's better than 'One Life to Live,' what goes on at your house. Some people on the block are nervous that it might be catching, like a virus. But I subscribe to the theory that it's hereditary. Like mental illness."

Joy blanched. "Let's go," she said to Molly.

"Oh, aren't we in a friendly mood," Barb snapped. She put her little hands on her hips. "You know, I never would have sold you this house if I had known you better. But your husband was so nice, I never thought . . ." Her voice trailed off and she shook her head.

"No matter what happens, I'm moving," Joy said to Molly once they were in the car.

"You can't move unless you take me with you," Molly added as she pulled out of the driveway.

Joy closed her eyes and let herself be lulled into a daze by the rhythm of the car. An hour later, when the motor switched off, her eyes popped open.

They were parked in front of Lanny's old house on Dowling Place. The street was deserted but for two young children sitting in miniature cars on Joy's old front walk. Joy got out of the car and walked up to them, stooping down next to the five-year-old boy who was eyeing her suspiciously. "Do you live here?"

"Yes, but I'm not allowed to talk to you," he said soberly.

"My grandma lives over there," the blond girl said, pointing to what was once Lanny's home.

"What's your name?" Joy asked the girl.

"His name is Jeremy, and I'm Shannon," the little girl offered.

"I used to live in your house, Jeremy, when I was your age." Joy looked over his head to the front porch of her old home.

"You did not," the boy said, squinting his eyes, looking annoyed. "It's just me, Mommy, Daddy, Sol, and sometimes Uncle Rob."

"Is your mommy home?" Molly asked the boy.

"No, she's at work so I can have more toys," the boy answered.

"My grandma's home, but she's on the phone," the girl said. "She's always on the phone. You want to see?"

Joy looked over at Molly.

"Let's go," Molly said.

The little girl took Molly's hand and pulled her into the house. Joy followed them into the foyer. She stared at the painted blue walls where clusters of botanical prints hung together like bunches of grapes. But her eyes didn't register the prints, or the blue walls, or the bleached wood floors. She saw Lanny's foyer. She saw moss green carpeting and green and beige wallpaper with ducks and rifles. Against one wall she saw a long table, covered with Lanny's books, piles of bills, and a glass bowl filled to capacity with pennies. It could have been yesterday she had been here, dragging Buddy home for dinner.

"Grandma," the little girl called. "This lady wants to see the phone."

Her young grandmother appeared in the hallway at the end of a twenty-five-foot phone cord. She motioned for Joy and Molly to follow her into a large country kitchen. "I'll be off in a second," she said, covering the mouthpiece.

A large saucepan filled with chocolate pudding sat on the island in the middle of the room, but Joy saw the pot of oatmeal that Lanny cooked every morning, that hardened through the day until it was time for the dinner dishes to be done.

She looked at the window that faced her house. A small butcher block table sat in front of it now, but she could still see the round table that used to be there, the orange linoleum top cluttered with appliances, half taken apart.

Her eyes wandered to the mud room off the kitchen, where raincoats hung from low hooks, boots were lined up in order of size, and garbage was stored before being thrown outside. Then she saw the door to the garage. She walked closer. It was the only thing unchanged. It was the same door, black steel with a rusty lock. The door opened, and Jeremy walked into the kitchen.

"Hold on," the woman said into the receiver. "I told you not to come through the garage," she yelled at the boy. He let go of the heavy door, which slammed shut with a bang that sent Joy reeling flat against the wall.

"I'll have to call you back later," the woman said to her caller. As she hung up the phone, she stared at Joy who was stuck to the wall, her cheeks bright red, her heart racing.

"How can I help you?" the woman asked as she wiped her hands on a towel she had tucked into the front of her navy pleated skirt.

"If it's a bad time, we'll just leave," Joy offered, backing up toward the hallway. She wanted to leave. She was desperate to leave.

"No, stay," the little girl whined.

"Shannon, go outside and play with Jeremy." The woman pushed her granddaughter toward the front door and Jeremy followed. "When I call you, we'll have the pudding."

"Yea," Shannon said as she ran out of the house, pulling the little boy along by his hand. "I'm going to have chocolate pudding."

"Jeremy is, too," the woman yelled after them. She closed the door with a sigh and gestured for Joy to follow her into a small sun room filled with green wicker chairs.

Joy looked at the square room, with its baskets of chrysanthemums. When Lanny had lived there, the den had had uneven pine shelves along two walls stuffed with trucks, trains, and tiny plastic soldiers. Buddy had the soldiers, too. They'd ordered them from the back of a box of Cocoa Puffs, one hundred soldiers that came in a plastic bag and ended up everywhere, sprinkled around the house like dust.

The woman waited and Molly waited until Joy realized they were waiting for her.

"Sorry," she said. "My name is Joy Bard."

"Mrs. O'Neill," the woman said as she crossed her legs and her hands and closed her mouth.

Joy took a breath and went on. "I used to live next door,

where Jeremy lives, and I'm here because . . ." She stopped and looked out the window at the garage. When she turned back into the room she saw a young Lanny sitting on a red vinyl couch that was split down the middle, with foam rising up through the crack. She could see herself telling him something. She could see him laughing.

"She's here because she's trying to find out some things that happened when she was a child," Molly explained, trying to make it sound light.

"Oh," Mrs. O'Neill said, looking from one to the next.

"Would you mind if we looked around your house?"

"Oh," Mrs. O'Neill said again. "I don't know. I mean, I don't know you. And things happen. I'm sure you're perfectly nice people, but I don't know you. I don't really know."

Joy stood up. "It's all right. I understand. I wouldn't let two strangers walk through my house, either." Her eyes were stuck on the garage.

"Oh Mother Mary," the woman said suddenly, her hand rising to her mouth. "This is about the boy who was kidnapped, isn't it?"

"Yes," Joy said quietly, without thinking.

The woman whispered, nervously. "When we bought the house, of course we didn't know. And then we heard stories. About a kidnapping. And then, you know how people talk. We heard other stories. Some people on the block insisted there was no kidnapping. That the boy just died. But his body was never found. Did you know him?"

Molly shook her head quickly and looked over at Joy, but Joy wasn't listening. She was staring out the window at the garage. She turned pale suddenly, like a ghost.

"Can I go in there?"

The woman looked from Joy to Molly and back to Joy. "I don't know," she said slowly, sizing up the danger, not wanting to be rude. "I suppose it would be all right to go in the garage. Just the garage," she added, emphatically.

She stood up awkwardly, then grabbed a set of keys off

a bookshelf near the door. "Let's go out this way so I can tell the children." She led them out the front door.

"Shannon, why don't you and Jeremy go wait in the house. I'm going to take these ladies to look at the garage, and when I come back in, we'll have the pudding."

"Just me," Shannon called.

"Both of you," Mrs. O'Neill insisted. She watched the two children climb out of their toy cars and walk up the front path and into the house.

"The police came twice to look in our garage. They didn't tell us why. My daughter always said it smelled. She refused to go in the there the entire time she lived here. We still don't use it, see?" She pointed to the car in the driveway, then put her key in the antiquated automatic garage door opener. The door rose slowly.

Joy looked straight ahead. She could see the blue Plymouth that wasn't there. She could see her brother behind the wheel, holding his fingers in his ears to drown out her voice. She could see the black metal door that went into the house, to the kitchen.

"Lanny never said anything about throwing up," she reminded Buddy.

"I guess I ate something bad for lunch."

"Well, I didn't have lunch yet. So how come I feel like throwing up, too?"

"Because you're my stupid sister who wants to do everything I do. So just shut up and wait for him."

"I'm getting out of here," she said.

"Get back in here. If you leave, you're out of the club."

"I don't care. It's a stupid club. You should leave, too. You don't look good."

"No way."

"Help me open this door."

"No way. Just get back in the car. He'll be here in a few minutes."

"I'm going in through the kitchen."

"Don't do it. His father's home."

"Come with me."

"Get lost."

"I'm going to tell Mom you're in here."

"You do, and you're dead."

"So come with me."

"Go flush yourself down the toilet."

"Fine. Fine. Stay here forever. I don't care. No one will care. I bet no one even notices you're gone."

"Do you know something? Do you know something that happened here?"

Joy heard the woman ask the question, but the voice sounded far away, as if it were coming across a great distance, a distance of time.

She raced into Lanny's house, smack into Henry.

"What are you doing?" he screamed as he double-locked the black door with a key he pulled out of the pocket of his low-slung pants.

It took half an hour to find Lanny. He wasn't in his backyard, or in the woods behind the house, or even up by the train tracks where they weren't allowed to go anymore. Finally she found him swaying slowly, standing on a swing in her backyard, looking at her through a pair of heavy binoculars.

When they got to the garage Lanny fiddled for several minutes with a bobby pin until the door rose slowly. There was Buddy, slumped in the front seat of the car.

Joy grabbed the car that wasn't there and fell to the floor.

"Oh, Mother Mary," she heard the woman say. "I'll call an ambulance."

"No," Joy managed to get out. "I'm okay. Just help me up."

"Mother Mary," the woman said quietly. "There was a sister. Who wasn't quite right in the head." She stared at Joy. "Are you the sister?"

"No," Molly replied quickly as she took Joy by her arm,

walking her over to the concrete steps, helping her sit down.

"I shouldn't have let you in," the woman said fretfully as she opened the door leading into the kitchen. "My Joseph is going to kill me if you sue."

She disappeared into the house where they could hear her scream at the children for devouring whatever chocolate pudding hadn't dripped onto the floor.

Molly sat down next to Joy on the steps and put an arm around her. "Are you okay?"

"He wasn't kidnapped," she said, holding back the tears that were straining to explode.

Shannon and Jeremy came rushing into the garage through the kitchen door.

"What happened?" they asked in unison. They looked at each other, laughed and hooked pinkies. "Owe a coke, owe a coke, jinxo man. Stab me in the belly if I don't step on a can." They pulled their pinkies away from each other, like human wishbones.

Joy shot up as if she'd been kicked. She grabbed Jeremy by his shoulders.

"Where did you learn that? Who taught you that?"

"Let go of him," the woman shouted, appearing at the doorway in her chocolate-stained clothes.

Joy dropped her hands. "Where did they learn that? We used to say that all the time, 'owe a coke, owe a coke, jinxo man.' Where did they learn that?"

"It's in her clubhouse," Jeremy said quietly, unsure of what was going to happen next.

"Buddy and Lanny's clubhouse," Joy said quietly.

"Shannon's clubhouse," Jeremy corrected her, his lips pressed tight.

"Do you want to see?" Shannon offered.

Joy looked at Mrs. O'Neill, who said, "It's nothing to see."

"Please Grandma," Shannon pleaded. "Can't we show her?"

"All right," the woman capitulated. "But that is it. You look at the clubhouse, and then you go."

The three women followed the children to the backyard, to the shed where a pair of faded red handprints peeked out from beneath the overgrown ivy.

"It's written on the wall inside," Shannon boasted. "That man read it to me."

"What man?" Joy and Mrs. O'Neill asked in unison.

"Owe a coke, owe a coke, jinxo man. Stab me in the belly if I don't step on a can," the children chanted again.

"The man who came this morning," Shannon explained. "He used to live here, too."

"You didn't tell me," Mrs. O'Neill said. "Why didn't you tell me?"

"He said we couldn't," Jeremy pronounced with great solemnity.

The woman shook her head. "I don't like this at all. Go on inside the clubhouse and look at whatever it is you want to see," she said to Joy, "and then I want you to leave."

Joy forced herself to cross the threshold. The furniture was all gone. The worn couch, the faded rug, the purloined lamps. All the garbage, other people's garbage, that the boys had collected like treasures, was gone now. It was just a shell.

Shannon appeared at her side. "I hate it in here." Then she began jumping up and down on the wood plank floor, the hollow noise echoing loudly in the tight space.

Joy raced out of the clubhouse, ducking her head as if the roof might cave in on her. As she ran across the front lawn to the car, Molly frowned, ignoring the puzzled looks they left behind.

When the car turned the corner onto Lily Lane, Joy asked Molly to pull over. But before they stopped she'd rolled down her window and retched over the side of the car—just like she had, she suddenly remembered, the day that Buddy died.

CHAPTER
THIRTY-FOUR

EVERYBODY WAS CROWDED in Lanny's office, and he was playing all the parts.

"Your honor," he said to his empty desk chair, "this deal is more than fair. The target board has full discretion. We are simply offering the better choice."

"Way to go, Lanny," Ray cheered him on. But Lanny could barely look at Ray. Because Ray was a jerk. Because who else but a jerk would call his boss's wife and leave a message on the machine? Who else but a jerk? He pushed the thought out of his mind, to be dealt with later, and went back to the glory at hand.

"Then what did the judge say?" Ray asked, sweaty and eager as ever.

"I will rule now, with an opinion to follow," Lanny continued in the judge's baritone register, playing to the crowd. "I rule in favor of Catco."

O'Connell, the mergers and acquisitions attorney in charge of libation, popped open a bottle of champagne. Everyone cheered. Three of Lanny's colleagues whispered in his ear that he'd done okay, that he'd saved his ass, and some others as well.

Along with a few other secretaries, Kelly wandered in holding a cone-shaped paper cup she'd brought from the bathroom. The mood was light, a good impromptu office party, until the phone rang. Kelly answered, hushing the crowd, mouthing that it was Berger calling. The room emptied as if a skunk had walked in and dropped his scent.

Lanny followed Leslie, Berger's secretary, into the softly lit office. Berger, a man of little movement, sat behind his bare glass desk giving out no clues to his mood.

"Congratulations," he said finally, his eyes pointing Lanny to a chair, to sit down. "I knew you'd come through."

Warmed by the praise, Lanny started to give the details of his day in court, but Berger interrupted. "I'm not talking about that. I just got off the phone with Ed Robinson, who told me the Catco board has voted unanimously to recommend their shareholders vote for the merger."

Lanny held back his smile. He'd done it brilliantly. But he had to stay modest. Berger didn't like arrogant sons of bitches, so he had to stay modest.

"I want you to know, Lanny, he gives all the credit to you. He says you were the one who kept it all together."

"Thank you, sir, but there were a lot of people on board this one. Ray did a damn good job in San Francisco, for one. Then there was Leonie, and Bill Martin. We had quite a crew."

"That's just the point. Robinson wants you to sniff around. He wants to know who leaked the deal. You brought this one in, but you brought it in on a leaky boat. Now you've got to find the hole."

"No problem, sir," Lanny said, but he was thinking, I'm fucked. I don't know where the leak is. It could have been Ray. It could have been anyone. Someone at Catco. Or Albacon. Some secretary or an elevator operator who overheard something. It could have been Joy. He looked around the room, feeling set up, trapped. Someone was out to get him. Someone was getting ready to shoot him down.

"Dinner, Thursday night at eight o'clock," Berger was saying. "Robinson and Catco will not have their wives with them, so neither will we."

"Fine," Lanny said, trying to catch up to him, trying to figure out exactly where he stood.

"And then I want you to pick out a week for vacation. Leslie will make arrangements for you and your wife to stay at our condo in St. Croix. I know it's a difficult time for you now, so whenever it suits you, the week is yours."

Lanny couldn't keep up. He didn't know which parts were real and which were a crock of bull. He stood silently, his head tipped, deferential.

"I must tell you, you've earned my respect on this one. Everyone here thought it was over when Albacon arrived on the scene. Everyone but you." Berger leaned back in his chair and started dialing. Lanny was dismissed.

"Thank you, sir," he said. But he was busy thinking. Was he being set up? Or was he the golden boy again?

Berger covered the mouthpiece of the phone. "One more thing. I'm going to have Victoria call Joy. Now that we're neighbors, we'd like to have you up to the house for dinner." He looked away and bellowed into the phone. "Hello, Thomas."

Lanny glided out of his office. Invited to dinner. Now he knew. He'd made it to the magic circle. He might even end up one of Berger's closest friends.

"Mr. Bard?"

He turned to see Leslie running down the hall after him.

"Here are the dates when the condo is available over the next two months. Just let me know."

Lanny grabbed the list and kissed her cheek. As he ran down the hall, he turned once more to see her watching him, smiling.

"How about I take you to lunch at the Four Seasons?" he asked Kelly when he got back to his office. She booked a table in a loud voice, making sure all her friends heard.

He realized he was on edge when he snapped at the maître d', for keeping them waiting five minutes before seating them. After excusing himself to apologize, he returned with two glasses of champagne.

"I hope I can convince Joy to come with me to the condo," he said after draining his glass. He wrapped some gravlax around his fork.

Kelly took another sip of wine. "Why wouldn't she want to go?"

"Well, she's been unwell. She's not herself."

"Gee. I would give anything for a week in St. Croix."

Lanny looked at her and smiled. She had skin like a baby, smooth, unlined. It was time for him to start thinking about his future. He ordered her a second glass of champagne.

They came back to the office laughing. Lanny shut his door to return phone calls, to kid with clients in the gregarious way they loved. He was in the middle of a call when Ray let himself in and sat down across from him.

Lanny managed to disengage the client and hang up the phone. "What's up, Ray?" he asked. He didn't like that Ray breezed right in without knocking. He didn't like how comfortable Ray had become. He didn't like Ray calling his wife.

"I guess I'm still flying from that Catco deal." Ray smiled but dropped it when Lanny didn't respond. "The thing is, I called Joy today. To get her input on that Christmas party. Did you know Berger stuck me with it again? It's nuts because I know no matter what I recommend, he'll still just have us all over to his house for drinks. But no, I have to go through the motions—getting Leslie to call for prices at Windows on the World, the Rainbow Room, Twenty-One."

Lanny stared, steely-eyed.

"So," Ray went on, clearing his throat, "I called Joy 'cause I figured what the hell do I know anyway about places to have Christmas parties? I thought Berger hated my suggestions last year, but guess I was wrong on that one."

Lanny raised his eyebrows, waiting for the point.

"The thing is, Joy didn't have any ideas, either. But I wanted to let you know. She mentioned she's giving it up. That thing you were telling me about."

"Oh?" He dug his fingernails into the bottom of the wood desk.

"You know. What you told me—how she's all worked up all the time, about her brother. Well, you don't have to worry anymore." He smiled again, happy to be delivering good news. "She told me she's going back to Toney's

River, or wherever it is you guys grew up. She's going today. By tonight, that's it. She's giving it up. She's done."

"She told you that?"

"She did. I swear. She's done with it by tonight. You don't have to worry."

"She told you she's going to Toney's Brook and then she's finished with it?"

"You got it." He grinned, waiting to be thanked.

Lanny didn't move. How the hell did she manage to drag Ray into this, he thought. And then he thought of her in Toney's Brook again, mucking things up.

Ray stared at him, waiting for him to say something, but Lanny was gone, lost in thought.

"Okay, then," Ray said, backing out of the office. He closed the door behind him and let out a low whistle. It hadn't quite gone as he'd hoped.

At five, Lanny left the office to the sound of applause. His co-workers, still reveling in the glow of his success didn't notice he was somber, sad, resigned to what lay ahead for him and for Joy.

CHAPTER
THIRTY-FIVE

A LONG FACE stared back at her through the windshield. Holding her breath she slid her hand, noiselessly, to the metal door handle. She unlatched it slowly, had one foot on the pavement, when she noticed the person on the other side of the glass was moving, too.

Afraid to look straight at him, she caught a glimpse out of the corner of her eye that made her feel it was someone she knew. She forced herself to steal another look. The anxious face gazing back at her came into sharp focus. She was staring at her own reflection. She put her foot back in the car and closed the door.

"Just come on in the house for a little while," Molly said, taking advantage of the sound of the closing door to break the silence.

Joy looked down into her lap. She had been counting on Molly all along, but now she wasn't sure. The ride home had been one long interrogation. Molly's questions came like gunfire, as if this was the payment she'd extracted for her help.

"Come on in, and we'll decide what to do over a cup of coffee."

Joy stiffened. This wasn't their problem. It was hers. No one's but hers.

Molly got out of the car and waited while Joy sat looking down the street toward her house. Every light was on. Lanny was home.

Squatting in front of the open car door, Molly tried again. "Come on. We'll have a cup of coffee, and then we'll decide what to do. We can call the police, if you want. We can call them here, or in Toney's Brook. Whatever you want. Let's just think it through."

Joy got out slowly, looking from Molly to her own brightly lit home. Then she followed Molly inside.

"Holy shit," Molly said, stopping dead at the entrance to the foyer.

Slowly, Joy moved to her side to see. The room was filled with piles of brightly colored Lego bricks, built into multicolored interpretations of houses, trees, and one-of-a-kind animals. Joy followed Molly into the living room where dozens of Golden Books were laid out across the floor like a patchwork quilt.

"Trina did not do this alone," Molly announced. "This has the signs of my mother's hands."

Joy looked on through glazed eyes. She couldn't make small talk with Molly now. She had forgotten how.

In the kitchen, Trina's troll dolls had taken over. Two sat at the table, two were coupled on the floor, two were perched over mixing bowls, and one was upside down in a juice container. Joy cracked a tiny smile and flattened it out.

Molly lifted a note out of the spring-set mouth of the Mickey Mouse magnet on the refrigerator door. "Well," she cheerfully announced as if she and Joy had just returned from a day of shopping. "Seems my mother decided to deal with the mess by taking Trina out to dinner. Can you imagine what the restaurant looks like by now?"

Joy's reflexive smile did not return. She was drifting, running over the day's events, unwilling to let them go. She was a hoarder now, holding on to each memory as if it were an overfilled balloon, threatening to fly away.

"Boom, boom, ain't it great to be crazy," a sugar-coated voice sang out from the cassette player in Trina's room.

"They're back," Molly said, annoyed. "Do you want to come up and watch me have an argument with my mother?"

"No, thanks, I'll wait here," Joy mumbled as Molly disappeared up the stairs.

She picked up the Golden Books from the floor and placed them in a pile on the coffee table, then sat herself down in a corner of the couch. Wearily lifting up her swollen feet, she stretched her legs out in front of her. Her eyes closed but just for a second, like a slow-motion blink. It was too risky. She couldn't afford to sleep now. She had too much to do.

First she had to get back home. She had to get some money and pack a small suitcase of clothes. She'd take the photographs she had of Buddy. And her grandmother's watch. It wasn't much. When she thought about what was precious to her, it wasn't much at all.

Molly thought she should call a lawyer. But a lawyer would only advise her not to leave. She'd heard enough stories from Lanny and his friends to know that was standard advice. Stick it out and keep the house and half the money. Leave and get nothing. But she didn't want the house, and she didn't want the money. She wanted to get away, clean and fast, with whatever she could easily carry. That was all.

"Call your mother," Molly had advised. But that would be no help. Somewhere along the way Lanny had gotten to Dorothy. Somewhere along the way he had made Dorothy more his mother than her's.

As for Molly's suggestion that she call the police, that was out of the question. How could she tell the police her brother's body was buried in the dirt under the old clubhouse? How could she explain why she hadn't told them in all these years? What would keep them from thinking that she had killed her brother, that she had buried him there herself? When it came down to her word against Lanny's, she didn't think it likely they would choose to believe her.

The phone rang. Joy stood up. She would ask Molly to come home with her. Lanny wouldn't do anything in front of Molly. She was a beautiful woman; he'd keep busy trying to charm her, to impress her, to win her like a civil suit.

The phone rang again. She walked to the foot of the stairs. She would ask Molly to stay in the living room with Lanny while she went upstairs to go through her things. As long as Molly was there she was safe. She would take a nightgown, a toothbrush, a change of clothes. She had to gather her slides and her portfolio. It shouldn't take too long.

The phone rang a third time.

"I'll get it," she called upstairs, and halfway through the fourth ring she picked up the receiver in the kitchen.

"Molly?" The voice was muffled as if the caller was cupping her hand over the receiver to be heard.

"No, this is Joy, Molly's neighbor."

"Oh, hello. This is Molly's mother, Muriel. You're the one having twins, right?"

"Yes," Joy said. And she thought, that's me. The one having twins. Soon to be the one having twins alone.

"Joy, darling, can I speak to Molly?"

"Sure, I'll get her," Joy said. Then she remembered. "I thought she was upstairs with you and Trina."

"Didn't she see my note? I left a note on the refrigerator to say I took Trina out to dinner. Oh dear, she must be worried. Could you please put her on?"

"Sure," she said, shaken, but Muriel didn't know her well enough to hear the fear in her voice. "Hold on."

She put the receiver on the counter and walked to the foot of the stairs. "Molly," she called up. "Pick up the phone. Your mother's on."

"The grand old Duke of York," the music played on.

"Molly," she called again, but the song was the only reply.

She walked back to the kitchen, slowly, listening for any hint of Molly, of anyone, in the house. She lifted the receiver off the counter.

"Did she pick up?"

There was no reply.

"Muriel, did she pick up?"

There was no reply. She shook the receiver, then put it to her ear again. "Hello?" she said weakly. But no one was there. The phone was dead. She gingerly hung it up and walked to the foot of the stairs.

"And when they were only halfway up, they were neither up nor down," the tape played on in Trina's room.

"Molly? Are you all right?"

The tape clicked off. The silence was suffocating.

On her way racing back to the kitchen to call the police, she remembered, the line was dead. She returned to the living room and looked out the window. She could run over to Sue's or Barb's. She could knock on Donna's door.

Then she remembered. Less than half an hour ago she had been frightened by her own reflection in the car. What if nothing was wrong? What if she was the one who had accidentally disconnected Molly's mother? What if Molly was in the bathroom? What if she had fallen? What if she was hurt?

"I'm coming upstairs," she yelled in a loud, tight voice. "I'm coming." The yelling brought some comfort, made her feel stronger and not so alone. "I'm coming to the bathroom." She walked down the quiet hall. "I'm coming to see if you're in the bathroom." The door was closed. She pounded on it, loudly. "It's me. Joy. Are you all right?" She turned the knob and the door opened. The bathroom was empty. She looked at the pale yellow shower curtain drawn over the tub. She held her breath and pushed the curtain aside. A collection of tugboats and rubber ducks stared back at her.

"Thumbelina, Thumbelina, tiny little thing," the tape started up again in Trina's room.

"I'm coming," Joy yelled. She walked slowly, holding on to the wall for support. She stopped in front of Molly's bedroom and looked in. The drawers were open, the clothes emptied on the floor. The dresser top was cleared. Molly's jewelry pouch lay upside down on top of a pile of stockings and sweaters.

"I'm coming, Molly," she called, tears beginning to fall down her cheeks. "I'm almost seven months' pregnant," she said quietly, in case the intruder could hear her, in case he was sentimental. "I'm seven months' pregnant with twins."

"Though you're no bigger than my thumb," the voice sang on.

She stood at the threshold of Trina's room. Toys were everywhere. Books, crayons, dolls, and a toy tea set, dumped on the floor. Trina's small, delicate clothes were scattered about, half-in, half-out of the open drawers.

"Sweet Thumbelina, don't be glum."

Joy heard a soft tap from the closed closet door.

"Don't be glum, don't be glum, don't be glum."

She walked to the door. The tapping was clear. Gentle. Steady.

"I'm going to open the closet door," Joy whispered softly. "I'm pregnant with twins. Please don't hurt me." Her voice was barely audible.

She pulled the doorknob. There was no resistance.

"When your heart is full of love you're nine feet tall."

She opened the door, staying behind it.

"If you're happy and you know it, clap your hands."

She walked to the edge of the door and peered around.

A groan came out from deep within her as she rushed into the closet to Molly, who was slumped in a corner clutching one of Trina's small plastic hangers. She looked straight at Joy, almost through her. Her wrist moved the hanger back and forth as if she was still tapping on the closed door.

"What's happened?" Joy asked. Molly's eyes rolled back in her head, and her eyelids fell.

"Please, no," Joy whispered, grabbing Molly by her feet. She dragged her out of the closet. Her body was heavy, and she slipped out of Joy's tight grasp. Joy looked at her own hands. For a second she wondered how they had gotten covered with paint—then she realized it was blood. Her eyes raced across Molly's body until she saw it, a large butcher knife extending out of her stomach.

She dropped to the floor and lay on her side, awkwardly shifting her weight to find a position where her stomach wouldn't interfere with getting close enough to Molly's mouth to feel if she was breathing. A soft weak intake of air just discernible, Joy managed to give a few mouth-to-mouth breaths before leaving Molly's side to find the phone. She was sure there was a phone in the bedroom.

With her friend left prone in the hallway, Joy stepped over the clothes on Molly's bedroom carpet, making her way to the phone on the nighttable. She tried to remember Edgebury's emergency number, but she couldn't so she pushed "O." She put the receiver to her ear, then remembered. The line was dead.

She returned to Molly, kneeling beside her. "You've got to keep breathing," she said. "I'm going for help."

She looked at the knife in Molly's stomach and the blood caking on her shirt. She tried to remember if she was supposed to pull the knife out or leave it there. She clutched the handle and pulled gently, but it resisted. She let go and stared. Her hand had fit around the worn edges of the knife's handle as if she knew it well.

"That's my knife," she said out loud, her eyes widening.

She heard the front door slam. "Who's there?" she called out as she plodded down the stairs.

"Hello?" she called again as she rushed to the foyer. But she was alone.

She pushed her heavy body back up the stairs to Molly. "I'm going to get help," she said, squeezing Molly's hand. "If you can hear me, just hold on. I'm going to get help."

When she opened the front door Trina was standing on the steps. Muriel, Molly's mother, was reaching for the bell.

"We brought our dinner home," Muriel said cheerfully clutching a white grease-stained bag. Then she saw Joy's bloody hands and the red streaks down her face. She dropped her dinner to the ground, a soggy cheeseburger poking through the torn bag.

"Frère Jacques," the music called from upstairs.

"Mommy," Trina yelled as she darted around Joy and started upstairs.

"No," Joy called out. She raced after the little girl and grabbed her by the hand, dragging her back to her grandmother.

"Molly's been hurt," she said quietly to Muriel as she guided them out of the house. "I'm going to call an ambulance. Then I have to call the police."

"Where's my baby?" Muriel called out.

"I'm here," Trina chimed in. "Where's my mommy?"

Joy slammed the front door closed. "Please stay out here," she pleaded. She looked into Muriel's eyes. "I'm going to call an ambulance. Please don't let Trina go in."

She sat a limp Muriel down on the front steps. Trina quieted instantly, hiding herself in her grandmother's chest.

Racing next door she rang the bell. She had never been formally introduced, but she'd seen the old man who lived there getting in and out of his old white Buick. She rang again. The lights were on, but no one answered. She rang a third time, and still no one came. She ran across the lawn to the next house. A car was parked in the driveway. She rang the bell. The blue light of a television set was visible from the window upstairs. She pressed the bell again, holding her finger on it.

"Anybody home?" she yelled. "I need help. Please answer the door."

There was no reply.

She ran across the street to Donna's house, but even before she lifted the heavy brass knocker, Seth opened the door.

"I need to use your phone," she said breathlessly. "There's been an accident."

The boy didn't move. He just stood in the doorway, smirking.

"I've got to use your phone," she demanded, her voice shrill and urgent.

"It's broken," he said, slamming the door in her face.

She walked into the middle of the street and screamed, a deep, mournful cry. Then she faced the blazing lights of her own house and went inside.

CHAPTER THIRTY-SIX

THE DOOR WAS unlocked and ajar. She kicked it gently, and it swung open. Stepping inside, she listened for him.

At first she heard only her own rapid breathing, but then her ears caught the sound of arguing coming from the living room. She grabbed an umbrella from the cast-iron stand next to the door and held it in front of her like a sword.

As she passed the open closet door she saw a pile of coats lying tangled on the floor, signaling that someone had grabbed a coat off a hanger too fast. Using her umbrella like a fireplace poker, she pushed the coats around revealing her squashed raincoat, his denim jacket, and a wool baseball jacket she'd never seen before.

Then she heard it, a male voice, harsh and muffled, difficult to make out. Slowly making her way to the living room, she strained to hear more. Words began filtering through. Gunfire. Stand-off. Hostages. It was Tom Brokaw on the seven o'clock news, turned up too loud.

Holding the umbrella straight in front of her, she strode into the room, finding herself alone with Tom Brokaw's face flickering in and out of focus. She stared at his broken up head, the picture coming together and fading away. She lifted the remote control and pressed the button. The TV went dead. Still she heard voices.

She followed the sounds into the kitchen where Charlie and Dennis sat at the table, the butcher-block knife holder between them. Her eyes took a quick inventory. Charlie held the paring knife. Dennis held the carving knife. The large chopping knife sat erect in its slot. The butcher knife was missing.

"What are you doing here?" she demanded.

Charlie turned lazily. "We're waiting for you, Mrs. Bard. Mr. Bard asked us to sit here and wait with you until he got home." Then he noticed her blood-streaked face.

"Where is he?"

"He had to go out," Dennis explained, putting his knife down on the table, his dirty fingernails giving him away for what he was, a young boy.

"You can leave now," Joy said, keeping calm.

They both hesitated. They were supposed to stay and wait with her. Mr. Bard had given them ten bucks each.

Calmly she picked up the chopping knife. "You can leave now."

The boys didn't move.

Clutching the knife she grabbed the phone and pressed the emergency number.

"Police," the clipped voice said.

The boy's eyes stuck to her as she paced the room, then turned to them. "Drop that knife," she ordered Charlie, her voice fierce with newfound authority. Charlie lay the knife down and stood up.

"Who's speaking?" came the tinny voice of the dispatcher on the phone. "Hello? Who's speaking?"

"I need an ambulance. Someone's been stabbed."

The boys stepped away from her, afraid to move.

"And I need the police. Send the police."

Without taking their eyes off her, the boys backed out of the kitchen and ran out of the house.

"We're on our way," the dispatcher reassured her. "And ma'am?"

She had to strain to hear. She felt dizzy and nauseous and tired. "Yes?"

"Why don't you get into your car and drive the hell out of there."

She hung up the phone and splashed cold water on her face, using the sleeve of her sweater as a towel. Then she tried to catch her breath. She didn't have time to be afraid. She only had time to get some money and get away. The rest was his. The clothes, the jewelry, the books, the art supplies, the china, the stereo, the bicycles, and the tapestry her mother had given her. All the paraphernalia of their life together was his. She just wanted enough money to get away.

She walked back into the dining room to the straight back chair where she always left her purse. But the large black bag was gone. Not on the chair, not on the bookshelf, not on the table.

She walked to the foot of the stairs, and her eyes traveled up. She had just over a hundred dollars in an envelope in the desk drawer in her studio. Her checkbook was there, too. She eyed the staircase, and she eyed the front door. She held her breath and listened hard. But there was no sign of Lanny in the house. No creaking floorboards, no groaning pipes. She climbed the steps quickly. Reaching the studio out of breath, she threw open the door.

Tiny black cinders floated through the air and settled on her hair, her shoulders, her face. The windows were wide open, the wind making the cinders dance around her. The sweet smell of burned paper clung to the walls, lingering. Her eyes scanned the room. The shelves had been emptied. The drafting table was bare.

Her eyes caught a glimpse of one of the early Freds, peering at her from the wastebasket on the floor. She picked up the can and dropped it. It was hot. She looked inside. At the bottom were a few inches of cinders and several half-burned drawings. Clinging to one side, mean and ugly, was the singed face of Lanny's father, looking up at her. She kicked the can across the room and waited, ready for Lanny. She pulled the chopping knife closer to her and saw the blade of her small X-Acto knife lying on the floor. She picked it up, snapped on the plastic cap, and pocketed it.

Her desk drawer was cluttered with sheets of art instructions and rough pencil sketches. She stretched her hand deep in back until her fingertips found the envelope where she'd stuck the money she'd earmarked for Lanny's birthday present. She pulled it out and opened the flap. It was empty.

"Bastard," she called out as she made her way down the stairs. She reached the first floor and ran to the kitchen, opening the silverware drawer, the junk drawer, the utensil drawer, looking for a stray dollar bill, but there were none. Then she spotted the little porcelain jar that sat next to her cookbooks, where Lanny deposited his pocket change every night. She spilled the contents on the table and counted out the quarters, nickels, dimes. It wasn't enough to get too far, but she could get to Dorothy's. She had to get to Dorothy's. There was no place else to go.

She ran to the kitchen, picked up the phone, dialed Dorothy's number, and put the phone to her ear. She checked her watch. It was seven o'clock. There was a train to the city every half hour. She could make the seven-thirty, if the police didn't come first. If the police came, it was over. She had found Molly. It was her knife. Her prints were on it. Molly wasn't conscious; she couldn't say what happened. It would be Joy's word against Lanny's. By the time Molly came to, it would be too late. And if she didn't come to—Joy stopped herself from thinking of it.

"Why isn't it ringing?" she asked out loud. She hung up, then punched in the number again. Again the connection didn't go through. She kept the phone at her ear and pressed down the receiver button. Nothing happened. No dial tone. No clicks. This phone was dead, too. This phone that she'd used to call the police. The police who told her to get the hell out. The police who didn't ask for her address.

She dropped the receiver, left it dangling to the floor, and ran out onto the porch. When she flung open the door she could see up the block to Molly's house, where Trina sat alone on the front steps, illuminated by the naked porch bulb, her small shape frightened and cold.

Joy ran back in the house. "Bastard," she screamed in the hallway. But the bastard wasn't there.

Her eyes caught the glimmering shape of keys on the front hall table. The engraved heart that declared Lanny's love for her lay on its back, and dangling from it, the keys to the car. She ran back outside.

"I'm coming, Trina," she called up the block. The little girl turned toward her. "I'm coming to take Mommy to the hospital." She couldn't tell if Trina had heard her.

She pressed the remote control opener and ran out to the garage as the door rose steadily on its tracks. The light came on and then blew out. She cursed the bulb and felt her way in the dark, running her hand across the car door until she found the keyhole. She stuck her key in and jiggled it in the lock. "Come on," she said to the key when the door wouldn't open. "Not now, come on." She jiggled the key again, and the lock turned. She opened the door and slid inside. Her belly grazed the steering wheel.

"We'll be okay," she said to her babies as she lay the chopping knife on the passenger seat and rubbed her hard stomach. She turned the key, and the car started up. A traffic report came blaring too loud, and she switched the radio off. She turned on the headlights, and the garage lit up in front of her. The brooms, rakes, and old hoses on the wall stared back, watching her. Her eyes flashed around, examining the shadows. The car sounded strange, like the engine was revving too fast, too loud. A red light on her dashboard announced the driver's door wasn't closed. She pushed the handle to open it. It wouldn't open.

"Keep calm," she told herself. She pulled the handle again, but the door wouldn't budge. She pushed up the electric lock button, but despite the sound effects, it remained stuck closed.

"You fixed the locks, you bastard," she said to an absent Lanny as she pushed the knife to the floor and heaved her body across the seat to the passenger door to unlatch it. She pulled the handle and the door opened, but just an inch. The car was parked right up against the wall. She couldn't fit her pregnant body through the narrow opening, not with her belly protruding in front of her like a lopsided watermelon.

As she clumsily slid back into the driver's seat, she heard a noise and turned just in time to see the automatic door descending. Lanny stood in the driveway, watching her. Then he was gone. The door was shut. He'd closed her in, surrounded by the hum of the engine racing too loud.

"Not now," she cried out, grabbing onto the ignition key. She tried to turn it off, but it wouldn't move. The key was jammed in. The car was stuck on.

In a flash she thought of Lanny's trips to the garage, of his grease-stained tool kit. "You fixed the car," she screamed. She pressed down the electric window opener, but the window remained shut.

She pulled off her sneaker and pounded the side window. But the soft canvas Ked flopped against the glass like a sock. She dropped it and flung open the glove compartment pulling out maps, broken pencils, stained memo pads, the owner's manual. Then an ice scraper tumbled onto her lap.

It was the size of a small hairbrush, but she wrapped her hand around it as if it were a sword and smashed it into the window. The plastic handle split in two. The window stayed intact. She wiped her bloody hand on her cheek, then frantically felt around inside the glove compartment again. It was empty.

She sat for a moment, catching her breath, until she noticed the chopping knife, lying on the floor. Grabbing it, she thrust it at the side window as if she was jamming it into

Lanny's back. It took three blows before the window shook, then shattered into a hundred cracks, like a giant spider web. Using the wooden handle of the knife she pushed the cracked window out, until it tumbled to the ground, crumbling into a thousand glass pebbles, the knife falling along with it.

She hoisted herself up, but she couldn't fit. Her stomach was too big. She turned to the huge windshield in front of her.

The knife lay on a cushion of glass on the garage floor. She needed to find something else. She pulled at the steering wheel, the door handle, the radio. The ashtray came out in her hand. She banged it against the glass, but the ashtray cracked into three sharp pieces. She touched the sharp edge of the biggest piece, pricking her finger, then stifled a yawn. She pounded her hands against the steering wheel, pounded the horn, holding her fist on it until she couldn't bear the noise anymore. She felt like puking. She yawned again. Surely someone had heard the horn. She closed her eyes to rest while she waited. She started to drift to sleep, then caught herself.

"No!" she screamed, sitting up straighter, swallowing another yawn. "No." She shook her head to shake off sleep.

Her eyes raced around the car, the garage walls, the broken chairs dangling from the rafters above, the old wood planks, the gardening tools. She slid across to the passenger seat and pushed open the door, squeezing her thin arm through the narrow opening. Her hand grabbed a wooden pole, and she twisted and pulled until she drew it into the car. Her breathing slowed as she tugged the tool in. The handle was old and split, but at the top of the neck lay the rusty head of an ax.

She heaved it against the windshield, once, twice, and then the glass turned into a window knit of a thousand cracks. She threw the ax at the center of the window, and the plate glass fell, in one malleable piece, onto the hood of the car.

Pushing herself over the dashboard, she swung her legs out and dropped herself over the hood. She pressed the button activating the electric door, but she knew right away it was disconnected. In a daze she stumbled back to the car, reached through the window, and grabbed the remote control door opener. Still the door wouldn't budge.

Leaning against the car she yawned again, and again, and again. The yawns were dissolving, one into the next, deeper and deeper. She stumbled to the corner of the garage where a dusty folding chair sat open. She sat down suddenly, to rest, just for a moment. If she could only rest for a moment she could think more clearly.

Exhausted, she closed her eyes. The spinning started. The garage danced around her head. Her stomach reeled. She leaned over and puked.

"No," she shrieked, when her stomach cramps subsided. She pushed herself up and kicked the chair over on its side.

"Help me," she called out. But no one could hear her.

Bypassing the watering cans, hoes, and rakes, she picked the heaviest shovel she could find and lifted it above her head. She heaved it against the garage door. It bounced back at her, falling at her feet. She leaned against the wall, stuck in an endless yawn. The car droned on. She slid down the wall and sat on her heels. She heard a tapping noise, a knocking.

Rushing to the door, she threw herself against it, pounded with her fists and screamed, "Help me. I'm locked in here. I can't turn off my car. Please, help me."

The tapping grew louder. She raced back to the car and reaching through the window, held her hand on the horn, blaring it. When she stopped, the room started to spin. She stumbled back to the door and pressed herself against it. "Can you hear me? I'm locked inside. Can you hear me?"

"Help me. Help me," Lanny's sing-song voice came at her through the door. "My wife is locked inside. Help me."

"You bastard," she screamed, kicking the door. She collapsed on the floor. "I hate you," she spit out. She felt her lids closing, then pushed herself up and forced herself back to the car. Stretching her arm through the window she tried again to pull out the key.

"Help me," she heard Lanny saying. "Help me."

She lifted herself onto the hood of the car and dropped her legs inside, ducking her head under the roof. Half climbing, half tumbling, she fell onto the seat and squeezed behind the wheel. She threw the car in reverse and released the emergency break. Then she stamped the gas pedal flat to the floor.

The car burst through the thick door, raced backward down the driveway, and smashed into the hundred-year-old oak tree across the street before lurching to a stop. For a moment she sat perfectly still. Then she leaned out the window to vomit again. She forced herself to breathe through the pain of her cramps. She surveyed the car, looking for something to use to defend herself against Lanny when he came.

But he didn't come. Her stomach settled slightly. Her yawns became more shallow and infrequent. He didn't come. She took a deep breath. She climbed out of the car and looked around. Lanny was nowhere in sight.

Up the block an ambulance and three police cars were pulling away from Molly's house, sirens blaring. The police would be looking for her soon. She could see the crowd gathering, people bunched together trading nuggets of information.

She felt inside her pocket for the change that weighed her down like cinder blocks. She checked her watch and buttoned her coat against the wind. Then, walking in the middle of the street, she took the long way to the train to avoid passing Molly's house, looking behind every few seconds to make sure no one was following.

CHAPTER THIRTY-SEVEN

THE MAN RANG the bell, knocked, and rang again. Lanny hung back against the wall, in the dark, watching. Waiting.

The man said a few words to the policeman and then looked off to the distance, thinking. But Lanny could tell. The plainclothesman was the one in charge. He was in charge of the whole thing. He could tell by the way the man held his head and how his arms hung relaxed at his side, while his hands moved slightly, ready to grab for his gun.

Lanny watched from the shadows as the man pointed to the front door and then across the street to where the car sat, smashed into the tree. Then the man looked at his watch like he had somewhere else to go. He pointed his finger at the cop, giving him last-minute instructions. Lanny strained to hear, but all he could make out was the sound of hard shoes jogging up the block.

So now he had a cop standing on his front steps, with his legs spread slightly and his head stiff, staring straight ahead, waiting for him.

When he got to the bedroom Lanny dressed slowly, in the dark. As he crept downstairs he ran his thumbnail over the lifeline of his left hand, until he pierced the skin, drawing blood.

And he thought, I should have known. I should have known she'd find a way to get away. Why didn't I know? Why did I think she'd be like Buddy? She never was. She never was like Buddy. Not at all.

He left by the basement door, which, through understaffing or neglect, the cops had left unwatched. Then he cut through the yard, using the trash can to climb over the fence. He knew exactly where she was going. There was only one place left for her to go.

At Mike's Deli the phone was free. His luck still held. He placed his call.

"Hey, there," he said when she answered. "I've got a surprise for you."

"Who is this?" she asked coyly even though she knew.

"Your favorite boy," he played right back to her. "Your one and only favorite boy, and I'm calling with a surprise."

"Lanford," she said in a voice that told him someone was there. "Where are you?"

"We're at our friends, in the Village. And we want to take you out. You have to get rid of whoever's there, put on your best dress, and take a taxi to the Russian Tea Room. We'll meet you out front. We've got some great news. We can be there in than half an hour."

"Well." She was hesitating. He couldn't let her hesitate.

"Why don't you wear that red suit? You look great in your red suit. And it's a special occasion, Ma. You're going to be so happy for us. You have to meet us. Right honey? Joy's nodding her head, Ma. She says you have to meet us."

"Well, all right, then." And he knew she was already thinking, which shoes, which hat, which bag.

"You're the best," Lanny said. He hung up before the automated operator had a chance to ask him to put in more money, giving him away.

CHAPTER THIRTY-EIGHT

JUST AS SHE reached the top of the stairs, the train pulled away. Now she'd have to wait for half an hour. Shivering, she paced the deserted platform. The wind carried away the sound of her cough. The street traffic below echoed fiercely, like airplanes taking off close by. Pigeons gathered out of sight, cooing. With her feet at the edge of the platform, she leaned in and strained to see down the tracks, as if that would make the train come faster.

At street level, next to the station, a small antique store was open late. The sleigh bells hanging on the door jingled every time it opened. That's where she would run if Lanny came. She would run there, and they would help her.

The platform was dimly lit. She stepped back to the wall, listening. Her body tensed as she heard the soft tap of footsteps approaching. She listened for the sleigh bells, but they didn't ring. The footsteps continued toward her. Someone was coming up the stairs.

Hanging back against the wall, she held her breath while looking for something to use as a weapon. But there was nothing to find. Not a squashed beer can, not an empty bottle, not even a small piece of dislodged cement from the cracking platform. She cursed the town for keeping the station so clean.

The slow footsteps padded closer, but the echo from the overhang made it hard to know where the sound was coming from. Suddenly a figure emerged on the opposite side of the tracks. It was an old man, stooped and frail, bundled into a heavy tweed coat. A bright red scarf was wrapped several times around his neck, and a black fedora sat low on his head, keeping his face in the shadows of the dim station light.

She couldn't see his eyes, but she could feel him stare. His mouth opened into a smile.

She smiled back, faintly. There was no way this old man could help her. He was on the other side, out of reach, and besides, he was too old. She craned her neck to look for the train. Then he called to her.

"Pardon?" she yelled.

Her question was carried off by the wind, his reply drowned out by the rumble of an approaching engine. He called again, louder, just as his train pulled into the station, blocking him from her view. When the train pulled out he was gone, three people left in his stead. Like mice, they scurried down the stairs, hurrying home, late for dinner. Again, she was alone.

She paced, and then another set of footsteps joined the sound of hers. When the sleigh bells didn't ring, she checked her watch and realized the store was now closed.

The footsteps came closer. She watched the top of a

black cap come up the stairs until she saw the full-figured shape of a woman clutching a small shopping bag. Then she saw it was a pregnant woman. Another person who offered no protection. Still, it was someone nearby. Her shoulders relaxed slightly.

Joy tried to make eye contact, but the woman had her back to her as she checked her purse. She walked past, dropping her cigarette at Joy's feet. Joy stepped on the smoldering butt with her sneaker and noticed she only had one Ked on. The other was still in the garage. The white sock on her shoeless foot was charcoal gray.

As the woman stepped farther away from her, Joy saw herself through the woman's eyes. One shoe missing, the sleeve of her coat torn, her lapels speckled with dried vomit. Her hair was a tangled mess, shooting out around her head like a fright wig. She could feel lines of dried blood streaked across her cheeks like war paint. She licked her hand and rubbed her cheeks to wipe off the blood. Now her hand was bloodstained, too. Ashamed, she turned away as the rumble of the next train approached. Pretending to cough, she hid her face in her hands until the bright lights of the engine had passed and the train screeched to a stop.

It was a small train with only three cars, only one set of steps. The conductor helped the other woman up and then extended a hand for Joy.

"Pretty fertile water in this town," he joked before looking at her. As Joy climbed the steps, he turned his back and walked away.

She watched the woman take a window seat in the middle of the nearly empty car, so she took the window seat on the aisle across, a few rows up. She would try to explain. She would tell her everything. But the woman kept her head turned away. Away from the unpleasant sight Joy made.

So Joy turned away, too, to her own dirty window, to the empty platform. It was taking too long. If the train didn't move soon, she wasn't going to get away. They would get her. Someone would get her.

The train jerked forward as the brake was released, and

it rolled quickly to a cruising speed. As it turned the curve Joy looked back at the station one last time and saw a glimpse of a figure in blue running down the platform. But she couldn't tell if it was a policeman, or Lanny, or just someone who was late for the train.

At the next stop a teenage couple got on, the boy draping his arm over the shoulder of his girlfriend, who leaned into him as if she wanted to disappear inside his bomber jacket. When the train stopped again an old woman carrying two plastic shopping bags walked down the aisle, muttering to her feet. The third time the train stopped, no one got on or off.

Joy unwound another notch. Her hands rested on her belly as a baby punched her from inside with an elbow or a knee. She rubbed the hard misshapen mound and closed her eyes. But they popped open wide when a bang cut through the silence. As the train chugged along she caught a glimpse through her now cracked window—two boys leaning over a metal railing, cheering as they jumped up and down. Their rock had made a direct hit. The cool October air leaked through the tiny hole in Joy's window, marking the rock's impact.

Joy leaned back, drenched in sweat, trying to recover her composure. She looked around to see if anyone else had seen the rock hit. The pregnant woman turned toward her. Their eyes met, and locked. The pregnant woman was Lanny. Lanny in Joy's old black wool coat. The tiny red-blonde hairs on her arms stood erect as she saw Lanny's feet hanging half-out of her own patent leather sling-back shoes. She stifled a scream.

The door to the car rattled open. The conductor walked in. He seemed to move as if underwater, too slow, stopping first at the teenagers to collect their fares. Joy stood up on shaky legs. Clutching the seats on either side of her she wobbled down the narrow aisle.

"What's the next stop?" she whispered.

"Say what?" the conductor shouted, leaning closer. "I only got one good ear. "Speak up."

"What's the next stop?" she whispered directly into his good ear.

"Ma'am, where you want to go?"

"I want to know what the next stop is. I want to get off at the next stop. And I don't want you to tell anyone where I've gone."

He stepped back to get a better look. She smelled of vomit. She looked insane. "Lady," he said, keeping his voice low. "No one cares where you're going. Don't take this personal. But trust me. So long as you got two dollars and forty-five cents, you can tell people whatever you want."

She dug a mountain of change out of her pocket and opened her palm. The conductor counted out her fare, rolled his eyes, and continued down the aisle to the woman who was Lanny.

Joy turned her head just enough so she could watch the conductor as he bent down close to Lanny. The conductor listened, then looked back at her, his eyebrows raised. He walked up the aisle, stopping alongside her row.

"You gave me too much change," he said loud enough for everyone in the car to hear. "Listen to me," he said under his breath. "That lady back there, in the cap—she asked me where you're getting off."

The downy hairs on the back of Joy's neck stood up.

"Now, don't worry. I told her Grand Central." He leaned down like he was picking up an old ticket from the floor, and he whispered quietly. "But if you ask me, that ain't no lady, and I would watch myself." He stood up and looked at her again. "You need the police?"

She thought of the questions the police would ask. What happened to Molly? What happened to Buddy? She thought of the babies she was carrying inside her—of losing them. Then she thought of Lanny, sitting across the aisle, wearing her sling-back shoes.

"Yes," she whispered.

She followed the conductor down the aisle as the train slowed to a halt.

"Don't worry," he whispered to her as she paused at the top of the narrow staircase. "You get on your way. I'll call for the cops to talk to that woman. That man," he corrected himself.

Her feet banged on the perforated metal as she ran down the steps, so she didn't hear Lanny scurry up the aisle after her. She didn't hear him call out to the conductor, pretending he was hurt, didn't hear him hobble to the metal platform between the cars. She didn't hear the conductor ask, "What's wrong?" before being struck on the back of his head.

The platform was deserted, so no one was there to see the blood that trickled down onto the tracks as the train pulled out of the station. No one was there to see the woman jump from the train only to take off her wool coat, her black cap, and her sling-back shoes, revealing herself underneath as a man in a navy blue suit.

Lanny rolled down his pant legs and shoved his feet into the sneakers he'd carried in his shopping bag. Leaving Joy's clothes strewn about the platform, he raced down the steps to the taxi stand just in time to see her duck into a cab. He hid behind a lamp post, out of sight, until she slammed the door, and her cab pulled away. She didn't see that half a minute later Lanny hailed another. She didn't see because her eyes were closed. She'd closed them now because she was safe. The conductor was calling for help. It would all be over soon. The police would find her at Dorothy's. A tear dripped down her cheek.

CHAPTER THIRTY-NINE

THE CABBIE TRIED to look as if he hadn't been sleeping, as if his head hadn't been tipped back on the seat, his mouth hadn't been hanging open, when Lanny got in and slammed the door.

"How you doing?" the cabbie asked into the rearview mirror.

Lanny stared at the fat neck in front of him, at the ears that stood straight out revealing decades of dirt in their creases.

The cabbie stared back in the mirror. "Where to, Bud?"

Lanny answered quickly, "Seventy-seventh and West End Avenue in Manhattan, and—"

"I know," the cabbie interrupted. "And step on it. I know. I know. I always get you guys. Everybody's in a rush. Everybody's got somewhere important to get to but me."

The cabbie blathered on, but Lanny kept his face blank. He didn't want to be rude. He didn't want to be friendly. He didn't want to be remembered.

"Here's fine," he called out when they stopped at a red light at the corner of Seventy-fifth and Riverside Drive. He tipped exactly fifteen percent and bent down to retie his perfectly laced sneakers until the cab was out of sight.

No one was in the lobby, and he rode up in an empty elevator, under the bug-speckled fluorescent light. Quiet as a dead man, he put the key in the lock and swung the door open to find Dorothy buttoning up her cashmere coat, about to leave.

"Lanford," she said. "I was just coming to meet you. Everything's gone wrong. That's why I'm late. I wanted to call, but the phone is out. Were you waiting at the restaurant forever? Are you angry with me?"

He didn't expect her to be home. She was talking too fast. He tried to keep up, to figure out what to say.

"No." It was all he could manage.

"Well, should we go? Is Joy waiting for us?"

But he was thinking, Joy should be here. She should have been here for a while.

"I don't know." It was all he could say.

"Do you want me to call the restaurant?"

He couldn't concentrate. The words weren't penetrating. He could tell from her tone she'd asked him a question, but he couldn't figure out what it had been. And he was thinking, why isn't Joy here? Where did she go?

"Okay," he said to whatever it was Dorothy asked. But his eyes were flicking everywhere, wondering, is she here? Where else would she be? Is she here?

"Is she here?" he asked.

"Pardon?" Dorothy was standing on the other side of the room, next to the little phone table. She had the receiver in her hand and one long finger on the dial. But she had just told him the phone was out. So the lies had already begun.

"Where is she?" he asked. He was calmer now.

"I'm calling the restaurant, dear. Isn't that where she is?"

As if the world had snapped into focus he saw her hand trembling. He saw the slow steady movement of her jaw, as she chewed the air in her mouth. He saw her fear.

"Go ahead and call then." He sat down on the couch next to the phone.

"All right," she said, but she didn't move.

"Go ahead. Call the restaurant. See if Joy is there."

Her hand shook as she dialed. She saw him notice.

"Don't be harsh with me," she pleaded.

"Harsh with you?" he said gently. "I just want to help you." He took the phone from her. She backed away, slowly. "The first problem is, you're trying to use a phone that you just told me doesn't work." She stepped back farther. He heard the bedroom door shut quietly. Joy.

"If you want to call someone," he went on, "and your phone is out, the first thing you have to do is this." He yanked the phone line out of the wall.

"Then you have to do this." He threw the phone across the room into the glass doors of the fireplace, which broke into long sharp splinters.

"Then you make your call." He cupped his hands over his mouth like a megaphone and yelled in a shrill, high voice, a bad imitation of Dorothy. "You can come out now, Joy. Everything is okay."

"Now, Lanny," Dorothy started in.

"No," he screamed, the power of his voice knocking her down on the couch. "I'm sick of this," he shouted. "I'm sick of people who want to throw me away like yesterday's garbage."

"No one wants to throw you away," she said softly.

"And you," he shouted back. "You were supposed to be my mother. Well, fuck you, Mother."

"Lanford," she said in her little-girl voice.

"Don't try. Don't even try. Because this time you're not going to dump me."

"We don't want to dump you," she continued in her saccharin voice. "We love you," she said. She stood up and approached him slowly. "Joy loves you. But you're ill right now. You need help. That's all. You just need some help."

"I think you've got it backward," he spit at her. "You're the one who's going to need the help."

"We both love you, Lanford. We do." Her voice was getting higher. She opened her arms, and he saw they were shaking.

"Come to me, Lanny." She opened her arms wider.

He looked around the room. Joy was nowhere in sight. He let Dorothy wrap her trembling arms around him. He dropped to his knees, taking her with him into the pile of broken glass. Tiny shards pricked his skin like little bites, but the pain was good. It kept him alert. He was aware of every movement. Dorothy's nostrils flared as she took a silent breath, readying herself.

"I don't want to kill you, Ma," He said to her as she started to pat his back like he was a baby.

"There, there," she said. "There, there."

It felt so good. Almost like she meant it.

"I don't want to."

"Shhh," she said, stroking his head. "Shhh," she said rocking him. Then he felt her move her arm.

"I don't want to kill my ma," he said, a line of tears streaking his face. "I don't want to." He pushed away from her and looked her in the eyes. "But what choice do I have, really?"

He squeezed her throat, and her eyes widened as her body jerked about. Then he felt it. A pinch, like a bee sting, in his back. When her hand came around the second time he saw the shard of glass.

It didn't take much effort to disarm her. He laughed as he did it, increasing the pressure with his thumbs until the glass dropped out of her bony hand, hitting the pile of shards with a delicate clink.

She looked at him, pitifully. He closed his eyes, and squeezed his thumbs tighter still, her arms flailing like she wanted to fly away.

When he looked again, her face was reddish blue. Then a noise came out of her throat, the sound of sixty years of phlegm backing up, getting caught in the pipes. She shivered, convulsed, and her head flopped over, like a sock. With a quick shove he pushed her off him and walked down the hall, bleeding, for Joy.

CHAPTER FORTY

SHE LOOKED AT the heavy cabinet, considered pushing it against the door. She looked at her stomach and thought of the babies inside. She listened to the quiet, wishing she knew what it meant. Her mother might have gotten rid of him and gone for help. Or he might be lurking just beyond the door, waiting for her. As she strained to hear, there came a thump, then heavy footsteps. She recognized the gait.

Flinging open the drawers to the bureau, she looked for something heavy or sharp, but all she found were neatly folded sweaters and carefully rolled socks. She picked up a cedar block that lay on top of a pile of woolen vests, but it was too light. She tossed it to the floor.

She searched among the old shoes lined in the closet for one with a stiletto heel, but they were all sensible pumps. She had her hand in the desk drawer when Lanny threw open the door. She grabbed a thin paintbrush and clutched it to her, as if it could protect her.

"Hi, honey," he said cheerfully. She saw a spot of blood on the rug behind him. Her eyes rushed over his body, searching for signs of a wound, hoping to see a gaping hole that meant he would keel over soon. But there was no wound she could see. And there wasn't much blood. There was no way to know if it was his.

He plopped down on the bed. "What's new?"

"Please let me out of here," she said carefully, starting to back toward the door.

He jumped up and inserted himself in the doorway. "Why? Where do you have to go?"

"Where's mother?"

"Resting."

"If you let me out of here, I promise, I'll leave you alone."

"Why the sudden change of heart, anyway? I thought we had a pretty damn good marriage, all things considered."

She closed her eyes, wishing it was all a bad dream, but when she looked up again he was back sitting on the edge of her trundle bed, grinning like the Cheshire cat.

"You're a bastard," she whispered.

"Loosen up. Let bygones be bygones," he said breezily. "Besides, look who's talking. You're in this as deep as I am. Buddy couldn't have died without your help. And remember, you're the one who thought up the kidnapping. Your most brilliant moment, cleverly forgotten, I might add.

All told, I'd say you're in pretty deep shit." His voice was tightening, getting higher. She watched him pick a sweater off the floor, saw him fingering the sleeves.

"You're right. I'm as guilty as you are, Lanny. I'm more guilty. So let me go. I won't turn you in. I can't."

"What are you going to do with that thing?" His eyes were on her hand, gripping the long thin paint brush. "Paint a picture that will scare me to death? Or, I know, you can tickle me to death with the bristles. That would be fun. Go ahead." He got up. "Try it." He came closer. "Under the arms is a good spot. Or under the chin. Go ahead." He was inches from her face, daring her.

She held the brush tightly. They both stared at it. Then, with a groan, she shoved the sharp pointed end into his neck, beneath his Adam's apple. There was a sharp pop. Lanny stared at her dumbfounded. Then a cry, like a wounded animal's, gurgled out of his mouth.

He yanked the brush out of his throat, his eyes reddening as if the blood had risen to them. He grabbed her, the blood from his wound spurting onto her face.

"I should have killed you then," he growled, his spit hitting her cheeks, blood leaking and spurting, leaking and spurting, out of his throat. He flung the brush against the wall where it left its bloody mark. "But better late than never." Holding her still with one arm locked around her torso, he used his free hand to wrap the sweater around her slender neck.

She felt something pressing into her stomach and in a flash remembered what it was. Her ribs aching from his tight grip, she snuck her hand down into the front pocket of her maternity dress. Her muscles were turning limp. Her breathing was labored. Her fingers stretched, reaching down into the deep pocket, latching on to the slim metal handle of the X-Acto knife. She drew the knife out slowly, forcing off the tight plastic cap.

She exploded with her last burst of strength and speared him, shoving the thin triangular blade into his abdomen,

just above his groin, and slicing up, as if she was opening
a carton wrapped with heavy tape.

He groaned. His hold loosened slightly. She slithered out
of his grasp and ran to the hallway. She was halfway to the
front door when she heard the X-Acto knife hit the floor.
As she turned to see him, he came at her, running like an
injured ape, supporting himself with one hand on the floor.
Breathing heavily, with a raspy, sickening noise, he stumbled but kept on coming. Rocketing himself forward as if
he was inhuman, he outran her, latching on to her waist.

She swung around and spat at him. Stunned, he loosened
his grip long enough for her to twist her body and wriggle
out of his hold. He watched, weakened and frozen with
rage as she grabbed the Chinese lamp off the hall table, and
shoved it into the oozing hole in his stomach.

With Lanny at her heels she raced back to her room,
slammed the door in his face, and shoved the dresser up
against it.

Groaning loudly, Lanny threw himself at the door, his
voice collapsing into vomiting, gasping, ugly, rabid sounds.
For what seemed like a day she sat listening to him crash
all her mother's decorative objects to the floor. Then she
heard a rustling sound, Lanny pulling himself along the rug.
Suddenly, all was silent.

When she finally opened the door he was lying in front
of her, arms open, eyes open, mouth open, as if he was in
the middle of a question, asking what happened? What happened to you? What happened to me?

EPILOGUE

"WE CAN GIVE you the epidural, but Dr. Hammani and I strongly feel general anesthesia would be better, given the circumstances." Dr. Wayne towered over her, his hair hidden beneath a lime green cap, his hands gloved and ready.

Dr. Hammani leaned over her, adding in his thick mid-Eastern accent, "It is, of course, your choice. We're here to do whatever you like. Whatever you like is fine." He twirled the end of a hypodermic needle between his fingers.

The pain came racing back like a locomotive, crashing into her. The room disappeared. She was lost, alone with the pain.

"Breathe," she heard the labor nurse call out. "It's almost over." She felt a washcloth on her forehead. "It's going. The contraction is going."

Molly rolled her wheelchair closer, grabbing Joy's hand. Joy squeezed back, her mind flashing on the miracle of her friend's recovery. Then her pain brought her to the present.

"What do you mean, given the circumstances?" She asked as she came out of the contraction back to the room, back to the men standing on either side of her, surrounding her. "What do you mean?"

Dr. Wayne whispered in Dr. Hammani's ear.

"Excuse us, please," Dr. Hammani said as he motioned for the labor nurse to join him. "Not to worry. I'll make you a lovely pain cocktail when I come back." He took the nurse by her elbow, and they disappeared.

Another contraction came, the worst yet. She thought of dying, jumping out the window, smothering herself in her pillow. As the pain diminished she realized Dr. Wayne had been speaking to her right through it.

"The other baby is healthy. Focus on that. We're confident the other baby will be fine."

"What?" Another contraction was speeding toward her. She didn't want to disappear into her pain until she understood. She turned to Molly. "What is he saying?"

"Lanny and I only wanted to protect the healthy baby," the Doctor insisted.

"What the fuck are you talking about?" she screamed from deep within the hurtling pain of her contraction.

"Please, try to focus on the positive. You've lost one, but the other baby will be fine. Do you understand that? We feel the other baby will be fine."

He's still keeping secrets from me, Joy thought as the next pain came, and then, this time, quickly went.

"I have to push," she screamed suddenly, and she wished she could push Lanny out, too. Push him out of her mind, out of her history.

"Hank," Dr. Wayne shouted as the labor nurse and the anesthesiologist raced into the room. The last thing Joy saw was Molly rolling her wheelchair out of the way so that Hank Hammani could get close enough to put a mask over her face. Then blackness came.

She didn't know how many days she'd been lying there, floating in and out of consciousness, surrounded by a parade of nurses and doctors who came and went in identical green gowns with different faces staring out, different eyes, different shaped frowns. Pills were pressed onto her tongue, shots were injected, vials and vials of blood were drawn. But when she tried to speak she was hushed and patted down as if she were the baby. And she couldn't remember if there was a baby. All she could remember were Lanny's open eyes, staring up at her.

"Time to take him away," a voice interrupted. "Visiting hour starts in a minute."

Joy opened her eyes to see a tall, bony nurse standing over her.

"Say good-bye," the nurse ordered.

Joy looked at the bundle of white toweling in the nurse's arms.

"Is it a boy?" she whispered.

"Honey. They gave you too much stuff. You've been in one long cloud. That's your little son. Remember?"

The nurse uncurled the blanket, exposing the soft red down on the baby's head. Joy rubbed her cheek against it, felt the silken skin, took a deep breath of the fresh smell of new life.

"And we're tired of calling this little chicken Baby Bard. What's his name?"

"Bobby," she said, without thinking. That was Buddy's given name. Something Lanny had never known. A secret she had managed to keep from him to the end.

"Then say good-bye to little Bobby here, because I'm taking him to the nursery. People are piling up at the elevators like a heap of garbage waiting to get their hands on all these tiny bundles."

"Bring him back as soon as visiting hour ends," she called as the nurse left the room.

"Yes, honey. You're the only mother here who wants the baby back right away. You all think you're the only mother here." The nurse shook her head and smiled, as she wheeled little Bobby out of the room in his glass bassinet.

The halls filled instantly with the noise of grandmothers and uncles and friends exchanging hugs and compliments and happy cries. A steady flow of visitors passed by Joy's bed as they made their way to her roommate, their arms filled with flowers and fruit and chocolates. A single bouquet of fading yellow daisies sat on Joy's dresser, put there by a sympathetic nurse, leftovers from some other new mother with too many flowers to carry home.

She closed her eyes to avoid inquisitive stares.

"Joy?" The voice was tentative.

She opened her eyes and surprised herself by smiling.

Molly rolled her wheelchair close to the bed and grabbed Joy's hand. She turned around and called out to the man in the doorway.

"I'll just stay five minutes, Raoul."

The muscular, dark attendant winked and left.

Molly turned back to Joy. "I stopped at the nursery. He's beautiful, all cleaned up. He looks just like you."

"What color are his eyes?" Joy asked quietly. "I forgot to look at the color of his eyes."

"They're always blue at first, aren't they?" Molly clutched her hand.

"They're going to stay blue. Like his," she said. Then she turned away from Molly. "And what about the girl? Do they have a little glass bassinet all set up for my little girl?"

Molly touched Joy's cheek. "I'm sorry you lost the other baby."

"I have the boy," Joy said, because she'd heard the nurses say it. Even through her sleep she'd heard them say it. At least she has that little boy. At least she's got that chicken-sized little boy.

But she couldn't forget the girl, a tiny little girl with a tuft of golden hair and dimples in her cheeks. "Bobby's perfect," she reminded herself, conjuring up the image of her newborn son. She pulled the sheets up over her gown to hide the wet spots around her nipples, her breasts full and ready to nurse.

"You'll heal, you know," Molly said. "Just like me, you'll heal."

Joy looked at Molly sitting in the wheelchair as if she'd been sitting that way all her life. "Why don't you hate me?"

"Because," Molly said, staring at Joy in a hard long gaze. "It wasn't your fault."

Joy took a few shaky breaths and pushed herself up against the pillows. "Promise me," she said. "After I get settled in at home and after you get out of here, you and Trina will come live with me. I'll help you with your exercises. We can all take care of each other."

"Sure," Molly agreed, smiling gently.

They sat across from each other in awkward silence, Joy shredding a tissue into tiny bits. A streak of tears ran down Molly's cheek, wetting the collar of her robe, but she wiped it away before Joy noticed.

"I've got to go," Molly said finally. "My doctor says my survival skills are right up there with Robinson Crusoe, and that if I listen to absolutely everything he tells me to do, I'll be fine. Which was supposed to include staying on my own floor."

"Well, then, get out of here," Joy said, ignoring the tears congregating in the corners of her own eyes.

"Can we all fit in your mother's apartment?" Molly asked as she wheeled herself to the door.

"We'll have to. I know I'm not going back to that house. Even if it doesn't sell."

"I heard two people saw mine last week," Molly said as Raoul walked in the room and began to wheel her out.

"You take care of her," Joy told Raoul. "She's the only family I've got."

Molly shook her head and called out, "You've got Bobby now, too." Then Raoul wheeled her away.

Her eyes were closed; she was thinking of Bobby and of her little girl when a hand tapped her shoulder. She blinked, and Ray came into focus.

"These are from me," he said, handing her a cluster of strings that made up the stem of a huge balloon bouquet. "The candy striper asked me to bring you this." He set down a gigantic floral arrangement on the nightstand. "She said it didn't fit on her cart."

"Thanks, Ray."

He squeezed himself into the small chair beside her bed. "You want me to unwrap the flowers?"

She nodded, so he eagerly jumped up, tore off the plastic, and handed her the card.

" 'Congratulations on the birth of your child,' " she read. " 'Fondly, Barb, Donna, and Sue.' You keep the flowers," she said, handing Ray the card. "I don't want them."

"Get out. They're beautiful. Expensive, too. Look at all those orchids."

"I don't want them, Ray."

"Okay. I'll take them."

They sat, awkwardly.

"Why I'm here is," Ray said suddenly, as if he was answering a question, "I have a lot of free time now. You probably didn't hear, but they downsized the department." He laughed. "Nice euphemism for getting canned, right?"

"Sorry to hear it, Ray."

"What am I saying? So what, I lost my job, right? Look at you. With what you've been through, I'm bothering you with my dumb story about losing my job. I'm sorry. I'm awfully sorry."

"It's all right, Ray. But I'm really tired. Do you mind if I just try to get some sleep?"

He leapt up, nearly knocking over the lush flowers. "Sorry. Of course. You had a baby. I didn't even see the baby."

"Why don't you stop at the nursery on your way out? He's the tiny one with the wispy red hair."

"I'm awfully sorry, Joy. I didn't know how bad things were. If I had known, I would have done something."

It was going to be tiring, this new job of reassuring the world she was okay. "Go say hello to Bobby, Ray. I'll call you when things are settled down."

"Please. Any time you need me," he reiterated. "I've never changed a diaper, but I'm a quick learner."

"Thanks, Ray. For now, just take the flowers."

He sighed heavily as he left the room carrying the oversize arrangement.

The sounds of her roommate's friends faded as she lay back, thinking about Bobby and what it was going to be

like, raising him on her own. She imagined him, lying on
his back in his crib, staring up at his black and white mo-
bile. Then she thought of the other crib, where her little girl
was supposed to be, a beautiful little girl, with delicate fingers, tiny toes, and a gentle, wistful face.

She rolled on her side, away from the festive voices in
the hallway, and wept for the death of her second child.

When she woke the room was quiet. The nurse had
brought Bobby back. He lay, her angel, sleeping in the
glass bassinet against the wall. Ignoring her various pains,
she lifted herself out of bed and took him in her arms.
Holding him close, she carefully climbed back under the
sheets. As he opened his tiny sleepy eyes, she unbuttoned
her hospital gown and guided his lips to her nipple.

His mouth closed tight, and he sucked for a moment.
Then his lips fell open, and he seemed to smile. She recognized the smile and knew that, by the time Bobby was a
year old, he would look like Lanny. His smile would be be-
guiling, a smile to fall in love with.

She closed her eyes and saw Lanny, grinning, sitting on
the trundle bed. She pushed the image away and opened her
eyes. Bobby, his innocent blue eyes clear and wide, was
looking up at her. Adoring her.